Helping out my Straight Neighbors

Kevin Davis

Published by Kevin Davis, 2023.

Table of Contents

Chapter 1
The Stray

The yelling outside woke me up. I looked at my phone, it was 1 am. I got out of bed and walked to the window. I could see my neighbor Evan and his girlfriend arguing. He was retrieving things she was throwing out of the house and scrambling to put them into his truck.

I felt bad for him. I didn't know them very well. Just seeing them in passing. I'd have been mortified to have my private life dragged out into the middle of the street like that.

She eventually stopped yelling and throwing things and went back inside. He sat on the doorstep for a while calling to her but eventually, he gave up and got in his truck and drove off. I got back in bed.

I'd seen Evan many times in front of his house working on his boat. He'd be shirtless with a sheen of sweat coating his thin but densely muscled frame. Lately, he'd taken on a more haggard look, his beard was long and scraggly, his mop of hair thick and wild looking. I'd often stand in my window and watch him work from a place of anonymity. I'd watch his muscles roll under his skin as he hoisted a motor or tugged at a stubborn bolt with a wrench. I'd reach into my pants and gently tug at my dick admiring this straight man's body, imagining what he kept hidden under his shorts. His ass was taut, not large, but filled his tight shorts. His package was readily apparent pushing out the front of his short shorts. His legs like the rest of him were thin but belied a strength in them, like steal cables of a suspension bridge seeming too small to hold up the weight of the roadway.

He hardly ever wore shoes as he scrambled up and down the boat, he was working on. He had a nervous energy about him like

1

a bee constantly buzzing from one project to the next never sitting still.

While walking in the park the next day I spotted his truck. When I approach I could see him curled up on his side across the back seat, his shorts riding down so that a few inches of his ass cleft hung out. Light blond hair trailed out of the cleft catching the morning sun. He held a ball of his clothes together as a pillow under his head. His morning wood appeared to be stretching the front of his shorts to the breaking point.

He must have somehow sensed my presence drooling at the window because just then he opened his eyes and locked their pale blue irises onto mine. He sat up looking embarrassed that he was caught sleeping in his car. I smiled weakly.

He moved to the door and opened it, dangling his legs down and rubbing his bare chest. His abs moved like ropes as he sat up and held himself in place.

"I saw what happened last night," I said trying to come up with something comforting to say.

"Yeah, she kicked me out," he said looking down at his flexing bare toes.

"Sorry to hear that," I said.

"Guess I had it coming," he said.

I didn't want to probe any deeper into why he said that, it seemed too private too personal for the kind of friendly neighbor relationship we had.

"Fuck I've got to piss, you mind," he said standing up in the grass strip by the sidewalk.

"Ah no," I said stepping back unclear what he was going to do.

I looked around, the park was mostly deserted this time on a Saturday morning. He held the door of his truck open and turned to face it. I caught the briefest glimpse of his semi-hard cock as he pulled and his large blond hair-covered balls over his waistband. I felt awkward though I desperately wanted to watch, so I turned away as I heard a stream of piss hit the soft grass. I acted like a lookout for him, all the while listening to that steady stream and wishing I was brave enough to turn and look at the source. I did manage to catch another brief glimpse just as he tucked it back inside his shorts, a bit of leftover piss seeping into the yellow fabric near the head.

He sat back down his feet up on the door frame, the smell of his piss rising on arcs of steam from the wet patch on the ground. I stood there not sure what to say.

He seemed to crumple, his head in his hands, his shoulders drooping. "I think she really means it this time," he said through broken sobs.

My heart went out to the poor guy. "It's going to be ok," I said though I wasn't at all sure that was or would be the case. He sniffed and looked up at me.

"You have someplace to go? You can't keep sleeping in your car" I said.

"No, I can't afford a hotel room, all I've got is right here," he said looking at the beat-up truck, his boxes of tools in the back, his clothes, and other few worldly possessions strewn around him.

I then said something I immediately regretted. "Why don't you come to stay at my place," I said.

He perked up sniffing back a tear. He looked like a dog at the pound who'd just been adopted.

"Just till you get back on your feet" I qualified the invitation. Did I really want this nearly destitute man living on my sofa indefinitely? I had a thing for lost causes and broken things. I had the hardest time parting with broken dishes. I'd feed a stray cat or nurse an injured bird. One day it was going to get me in trouble.

"You serious?" He said. This was the longest conversation we'd ever had and now I was inviting him to live with me. I couldn't back out now.

"Of course, I hate to see you pissing in the park and sleeping in your car," I said though I wouldn't have minded catching him doing the former. He pulled on a shirt and his shoes.

"We may want to bring along your tools, someone is liable to break in and steal them" I suggested going around to the back and opening the hatchback. I took one of the heavy toolboxes and he grabbed the other. He worked on boats, rebuilding motors, and repairing mechanical parts. These tools were his life and the only chance of him getting back on his feet.

"Thank you so much, you have no idea what this means to me," he said shoving clothes into a plastic shopping bag and tucking it under his arm. He closed up the car and followed me back to my house. His wife would be at work at the local hospital by now so there hopefully wouldn't be any drama returning.

"You can just put that over there for now, I'm sorry all I have is the sofa to sleep on. If that's not comfortable I can get an inflatable bed for you." I said.

"This should be fine! Thanks!" He said looking like he'd won the lottery.

"I'll get us some breakfast, you ok with bacon and eggs," I said.

"Yes, that sounds great," he said.

It had been a while since I'd had a partner or a roommate so having someone to share breakfast with was a nice change. While I enjoyed living alone and being able to do whatever I wanted whenever I wanted, I did miss sharing a meal and the day-to-day interactions of living with someone.

"Mind if I grab a shower, I don't want to get your furniture all dirty." He asked. I'd noticed the bit of motor oil on his arms and the dirt on his face and in his hair but hadn't said anything. He must have just come from work last night.

"Sure let me show you where it is," I said.

"These houses are all the same, if it's like our place I know where to go," he said getting up and pulling off his shirt as he climbed the stairs.

I heard the shower start as it was just above the kitchen. The image of him naked just above me flashed into my head. I pictured the water flowing down his body washing away the grime. I pictured him soaping up his crotch and tugging on his cock as it grew in his hand. The smell of burning eggs brought me out of my daydream. I looked down to see my sweatpants tenting out in front of me. I wished I'd worn at least some underwear today.

I heard the shower shut off and tried to busy myself to distract attention away from my dick.

"Hey," I heard from upstairs. I went to the bottom of the stairs and looked up.

"What's up?" I asked.

"Um, where do you keep the towels?" he asked.

"Oh shit, sorry I just did a load of laundry, they are still in the dryer. Let me grab you one" I said.

"Thanks!" He said from behind the bathroom door.

I ran down to the basement and pulled a towel from the dryer.

I knocked on the bathroom door.

"You can come in, I don't want to drip water everywhere," he said.

My heart pounded inside my chest as I pushed open the door and stepped inside. Evan was standing in the shower drip drying. The glass door was open. I held out the towel for him trying not to stare at his naked body but my eyes were naturally drawn down his chest, across a smattering of blond chest hair to the cut of his abs to his outie belly button. A drop of water, glassy and bright, defied gravity and hung suspended from the end of his cock. It took all of my willpower to resist the urge to drop to my knees and rest that drop on the tip of my tongue.

Evan coughed softly, and I realized I hadn't let go of the towel I was holding out for him. I quickly let go blushing my embarrassment at getting carried away. He smiled and looked down as he took the towel. I followed his gaze to my distended sweatpants and turned away from him. Precum was already seeping from my hard cock creating a dark patch on the light gray material

"Thanks," he said as I strode out of the bathroom without turning back.

"Breakfast is ready," I said in a shaky voice over my shoulder as I descended the stairs.

"I'll be right down," Evan said.

I dished up eggs and placed strips of bacon on each plate feeling my hand shaking. I had tried to tuck my dick down and clean up the wet spot with little success in either endeavor.

When I looked up there was Evan with just a towel wrapped around his midsection.

"Smells great," he said pulling up a stool at the countertop and sitting down. His hair was still damp and there was a patch of water droplets on his shoulder that he'd missed while drying off. I gulped and turned to the coffee pot, filling a couple of mugs. I put cream and sugar on the island and took the stool next to him tucking my unruly cock between my crossed legs.

We ate in mostly silence with me stealing glances down his body to the clear bulge of his cock and balls pressing into the terrycloth.

"She was pissed that I didn't get home in time to look after Alice before her shift," he said.

"Alice is your daughter?" I asked. I felt bad I didn't know his daughter's name.

"She means the world to me. What am I going to do?" he said resting his head in his hands.

"Give her some space, maybe you can work things out. She can't keep you from seeing your daughter" I said.

"I just got so focused on work, I didn't realize how late it was," he said.

"She kicked you out for that?" I asked.

"I guess it was just the last straw. I know I'm not easy to live with. I can't sit still for more than a minute and that drives her crazy" he said, and as if to illustrate his point, his leg began to bounce up and down from its resting place on the bottom rung of the stool making the towel vibrate. The knot at his waist loosened and slipped letting the towel fall open. I was treated to another quick view of his plump cock while he stood and retied the towel around his waist.

"I'd better go get dressed," he said apologetically.

"It's ok, no big deal," I said as my cock pressed against my leg trying to escape.

He sat back down and finished his breakfast washing it down with his black coffee. He held the towel with one hand this time to prevent it from shaking loose again. After breakfast, he went back upstairs and got dressed.

"So what are your plans for the day?" I asked when he returned fully dressed in the same shorts he'd been wearing and a tank top that was cut low down the sides. His strong pecs and abs were visible each time he moved and the material bowed out.

"I don't know, I have to go back to the boat I'm working on at some point," he said, "what about you?"

"I've got to work on some projects around the house," I said

"Need some help?" He asked. I was hoping he'd go to the boat so I could give my balls from relief.

"Sure, that would be great, I need to replace some rotting boards on the deck and I could use a hand with that," I said.

We grabbed some tools and I showed him the way up to the deck off the back of the house. As we worked the day warmed up considerably until I was sweating and my shirt clung to my chest. Dark patches appeared on my sweats not from precum this time. I'd finally managed to get my dick mostly in check as we focused on the work.

During a break, he pulled his shirt over his head and tossed it on a nearby chair. His back glistened with sweat. Each muscle group pulled and flexed as he moved a board into place and secured it with screws. I caught myself looking down the gap in his shorts to see the sweaty blond hairs filling in his crack. He also had a wet spot on his shorts that ran the length of his crack. I wanted to pull those shorts down and lick that sweaty hair and drill his tight pucker with my tongue.

"Got a mind of its own huh," Evan said looking back at me. I didn't know what he meant until I looked down and realized I'd gotten hard again.

"Oh shit, sorry," I said trying my best to tuck it away.

"Shit, I'm set to explode myself, Cassy and I haven't had sex since Alice was born." He admitted.

"Really! How old is she?" I asked.

"18 months," he said.

"Fuck that's a long time to go without," I said.

"I know, my only companion is my right hand," he said making a jerking-off gesture.

"That's a shame, a stud like you could get it anytime you want," I said.

"Oh I'm not all that," he said blushing.

"Seriously! You are in amazing shape. I know plenty of girls and guys who'd kill to get with someone like you" I said thinking, I'm one of them.

"Really? I've only ever been with Cassy. We met in high school" he said.

I pictured what Evan might have looked like back in high school. A few years younger without the beard or the rippling body. I decided I preferred this version.

There was a lull in the conversation as we got back to work. I tried to ignore my boner as I felt it brush my leg periodically. Nothing I did seemed to make it go down. Evan looked at it occasionally and smirked. It may have just been my imagination or wishful thinking but I thought the bulge in his shorts had gotten bigger.

"You seeing anyone?" he asked a few minutes later.

"I'm also currently in a dry spell," I said.

"What's it like?" He asked shyly a few minutes later.

"What's what like?" I asked not following his thoughts.

"Being with a guy" he finally said after several starts and stops. It was a hard question to answer. I wondered how he would have answered if I'd asked him the same question about women.

"I don't know. Something about two men fucking that is so animal, so primal." I said.

"Are you the girl or the guy?" He said and I was shocked at the question. He was clearly ignorant of gay culture.

"You mean am I a top or a bottom?" I clarified finding it hard to keep some annoyance at his ignorance from creeping into my voice.

"Sorry, I didn't mean to pry," he said picking up on my slight annoyance at the insinuation I was a girl. I've never been into feminine guys, give me a butch bear or leather daddy any day.

"It's ok, the question just surprised me that's all. I mostly top, but occasionally for the right guy I'll bottom" I said

"Oh, I've never known a gay guy before. I grew up in a very conservative state" he said.

"I'm sure there were gay guys there, they just probably hid it well," I said.

"Yeah, you're probably right," he said.

We finished up the deck and headed back inside to cool off and grab some lunch.

"I'd better work some more on the boat," he said after lunch.

"Ok," I said as my dick twitched again in anticipation of finally getting some relief once we had some privacy.

He got his tools together and headed for the door.

"Here," I said handing him a spare key. "This way you can come and go anytime without disturbing me if it's late"

"Thank you so much for everything," he said setting the toolboxes down and grabbing me around the waist. He pulled me into a hug resting his bearded chin on my shoulder. My dick inadvertently pressed into his crotch as he hugged me right. His body convulsed as I held him. Was he crying? He sniffed back tears as he let go and wiped his eyes and nose on his dirty tank top.

He turned and walked out carrying his tools with him. I stood by the door watching him go thinking what had I gotten myself into.

Chapter 2
Washing Up

I found his bag of dirty clothes and decided to run a load of laundry. As I took each article from the bag I was overwhelmed by his musk permeating them. I got to a pair of his briefs and took a whiff. I could smell his cock and balls on the pouch. There was a bit of something crusty on them. I realized he must have cum on them at some point. I imagined him in his car last night jerking off into his underwear before falling asleep.

I sniffed the crusty patch and stuck out my tongue. Sure enough, it had a salty bitter taste. My cock was rock hard and making more stains in my sweats. I pushed them down and let them drop to the floor. I grabbed hold of my dick and stroked it while I licked and sucked the material rehydrating his cum. I imagined I was sucking his cock and tasting the precum directly from its source. I could smell his crotch and balls and imagined I was licking them.

"Oh fuck" I cried as my load dripped down the side of the washing machine. It was one of the biggest loads I'd had in months. I scooped some of it up and licked it off my fingers.

I couldn't believe I'd just licked dried cum from Evan's underwear. I felt disgusted with myself. Was I that desperate?

I tossed my sweatpants and a combination of his clothes and mine into the wash. I held the wet underwear up and balled it in my fist. He wouldn't miss one pair, I thought.

I didn't bother getting dressed again, I figured he wouldn't be back for hours anyway. I preferred to do my chores in the nude anyway. I cleaned and vacuumed and made some dinner setting aside a portion for him to reheat when he got home. Home, I thought, I'm really getting ahead of myself there.

After dinner, I folded the laundry and headed up to take a shower before bed.

As the water ran over me, I idly stroked my cock again. I brought up the image of Evan's dick dripping wet right here where I was standing. I stroked my hard eight inches with the lubrication of some soap thinking again about his cock in my mouth and the taste of his cum from his crusty underwear.

"Oh shit sorry! I have to pee really bad" Evan said from the doorway. My eyes popped open and I let go of my cock. I'd not heard him come in. He smiled looking down at my dick bouncing up and down behind the glass.

He didn't wait for my permission, he stepped into the bathroom and hauled out his thick cock right in front of me with his right hand so I could see it clearly through the glass. A torrent of pee shot from his wide flared head and landed with a loud splash in the bowl.

"Fuck that's better," he said shaking and stroking the shaft to get the remaining moisture out of his urethra. It swayed and bounced as he manhandled it. It seemed like he took longer than typical to squeeze the last of his piss from his dick, letting it thicken in his hand.

He gave it one more tug then looked over at me as if realizing for the first time I was still in the room with him and tucked it away.

"Sorry to interrupt, carry on," he said with a wink as he turned and headed out the door. He didn't close it tightly behind him. The light spilled into the hallway but it was hard to tell if he was still there or if he'd already headed back downstairs.

I opened the shower door and stepped out into the rug. I looked at myself in the mirror and stroked my cock a few times to the view. I wasn't anything bad to look at either. Sure my "dad body" phase was creeping up on me. I'd have to start running and working out again if I wanted to preserve what I had.

I'd let myself go recently after injuring myself in a fall. It was the main reason I'd not started dating or hooking up again. I traced the scar along my shoulder where I could feel the plate that was holding the bones together just under the skin.

My confidence was shot seeing that ugly red line. I dried off and stepped out into the hallway in just a towel, I'd normally just walked naked to my bedroom.

The hall was empty and I could hear Evan busying himself in the kitchen.

"I left you some dinner in the fridge," I called down as I headed to my dresser to find some shorts and a shirt.

I found him sitting at the counter devouring the leftovers.

"This is so good!" He said with a full mouth of my ratatouille and smoked sausage.

"Thanks, it's one of my favorites," I said watching how he brought the sausage to his lips to take a bite. I had a flash of my cock between those full lips. I shook the image away and grabbed a beer from the fridge.

"You want one?" I offered.

"Sure," he said as I pulled the caps off two and handed him one. He washed down his meal with the beer and sighed a purr of contentment.

"That hit the spot," he said pushing his stool back. "Mind if I grab a shower before bed," he asked.

"Sure, towels are on the shelf," I said nursing the last of my beer.

I cleaned up the plates and started the dishwasher on delay then headed upstairs to go to bed.

Light streamed from a crack in the door to the bathroom. I could hear the shower running. As I stepped past I could see in, he'd left the door slightly ajar. I stood back in the shadows and looked into the bright bathroom beyond. Though he was obscured somewhat by the glass and the water running down it, I could make out his nude form and his strong arm flexing. I followed his arm down to find he was holding his cock in his right hand stroking it intently.

His hand was a blur as he moved it rapidly up and down what looked like a very impressive hard cock. It angled upward in his fist. He was turned to the side so I risked stepping closer to get a better look, though I'd now be illuminated by the ray of light streaming into the hallway. I could now make out his wide head as it bobbed up and down facing the glass.

"Suck it" I heard him say over the loud spray. I wondered if he was thinking of Cassy taking his cock in her mouth.

"Bend over and let me see that ass," he said, though his eyes were closed I nearly thought he was talking to me. He started to hump his fist, rocking his hips and clenching his butt with each stroke.

"You want this cock don't you," he said. Of course, I did, I thought.

I couldn't take it anymore, I slipped my hand inside my shorts and stroked my cock watching this stud pound his imaginary girlfriend in my shower.

I got bolder and pulled out my cock, feeling I was getting close.

"Fuck yeah take my fucking load!" He said as I saw streaks of white hit the glass and drip down in lines. I could see his cock head expand with each thrust as he deposited a new stream onto the glass. My body rocked as I painted the door frame with my load. I saw his eyes open and I jumped back into the darkness. He peered out through the glass for a moment before he grabbed the sprayer and hosed his cum from the shower door. I lingered a moment longer to catch him stepping out of the shower to grab a towel. His still half-hard cock bounced in front of him, its wide head an angry red. It had to be at least eight inches still. I conjectured it must have been at least 9 inches fully hard. Fear of getting caught leering at him forced me to retreat into my room.

I heard him flip off the light and his bare feet on the stairs as I drifted off to sleep.

Chapter 3
Rooftops

The next morning, I woke with a start, remembering my cum on the doorframe. I got up and went to the bathroom. The evidence was still there, but now dried and blended in with the off-white trim. I cleaned it up as best I could before returning to my room to get dressed.

I made my way downstairs to grab my laptop and make some coffee, so I could do some work upstairs while Evan slept in.

I found him on his stomach, one arm hanging over the edge of the sofa. The sheet I'd left for him was draped over his legs but had pulled off the rest of his body. His naked ass was visible just above the hem of the sheet.

The sunlight streamed through the window, illuminating each muscle grouping on his back in light and shadow. His two round ass cheeks stood out. They were covered in soft blond hair that caught the sunlight, making them glow like golden threads. The hair got darker the deeper it went into his ass crack, until it nestled around his obscured hole. The top of his ball sack was just visible under the edge of the sheet. A line traced the separation between his two balls in the sack, like stitching on a softball. They were a darker shade than his tan skin. His shoulders were freckled red from the sun while his ass was lily-white.

I pictured what it would look like to have my dick slipping between those pearly cheeks and sinking into the soft blonde hairy hole.

The cheeks clenched together as he moved and stretched, rolling onto his back. His hard cock arched up over his tight abs and caught the morning sunlight like it was a spotlight trained on the main event. His soft pubes glowed in the light like they were on fire. He reached down and tugged on it, unaware of my presence.

I was afraid to move and give away my position, but also afraid that at any moment he would look up and find me there anyway.

He arched his back and reaching down to pull the sheet over him and roll to his side.

I was sad to lose the amazing view, but glad I'd not been caught enjoying it. I made like I'd just come down the stairs again and headed to the kitchen to start the coffee. As the aroma filled the room, I heard footsteps behind me. I looked back to find Evan in just his briefs leaning against the counter. His morning wood was tucked into the pouch but straining the fabric.

"Mmmm coffee" he said, sniffing the air.

"It'll be ready in a minute" I said, grabbing a couple mugs.

He grasped the mug in both hands like a sacred thing as he took a sip.

"Take these up out on the deck?" I suggested. It looked like the start of another hot day, so it was good to enjoy the coolness of the morning while we could.

The stairs lead to a door onto a second floor deck, then up a staircase to the roof. The rooftop deck was arranged with potted plants around the parameter, creating an urban oasis. I set my coffee down by the outdoor sofa, while Evan took a seat across from me on the rocker.

He hadn't bothered to put on anything else, so he sat there in just his white Calvin Kleins. Being up here away from the street with nothing around, you could imagine you were alone. After a run, I'd come up here and slip off my shorts and stretch out in the nude. It was nice to feel the warm sun on my bare skin and the breeze wicking away my sweat.

"This place is great! So private" he said.

"Yes, it's great, no one can see us up here. I'll sometimes come up here and nude sunbathe" I admitted.

"Nice! When I'm out on a boat, I'll strip down when no one is around. I'd work naked if I could get away with it" he said. I'd pay him to work naked, I thought.

We sipped our coffees, relaxing until my phone buzzed. Work was attempting to draw my attention away from the stud across from me. I felt like calling out sick and spending the day nude sun bathing with Evan.

"You mind?" he asked, standing up and shucking his underwear before I could respond. I nearly choked on the mouthful of coffee, spraying it all over myself as I marveled at his body. He stretched, then laid down on the outdoor rug in the full sun, closing his eyes. I soaked up the sight, providing me more fuel for my spank bank.

"Wanna join me" he said, squinting up from a furrowed brow.

Fuck work, I thought, putting down my phone and slipping my shirt over my head. My overstimulated dick was already semi-hard as I looked around, then dropped my shorts. Evan was still looking up at me with one hand shading his eyes as I sat down next to him.

"What happened to your shoulder?" He asked, pointing to the scar on my shoulder.

"I had a bad tumble on my bike, broke my clavicle. They had to put in a plate to keep the bones together" I said. We were so close now our dicks could have touched if I rolled onto my side.

"Fuck, that must have hurt," he said.

"I think I was in shock because honestly, I don't remember it hurting much at the time," I said.

"This hurt like hell, the bone was through the skin" he said, lifting his leg and showing a thin scar and line of round marks where I assumed they must have had pins to hold the bones in place.

"Fuck!" I said.

"Yeah, was off my feet for months, I was going nuts! Haven't been on a motorcycle since" he said.

There was a strange sort of intimacy in comparing our war wounds, that seemed to bond us.

"Thanks" he said softly after a while of us laying in the sun, eyes closed, enjoying the warmth and soft breezes.

"For what?" I asked, turning my head to face his handsome bearded face.

"For everything, you didn't have to invite me to stay with you. You came to me at my absolute worst moment. I really had no idea what I was going to do. I'd seriously considered ending it all" he said, rolling onto his side to face me.

"It'll work out," I said.

"I think you're right. I never sit still like this ever, I feel so relaxed around you" he said.

A warmth grew in my chest as a laid back and closed my eyes, seeing the sun as a warm glow behind my eyelids. If I wasn't careful, I could fall for him hard. I knew in the back of my mind he was straight and totally out of my league. There was absolutely no way it was going to happen.

Then, just like that, he leaned in and kissed me. His wet lips touched mine and my eyes opened wide. I was stunned. I felt his hand glide his palm over the underside of my hardening cock. It sprang to life instantly, pushing against his touch. He wrapped his fingers around it, looking down and grasping it tight between his fingers.

"This is so fucking weird" he said as he held up his cock in one hand and squeezed mine in the other.

"Good weird?" I asked.

"Different than I expected" he said, pulling the loose skin up and down on my shaft. I immediately started to leak down the shaft onto his fingers.

I reached out and grabbed hold of his shaft and he let go. We stroked each other's cocks, looking into each other's eyes as I grew closer to orgasm.

He traveled down my body, licking my skin as he went, until he reached my cock. He held it in his hand for a moment, looking up into my eyes before sinking it into his warm wet mouth.

Chapter 4
Catching Some Rays

"We should head in before we get too burnt," he said, casting a shadow across my face. I looked up to see he'd put his underwear back on. I suddenly felt very naked with my hard cock pulsing as it rested its heft against my leg.

"I must have dozed off for a minute there" I said.

"Having a good dream" he said grinning and nodding at my hard dick.

"You could say that" I said grabbing my shorts to cover myself up turning redder than the sun was making my face.

I reluctantly slipped them back on and followed Evan back inside.

"Guess I should get to work" I said.

"Me too," he said, gathering up his tools.

"See you tonight," I said.

"You sure it's ok, I'm not too much trouble?" he asked.

"Not at all, I haven't had a roommate in a while, and it's nice to have some company for a change," I said.

"I don't have many guy friends, all our friend are hers, mostly couples she knows," he said looking a bit like a lost puppy.

I didn't see Evan till late that night when he came in smelling of diesel fumes and covered in grease and grim.

"I'm going to hop in the shower" he said.

"Ok, I'll heat you up something to eat." I said as I headed to the kitchen and pulled out a container.

"Something smells good!" Evan said. I turned to find him standing in the middle of the kitchen naked. I blushed.

"Hope you don't mind, just didn't feel like getting dressed. Nothing you haven't already seen anyway," He winked.

Of course, I don't mind, I screamed inside my head.

"It's fine by me," I tried to say nonchalantly, but my voice cracked like a hormonal teenager.

I dished some on his a plate and handed to him. He turned and headed back to the island while I got a good look at his ass shifting back and forth with each step.

Fuck that's a nice ass, I nearly said out loud. As he set his plate down his fork fell off the plate and onto the floor.

I audibly gasped seeing his tight puckered ass ringed by dirty blond hair as he stooped down to pick it up.

He sat down seeming oblivious to the effect he was having on me. Any more of this and I might lose my resolve and bend him over the island and fuck his beautiful ass.

"Join me" he said sitting down at the countertop.

"I already ate" I said.

"No I mean ..." he looked down at his nude body and over at my fully clothed one.

"Oh" I said.

"Hope it's ok, I used to go around the house naked all the time till Cassy complained about it after Alice was born. She didn't think it was appropriate to be naked around her. I guess I see her point, but I've missed the freedom" he said.

Who knew my hunky neighbor was a closet nudist.

"It's funny you say that, I like to strip down and go naked when I get home," I confessed.

"I know" he winked.

"What do you mean?" I asked.

"You can see in your front window, I've seen you in here walking around naked, I think half the neighborhood has seen you." He laughed.

My face reddened. Guess I should get some curtains.

"Hey, if you've got it flaunt it," he said grinning.

"Oh please, I'm not sure anyone wants to see this" I said rolling my eyes. I hate receiving compliments. Did he really compliment me? I wondered what the neighbors would think if they saw him here now.

"Why not? You've got a great body." He said.

"Maybe I used to, since the accident I've gotten out of shape" I said.

"You seemed alright from what I saw earlier. Come on join me, I feel weird being the only one." he said egging me on. I slipped off my shirt then dropped my shorts stepping out of them. Evan smiled and I blushed in embarrassment. I felt awkward in front of him though normally, I never thought twice about walking around my house naked.

I took up a stool next to Evan and sipped a beer as he finished his dinner.

"Got any movies?" He asked after he cleaned up the plates and loaded the dishwasher. I grew hard watching him bending down to put the plates in the lower rack, picturing my tongue licking his hairy hole.

"I've got most of the streaming services you can scan through them if you want, I'll be right in." I said keeping my boner hidden under the overhang of the counter.

He walked past and took a place on the sofa picking up the remote.

Once I had my dick under control, I walked over and sat down on the far side of the sofa next to him. His dick rested against his leg looking plump but not hard. Mine was only semi-hard thankfully.

"This ok?" He asked nodding to the screen which displayed an action movie title.

"Sure that's fine" I said, I know I wouldn't be paying much attention to the action on the screen anyway.

As we watched the movie, I kept stealing glances over at him taking in his body and dick when I could without being obvious. I thought I felt his eyes on me every once in a while. At one point in the movie there is a sex scene and I noticed Evan's dick stir and fluff up a bit. He moved his hand to it and idly tugged it a few times before just resting his hand over his dick. I struggled to keep my dick in check, but it was a losing battle.

"Got anything else?" he asked rubbing his dick which twitched to life as he manhandled it.

"We can watch something else, you got the remote" I said.

"No I mean, you know" he said glancing down at his now nearly hard cock.

"Oh" I said visibly shaking. Is he really asking if I have any porn?

"A buddy of mine and I used to watch porn together all the time" he admitted.

"I've got a few old dvds, but I doubt those would be your speed. There's always the internet" I suggested.

"Anything is cool," he said leaning back and resting his hand on his cock. I wanted to know more about this buddy and what they might have done besides just watch porn, but I was too afraid to ask.

I pulled up a porn site on my phone and did a search for some straight porn not sure what he liked. I found a clip with a guy I thought was cute and streamed it to the tv.

"Fuck!" he said, his eyes glued to the screen. A woman with dark hair and full breasts was looking up with a massive dick hanging over her face. Her small hands could barely reach around the thick cock as he held it up and licked the head. He watched the screen while I mostly watched him out of the corner of my eye.

At first, he just rested his forearm against his cock as it grew. I couldn't see it well with his arm in the way. I was fully hard already, but I also tried to hide it from him worrying I might weird him out.

My dick ached for attention, but I let it just hum with a steady blood supply.

I caught movement out of the corner of my eye and spotted Evan's hand move up his shaft rubbing it overhand while also furtively covering it.

"This ok?" He asked looking over at me with his fist around his cock.

"Yeah, sure," I coughed out getting a better look at his thick member.

I grabbed my dick and stroked it with my left hand, so he could clearly see me. His eyes remained locked on the screen.

His dick jumped and dribbled a stream of precum onto his abs. I looked back at the screen to find the woman was now on her knees with the guy getting ready to plunge his massive cock into her pussy from behind.

"Got anything else?" He asked.

"I don't know what you like" I said.

"Let me take a look," he said, and I handed him my phone. I cringed at handing it off to him. Only touching my cock could be more personal than touching my phone. If he strayed too far he might find my photos which included plenty pictures of dicks many of which were my own.

"How do you get it to play on there?" He asked nodding at the screen. I scooted closer and tapped a button. The tv screen went blank for a moment then displayed a scene with a blond woman who somewhat resembled Cassy but with smaller breasts. A guy was eating out her pussy.

To my shock another guy came into the frame and fed his cock to her. The guy's cock could have been a clone of my own dick. Knowing my previous interest in only gay porn the search must have pulled up some mmf porn into the mix of options.

Evan set the phone down and grabbed his dick again tugging on it as a drop of precum oozed out of the piss slit.

"We can watch something else" I said feeling embarrassed when the scene switched to the guy who had been licking the girl's pussy was now sucking the other guy's dick while the girl sucked the first one's.

He didn't answer, he focused on the screen more vigorously stroked his dick. I sat back now close enough to him for our legs to touch. I could smell that same smell I'd caught a whiff of on his used underwear. I wanted to bend down and lick up the pool of fresh precum dribbling onto his abs. I wanted to smell the rich odor of his balls and suck them into my mouth. I was on the edge and knew I could cum at any moment if I wasn't careful.

Evan's mouth hung open slightly as the action shifted to the first guy licking out the girl's pussy while the second guy dropped to his knees behind the first one.

"Holy shit!" He called out as the guy licked out the guy's ass. He wasn't looking away in disgust like I would have expected. He focused on the close up of the guys tongue probing the hairy pucker.

"Fuck, anyone ever done that to you?" Evan asked.

"Many times, though I prefer to be the one licking," I said catching myself oversharing. "You?"

"I've never had a chick do that, what's it like?" he asked still not prying his eyes off the screen.

"Hard to describe really. If they do it right it feels amazing" I said.

On the screen the guy in the back stood up and lined up his dick behind the other guy's ass. He slapped his hole with his big dick and the first guy moaned and stuck his ass in the air while he continued to eat out the girl's wet pussy.

Evan suddenly stopped stroking his cock and let it hover untouched as it pulsed and leaked precum in a steady stream onto his abs.

"I can change the video if you don't like it" I said.

"No, it's fucking hot, I've never had a threesome" he said.

"I have. In fact, I've been in an orgy a few times" I said.

"No fucking way" he said venturing a sideways glance at me and then down at my dick.

"Yeah, a whole room full of fucking and sucking, I think I busted a nut in at least three asses and one mouth" I said.

"Fuck! I'm lucky to get it once a week much less four times in one day" he said stroking his dick with a closed fist around the shaft.

"One of the perks of being gay is guys are naturally horny and want to get off" I said.

"Too bad I'm straight" he joked.

"Hey, a hole is a hole right?" I said nodding at the screen. The middle guy was taking the other guy's dick like a pro while he fucked the girl's pussy.

Evan seemed transfixed at the closeup of that big dick disappearing into the guy's hole.

"Where is it all going?" He asked.

"You'd be surprised just how much dick an ass can take" I said, showing off my dick.

"Fuck! You do have a big dick," he said.

"Yours is way bigger," I said, nodding at his as he held it up from the base. His was probably only an inch or so bigger than mine, but he was at least 5 inches shorter than me, so it looked so much bigger on his smaller frame.

"Really? I think it's average," he said smacking it around.

"No way, you've got a huge dick," I said. He blushed at the complement.

He was nearly close enough that I could have reached over and touched it, but I was afraid I'd freak him out. I spread my legs a little wider and cupped my balls as we both seemed to forget what was going on on the screen and focused on each other's cocks.

Though I normally use my right, I stroked with my left, so he could see better. It also helped prevent me from blowing my load too quickly.

I felt his leg bush mine as he spread his legs apart. The touch was brief but electric. I held my leg out and let him touch it again if he wanted to. He pushed out his leg and our knees touched again. This time he maintained the contact. He was totally focused on my cock as he stroked himself while the girl on screen screamed as she fingered herself while the two guys fucked facing each other.

Evan grunted, and his abs tightened as a thick rope of cum shot up across his chest. I couldn't hold back any longer either, I grunted and shot a volley that landed on my chin. Evan rolled on his side and shot another volley that hit me in my side and dribbled down onto the sofa.

I jumped up and stood over him, launching the rest of my load across his chest as he laughed and rest of his load dribbled onto his abs. It became unclear whose cum was who's as the last of my cum mixed with his own.

Evan let go of his cock and looked down at his chest covered with our combined cum.

"Oh sorry" I said, stepping back immediately regretting taking it too far.

"Guess I deserved that," he laughed.

"We're cool?" I asked.

"Yeah, that was ... different" he said rubbing around our cum. "I'm going to get cleaned up".

I grabbed him a handful of paper towels, so he didn't drip cum all over the house. He did some triage before standing and heading upstairs. I couldn't believe what we just did.

"You coming?" I heard him call down.

"Um ok" I said getting up and heading to the stairs, my hard dick bouncing with each step. I expected him to switch into straight boy "let's never talk about what just happened" phase.

"You made the mess, seems only fair you clean it up," he said when I got to the top of the stairs.

Chapter 5
Saving Water

Evan was already in the shower when I stepped in. I grabbed the shower sprayer from its holder and turned to adjust the water temp.

"No, not with that" he said looking down at me.

"Then how?" I said naively.

"You know, like the guys did at the end just now" Evan said sheepishly.

I'd been so focused on him, I'd missed the last part of the video we'd been watching, so I wasn't following.

He scooped up some residual cum and held it between two fingers out for me.

"Oh" I said before a slipped his fingers in my mouth and licked off the mixture of our combined cum. When it was clean, he pulled his hand away and nodded down at his chest. I bent forward and licked his salty skin, feeling the light blond hair rake across my tongue. I licked up until I found his tiny pointed nipple and flicked it with my tongue. Evan moaned as I tongued the sensitive skin. I licked across his chest and found his other nipple and gave it a similar treatment. I felt Evan's body quiver as I bit down on the fleshy nub.

I continued down his chest, finding bits of wet saltiness as I went. I was tempted to go lower and lick the last pits of residual cum from his piss slit, but I thought that might be taking things too far. I stood up again once I was satisfied I'd sucked the last of our cum from his chest hair.

"Your turn," I said, pointing at a wet patch on my side where his cum had landed.

"Uh" he said looking around for an escape.

"Fair is fair," I said. He reluctantly leaned forward and raked his tongue along my side. I was glad I'm not ticklish, or I would have been squirming. He didn't stop at just the wet patch. He continued up my side under my arm. I raised my arm, and he licked up and into my pit. I grew weak in the knees as he licked and sucked my pit. I reached up and pressed his head into the hairy jungle. He pulled away standing up and facing me.

"We're even now," he said. I looked down, and his dick was hard again hovering in front of him all 9 thick inches of it.

"Looks like someone enjoyed that" I said nodding down at the impressive piece. He blushed realizing he was hard again.

"You too!" He said smacking my dick once playfully. It bounced up and down rhythmically. I couldn't believe he'd actually touched my dick. I figured he opened the door and two could play at that game, so I smacked his sending it down and up to smack into his abs with a wet thud. He laughed and went to smack mine again. I pulled my hips back just in time for him to miss.

"Too slow" I called out playfully as I got in another slap on his that sent him doubling over to defend himself. I had a clear advantage with my longer arms, but he managed to reach in and smack my dick once more but also caught my balls in the process. I doubled over in pain.

"Oh fuck, I'm sorry, I got carried away" he said resting his hand on my shoulder to see if I was ok.

I was doubled over but soon recovered still feeling a dull ache running from my balls to the base of my dick.

"You ok? Anything I can do?" He asked looking concerned.

"Kiss um and make um better" I said holding out my tender balls.

He looked down and laughed. "You wish".

"It's the least you can do" I said grinning from ear to ear.

"Alright, if it will make you feel better." He said stooping down, so he was eye level with my balls. My cock dangled in front of his face as well. He seemed to study them both for a minute.

"You don't have to, I was only kidding" I said kicking myself for giving him an out.

He leaned in and took in a deep breath and puckered up and kissed my right testicle. My dick brushed his face leaving a slug trail of precum where it made contact near his temple. He giggled and sat back.

"That better?" He said in a fit of giggles.

"Don't forget the other one" I said. He leaned in again and kissed my left one. He lingered there with his lips in contact with my ball, and then I felt his tongue lick it, and he sucked it into his mouth rolling it around on his tongue. His beard rubbed my inner thigh making my dick jump.

He spat it out and started laughing again.

"What's so funny?" I asked.

"I frenched that one" he said laughing hysterically. I couldn't help but laugh along with him. I tried to imagine what it was like from his perspective. Had he ever done anything with a guy before? I'd never known a straight guy to be so open to licking his buddy's balls before but then again I didn't know that many straight men.

"They do feel a lot better now" I said grinning.

"Just needed some TLC" he said reaching down and resting them in the palm of his hand like he was weighing out a ball of dough before kneading it.

"I didn't get yours did I?" I said reaching out and tenderly grasping his balls.

"Nah, they can take a beating," he said and to illustrate he grabbed them with one hand, so the sack was stretched to the limit, his balls pressing into the sack, so it looked shiny. Then he took his other hand and smacked them with a loud thwack. My balls tried to climb up inside me in sympathy.

"Fuck, how can you stand that?" I said as he did it again.

"Years of my wife busting my balls I guess" he laughed, then sobered at the mention of his wife.

He let go of his balls and let them swing free in their sack.

"Sorry ..." I said not sure how to navigate his rocky relationship.

"She'll come around in a few days" he said as if he was trying to convince himself more than me.

He turned and picked up the shower nozzle that I'd left on the floor of the shower and turned it back on spraying his chest with his back to me.

"I can let you you finish," I said turning to go. The abrupt change in his mood had me wondering if I should leave him to finish showering in his own. The last thing I wanted was for things to be awkward between us.

"Can you get my back?" He asked softly.

I picked up the scrubber and some shower gel and caressed it into his skin. His shoulders relaxed as I rubbed soap onto them. The soap ran down his soft skin and gathered in the light patch of hair just above his ass crack. I slowly moved up and down his back getting all the places that were difficult to reach. His skin was surprisingly soft and a freckled reddish brown from working out on the water shirtless. It sharply contrasted with the pearly white of his ass. I hesitated a moment at the top of his ass, wondering if scrubbing his ass was beyond my current mandate.

He shifted slightly, so his ass pushed out just a bit as if signaling it was ok to proceed. I ran the scrubber down his crack and back up getting in the deep crevasse. He audibly exhaled when my bare finger came in accidental contact with his hole. His ass involuntarily pushed against my finger as if it welcomed the invasion. I pressed a soapy finger into his opening just a little to gage his reaction. It puckered up and pressed down on my finger. I inched it in a little deeper. I couldn't believe he was letting me fuck his tight hole with my finger. He pushed back again and my finger slipped inside him. He grunted as if in pain and pulled away. It was like an invisible line had been crossed.

"All good?" I asked.

"Yup, thanks" he said turning to face me. His dick was rock hard and floating in front of him inches from touching my thigh.

"Turn around," he said taking the suds filled scrubber from my hand.

"You don't have to," I said, but he did a little twirl with his finger and I turned to face the wall.

I nearly jumped when his callused fingers touched my skin. I think he must have sensed how tense I was. He dug his fingers into my shoulders stepping closer to try to use some leverage to release the knots from them. Since he was shorter than me, it meant he had to get very close and stand on his toes to reach and push down. In the process, I felt the tip of his cock press against my ass. I could feel the heat radiating off it like a hot poker.

"God you are tense," he said trying to release the knots from my muscles. Ever since the accident I'd had varying degrees of pain in the shoulders. He hands felt amazing, soothing my aching muscles. His dick caught in my ass crack and pressed in closer to my hole. I don't normally bottom but at that moment I was ready to have him sink all nine thick inches into me.

"Oh fuck" I said involuntarily cringing when he hit a sensitive spot on my bad shoulder.

"Oh sorry," he said letting go and running a finger along the scar.

"It's ok, just maybe not right there where the plate is" I said. He moved down my back and his dick slipped away from my ass. I cursed the broken collar bone for cock blocking me yet again. He used the scrubber to scrub my ass once quickly then finished.

"All good?" He asked and I turned back toward him.

"Yeah" I said though my dick didn't seem to agree. He looked down at my dick and then back up at my face seeing the longing and expectation. His dick jumped a little as if he were contemplating something. I started to bend forward ready to take his thick cock in my mouth.

Before anything more could happen he switched off the water and stepped out of the shower leaving me dripping wet. I stood for a moment watching as he toweled himself off.

"Think I'll turn in for the night" he said hanging up the towel and heading downstairs leaving both my body and my dick dripping wet. I watched his naked ass flex as he descended the stairs wondering if I should follow.

A few minutes later the lights went out downstairs. I called down "goodnight" as I headed toward the bedroom, but I got no reply. What the fuck just happened? I said to myself slipping into my bed and tugging on my still hard cock. I'd not been this hard since I was a teenager, and it wasn't going away, no matter what I did.

I lay there wrestling with what to do. I nearly got up and went downstairs in hopes he'd invite me to continue. It would be awkward if he wasn't into it, though. "Ugh" I grunted frustrated by my indecision and the mixed signals. In the end, I just lay there falling into a fitful sleep.

Chapter 6
Restless

I felt the bed shift and something press in behind me. I pushed back, feeling skin come in contact with my skin. I felt an arm reach around and fold across my neck, pulling tight against me. I could feel hot breath on my ear. I felt something large press against my hole and violently push forward. I tried to scream in pain, but a hand went over my mouth, muffling the sound. My ass gripped the invading object, feeling bumps and ridges slip into me inch by painful inch. It seemed to never end. Just when I thought it was all inside me, more came looking for room.

A raspy voice echoed in my ear as I tried to struggle to get free, but something cut into my wrists and held them and my legs down.

"You want to fuck my husband, huh?" The voice asked, and I now recognized it as belonging to Cassy.

"I... I..." I tried to explain that nothing had happened. Not really, we'd just jerked off together. Was that really cheating? My mind raced. What was she doing? How had she gotten in here, and how was I chained to the bed?

Pain gripped my ass as whatever she had inside me was violently ripped out, then slammed back into me hard. I gasped for breath.

"This is what it's like to get fucked by Evan," she said while slamming the dildo in and out of my hole. My dick reacted to the pounding of my prostate by hardening and pressing painfully into the mattress.

"We didn't do ... agh" I started to say, but she jammed the dildo so far up inside me, I could almost taste latex.

"You will," she said ominously in my ear, holding the dildo in place as my ass quivered around it.

"He eventually fucks everyone in his life" she said, letting go of the dildo and leaving it hanging out of my ass. I struggled against my restraints, until I was able to roll onto my side. I felt myself falling off the edge of the bed.

I woke up with a start, my hands wrapped up in my sheet and sweat pouring from my brow.

"What the fuck!" I said as the dream began to fade from my mind. It felt like my ass was still on fire from the imaginary dildo that had just been inside it. My dick was rock hard, unfazed by the most disturbing dream I'd had in years.

I went to the bathroom and washed my face, still trying to shake the dream from it. When I ventured downstairs, the only trace that Evan had been there were the rumpled sheets on the sofa and the lingering scent of him in the air. I looked down and spotted a white stain on the sheet where some of his cum must have landed between us.

His tools and bike were gone, along with his backpack and clothes. I hoped he would be returning this evening, but the image of Cassy wielding the dildo made me shudder. Perhaps it was for the best that I didn't get mixed up in their marital strife, especially if she was going to continue to be my neighbor.

I went about my day as usual. I cooked dinner for two in case he did turn up, and if not I'd have leftovers for another night. I binged some tv and waited until it was time for bed, but he didn't return.

As I lay in bed, a went over everything that had happened. Was I too forward? As I recalled, it was him instigating things, asking about porn, smacking my dick. So why did I feel so guilty?

I tossed and turned all night, unable to sleep for more than a few hours at a time. I kept wondering what happened to him and waking up thinking I'd heard the door open. I'd even gone downstairs a couple of times to find the sofa empty.

It was around 3am when I sat down on the sofa and pulled the cum stained sheet to my nose, smelling his scent on it. I didn't realize how much I missed his funk wafting in the door when he arrived. It had only been a couple of days, and I'd already grown accustomed to it, but now it was gone.

I stroked my hard cock, smelling the dried cum and remembering the taste of our cum as I licked it from his chest. Pressing a finger in my hole, I imagined it was his big dick opening me up. I could almost feel his balls slapping my ass as he pounded me.

I continued to stroke myself, remembering how his hairy pucker felt with my finger clamped down inside it. The way the light blond hair matted down as the water ran over it. The feel of his hands gently holding my balls. I felt my ass clench down hard as hot wetness hit my face.

I rolled over and slept on the sofa the rest of the night, smelling his scent on the pillowcase.

I didn't see Evan for a few days. I already missed his company. I had a fridge full of leftovers for two, he hadn't eaten. I assumed he must have patched things up with his wife, which on some level, I was happy about.

I saw her and their daughter out for a walk one day, but he was nowhere to be found. Not that that was unusual, he often worked late and thinking back, I'm not sure I ever saw him walk in the park together.

A decided to go out for the evening Friday night to try to distract myself from obsessing over Evan and maybe have some fun with a more willing partner.

On the latter, I struck out. The bar was filled with young twinks ordering elaborate drinks and talking in loud, screeching voices that more irritated than turned me on. I left, grabbing a Lyft home before the bars even closed.

As I headed to the door, I spotted him. He was working on his bike in front of his house.

"Hey," I said, waving to him. He waved back, then dropped his tools and walked up to my porch.

"Hey, sorry I split the other day like that, I didn't have your number, or I would have called you." He said, looking up at me with blue within blue eyes.

"It's ok, patched things up with Cassy?" I asked.

"Nah, she still won't let me in, she's away for a couple of days and I needed some things." He said, nodding at the open basement window.

I wondered how ethical it was to break into your own home when your partner was out. I dismissed the thought as none of my business in the long run.

"Where are you staying?" I asked.

"On the boat I'm working on" he said.

"Oh, I guess that makes it easier to work on it" I said.

"Yeah, but it doesn't have a shower or anything" he said, smelling his ripe pits.

"You can use my shower, and you don't have to sleep on the boat" I said.

"But ..." he started to say.

"I won't do anything" I said, and he seemed to catch my meaning.

"It's just, I thought Cassy and I would ... you know" he said.

"I know you are hoping to reconcile with her, but in the meantime or if that doesn't happen, I'm just saying you have a place to crash if you need to." I said opening the door even if he was hesitant to walk through it.

"Could I at least get cleaned up?" He asked.

"Sure, come on in," I said.

"You know where it is," I said, heading to the kitchen for some water.

I heard the water turn on above me and wished I was up there with him. My dick pressed uncomfortably against my jeans, thinking about him naked above me in the shower. I was frustrated at striking out at the bar and longed to slip into bed and jerk off to fall asleep. I grabbed the sheets from the dryer, spread them out on the sofa, just in case he decided to stay the night after all.

I heard the shower turn off. I flipped through my feeds, seeing pictures of hot guys scroll past. I spotted one that looked a lot like Evan. I lingered on the set of pictures of the model, comparing and contrasting him to my memory of Evan naked next to me on this very sofa. I heard the stairs creek and looked up to find him descending them naked. I quickly hit the power on my phone and the image disappeared.

"You sure it's ok I stay?" He asked.

"The sofa is all made up for you" I said, nodding down at the sheet. He came over and sat down next to me, his soft dick resting on his leg.

"Ok, I'll let you go to bed" I said, standing up to head back upstairs.

"I'm still wired, you wanna maybe watch something with me?" he asked. My heart skipped several beats thinking about the last time we watched a movie together.

"Sure, I'm still wide awake" I lied, I was ready to hit the hay, but I couldn't pass up and invitation like that. "What do you want to watch?" I asked, fumbling for the remote.

"You know ..." he said, reaching down and grabbing hold of his own remote.

"Oh" I said, now much more awake, especially my dick. I handed him my phone and let him browse the selections on my goto porn site.

A moment later, the screen lit up with a beautiful blond with big tits sucking a rather large attractive cock. I wasn't sure if I should strip down or just remain clothed.

"Join me?" He asked, looking down at his naked body and up at me. I had my answer. I stripped off my shirt and shucked my jeans faster than I'd ever done in my life. My dick leaped to be free. I sat down next to him, closer than I probably should have, given how much available space there was. If I moved my leg just an inch, it would be touching his. He had his growing cock cradled under his hand, lightly tugging on it, hiding most of the shaft from view. His full balls pulled up with each light stroke. It took all my effort to keep from leaning over and licking them. I respected that he didn't want to cheat on his wife while they were still working things out, so I let him set the pace. The last thing I wanted was to be a home wrecker and the cause for their break-up.

When I looked back at the screen, I was shocked to find that the beautiful blond had an equally nice shaved cock arching up toward her abs. The guy who'd been getting the blow job was now licking the tip of her cock as she played with her wide nipples.

While it wasn't exactly my thing, I'm pretty open-minded about trans porn. Given the choice, I preferred a hot hairy trans man, though. But it was Evan's choice, so I wasn't going to complain.

"Holy shit! She's got a big dick" he said excitedly. Guess the fact that she also had breasts made it "ok" somehow ok to talk about her dick.

We watched in silence and furtively stroked our cocks. I was still much more interested in what was going on next to me than what was on the screen.

He'd begun to more openly stroke himself. I felt his leg brush up against mine. It moved away a moment later, then came back. This time it remained pressed against mine. The sensation was electrifying. I pressed my leg against his, mirroring his pressure.

We stroked as the tension between us mounted. I wanted to take it to the next level, but I didn't want to do anything he didn't want to do. As if reading my mind, he placed his hand on my knee, then slowly moved it up my thigh. My dick jumped and drooled, an excessive amount of precum down my fist. He looked over at me when his hand reached my balls. He lightly patted them and smiled.

"They've recovered?" He asked.

"Yup" I said, then wished I'd said they needed some more TLC, but the moment had passed. He gently rubbed them anyway, then moved up to the base of my dick. I let go, and he wrapped his fingers around my shaft, just feeling the heft of it.

"Damn you've got a big one" he said, shaking it around and slapping it against my abs.

I reached over and grabbed hold of his like he'd done with mine and did the same.

"You've got quite the monster here too." I said, playfully manhandling him.

"Feels weird holding another guy's dick" he said, but didn't let go.

"Feels good though" I said tentatively running my hand up his shaft and back down. He sighed and closed his eyes. He continued to hold my dick by the base while I stroked his cock a few more times. My precum combined with his, slicking up his pole as I worked it.

I felt his hand move up my shaft and looked to see his eyes were open again, and he was focused on my dick. His mouth hung open slightly, and his lips looked wet and inviting. I wanted to lean over and kiss those soft lips and feel his beard rub against my face.

He clumsily mirrored my strokes on his cock. His grip was just a little too tight for my liking, but I wasn't going to complain and risk breaking the spell. It was incredible just to have him touch me and let me touch him.

If he was willing to do this, I thought maybe he'd be up for something more. My mouth watered to get around that beautiful thick cock, to taste the soft flesh, to run my tongue around the ridge along that wide head.

"Can I suck it?" I asked, leaning in toward his dick. I sensed his dick would have welcomed my warm mouth around it, but his hand went up and held me back. I'd let my hormones get the better of me and taken it too far.

I sat back, still holding his cock. Perhaps, he was one of those guys that thought a hand job wasn't cheating, while anything more crossed an invisible line. I accepted his limits but continued to stroke him. He didn't let go of my cock but seemed to loosen his death grip, which was a good thing. I sensed there was now some awkwardness between us.

The video had stopped playing, having ended on the last frame of the blond's face and tits covered in great splotches of cum.

"Something else?" I asked. He looked up at the screen, seeming to just notice that the clip had ended. He nodded, and I grabbed my phone and thumbed through the list. I found a MMF threesome and hit play. It was straight into the action. A dark-haired woman was holding one thick cock in her hand, stroking it while she sucked on an equally large one.

He watched the action on the screen, avoiding looking at me and where my hand was or where his hand was. I resumed stroking him, kicking myself for making it awkward by asking to give him a blowjob. His dick jumped, and I looked back at the screen. The second guy had dropped to his knees next to the woman, and now they both were sucking the hairy guy's cock, trading off licking his shaft and balls.

I stroked him harder with a firmer grasp than I usually used on myself. Evan seemed to like this. Like he'd demonstrated with his balls, his dick didn't seem to mind a little roughness. He grunted softly as his balls tightened. He'd all but given up on stroking me, yet his hand was still clutching my dick. He would periodically squeeze it, coinciding with times when his dick would thicken as he got closer.

"Of fuck," he whimpered as the hairy guy inserted his dick into the ass of the smaller guy, while he in turn ate out the woman's pussy. Her fake sounding screams filled the room, drowning out the more subtle sounds of the guys grunting while fucking and being fucked.

I leaned forward and held my head over his dick but went no further. He gave me a worried look for a second, but his march toward orgasm had already begun, and there was no turning back now. I felt his dick expand in my hand and his balls press in against him tightly. I tugged at his balls hard just as he started to cum. I felt the first jet hit my cheek. It felt like hot candle wax dripping down my skin. I didn't have time to contemplate it as blast after blast hit me. It landed on my nose and my upper lip.

I opened my mouth wide, creating a larger target for the cum to hit. I was rewarded with a burst of cum dead center on my tongue. I savored the taste as his body shook with spasms. I held his cock tight in my fist at the base, stretching the already tight skin to nearly the breaking point. Evan grunted, and his balls pumped out another load that I greedily swallowed. His cum was bitter like a good hoppy IPA but also a little buttery and earthy. Before I realized it, my tongue had made contact with the head of his dick, and I was licking out his piss slit, probing for more nectar. He grabbed my head and pulled me back and away as he grew dangerously sensitive to touch. I reluctantly let go of his cock.

I was so enthralled with his dick, I didn't realize the effect his tight grasp was having on my member. It pulsed wildly as the waves of pleasure washed over me. Cum shot out and landed in the middle of my chest. Evan held on tightly as I continued to explode.

My eruptions began to subside and dribbling down my shaft and over Evan's fingers. Finally, he let go of my cock, holding his cum covered hand in front of his face.

"Sorry about that" I said, licking the rest of his cum from my lips.

"No worries, guess it comes with the territory," he said, then brought his hand closer to his face and sniffed it. For a moment, I thought he might lick up the cum, but he moved his hand away from his face and made to get up.

I stopped the video and went to the kitchen to get a towel. I heard Evan climb the stairs and head into the bathroom. It was very late, but thankfully I didn't have to work in the morning. Fatigue began to catch up with me. I headed upstairs to bed, passing Evan coming out of the bathroom.

"Good night" he said.

"Good night" I said, smiling. He turned and headed down to the sofa while I headed to the bedroom, wishing he was following me.

Chapter 7

Playground

It was nearly noon when I woke up the following morning. I heard one of the neighbor's out back running a circular saw. That was a typical sound for a Saturday morning, these houses always needed something done on them.

I went downstairs to find the sofa empty once again. I was a bit disappointed, and worried I'd scared him off again last night. Did we really jerk each other off? I had to check my browser history to prove to myself I'd not dreamt the whole thing.

I made some coffee and headed into the backyard to relax in the shade of the tree. I heard the saw stop and a head pop up over the fence.

"Morning, hope I didn't wake you" said Jake, the hunky father of two that lived next to me.

"No, it's all good" I said, sipping my coffee and wishing my fence wasn't so high. He was shirtless and had a decent body, with a hairy patch in the middle of his chest that formed into a neat line that disappeared into his shorts. He often worked in the yard or jogged around the neighborhood shirtless, so I called up the details from memory. My memories also included plenty of speculation about the size of the bulge in his short running shorts. On more than one occasion, I'd caught myself drooling over the package and the clearly visible cock head pressing into the fabric.

We were on friendly terms, meaning a "hello" when we passed each other in the street, but not much more.

He stayed at the fence, looking like we wanted to ask something, but was maybe afraid to.

"I saw Evan this morning ..." he started to say. My heart felt like it was in my throat.

"Oh," I couldn't help but blush before I was able to recover. "Yeah, I'm letting him sleep on my couch until he can work things out with Cassy."

"Oh ok" he said, "I saw him leave out the back earlier ..."

I worried that we'd become the subject of neighborhood gossip.

"I saw him sleeping in his car the other day and offered to let him crash with me," I said.

"Yeah, I heard them fighting again. You think they'll get back together?" He asked. In the back of my mind, I kinda hoped they didn't, and the odds were not in their favor.

"He's hoping they do" I said diplomatically. He wiped a bead of sweat from his forehead, and I imagined licking up the sweat running down his hairy chest and his ripe pits. It seemed like we wanted to say something more but left it at that.

"Guess I should finish before it gets too hot." He said.

"Whatcha building?" I asked, getting up and heading to the fence.

"A swing set for the girls" he said. I peered over the fence to find an array of lumber strewn around the yard. I watched his back muscles flex as he bent forward to pick up a 2×4 and place it on the sawhorse. He grabbed a pencil from behind his ear and measured before marking a line across the wood. The perspiration ran down his back, seeping into his light gray sweat shorts. The top of his crack and the wiry hairs in it were visible for an inch above his waistband. Below the waistband, a damp patch ran down his crack, making the material stick to his tight cheeks.

What was it with me and lusting after my straight neighbors? I was now thankful for the height of the fence, as it hid my growing arousal. An ear slitting whine commenced as he cut the 2×4, his biceps bulging as he held the saw steady.

"Hey, could you give me a hand?" Jake asked, pulling off the earphones and safety goggles. I fumbled for a minute trying to push my hardening dick into a position that didn't show. The manipulation only made matters worse. What a time to only be wearing a pair of thin jogging shorts.

"Ah sure" I said heading to my gate.

"Can you hold this up while I secure it?" He asked, holding a beam over his head and nodding to another set of beams. I grew weak in the knees when I saw his thick hairy pits and strong arms holding the beam. I was attempting to hide my semi-hard cock behind my hand, but I had to grab the a-frame piece with both hands to keep it from falling over. I began to blush, hoping Jake wouldn't see the clear outline of my dick in my shorts. If he did, he made no mention of it. He grabbed the cross-beam and lifted it into place. I felt the heat radiating off his body, as he stood close behind me, fastening a bolt in place and tightening it. I felt something graze my ass as he tightened the next bolt. The odor of his pits was nearly overwhelming as he reached up from behind me and tightened another bolt. I looked over to find his arm pit just inches from my face. I could almost taste the funky, salty sweat on my tongue. Once again, I felt something brush up against my ass. It could have only been one thing. I instinctively pushed my ass out and felt the heat radiating off his dick as it pressed into the thin material separating us.

All too soon, he stepped back as the last bolt was secured.

"Grab that one" he said, nodding downward. I turned and saw something else besides the a-frame he intended for me to pick up. His sweat shorts seemed to bulge out just a bit more than normal and now the rim of his helmet head was clearly visible along with a wet spot. The wet spot could have just been sweat running off his chest and down the front of his shorts, but I preferred to imagine it was precum forming at the tip of his cock.

I grabbed the a-frame and lifted it into place. Once again, Jake came up behind me and pressed in close as he put each bolt in place.

His dick felt like it was hardening as it rubbed along my crack. I wanted to pull down my shorts and let his cock rest between my cheeks. I longed for this straight god to bend me over the sawhorse and fuck me raw right there for all the neighbors to see.

"That's got it." He said, breaking up the vision I had of him plowing my ass. He stepped away and tugged at the structure to show it was securely fastened.

"All it needs now are the swings," he said proudly.

"Look's good," I said, but my attention was focused on anything but the swing set at the time. I was trying to make out if the imprint of his cock had indeed grown or if it was my lust fueled imagination. He noticed me looking and reached down to adjust himself.

"Thanks for your help" he said, wiping the sweat from his forehead and grinning.

"Sure, if you need help with anything else let me know" I said, hoping he'd take my offer to include helping him with the growing python in his shorts.

"I should be able to get it from here," he said, dashing my hopes but saving my knees.

I bid him goodbye and headed back into my yard. I sipped my now lukewarm coffee as I caught glimpses of him through the slats in the fence.

My cock continued to grow and snake down my shorts now that I was out of direct line of view. I was tempted to go inside and rub one out but hoped Evan would be back again this evening.

Instead, I ran some errands and returned later in the afternoon loaded down with shopping bags.

"Need a hand?" Evan said coming up the sidewalk. He unlocked the door and put down his tool boxes.

"Sure" I said, handing him the bags I had and turning to grab the rest from the car. I returned with the rest of the groceries and set them on the counter. He was already stooping down to put the frozen items in the freezer. I gazed longingly at the inch or so of hairy ass crack peeking out from his shorts. He turned to grab some more items. Bits of grime and motor oil stained his arms and bare chest. His shorts left little to the imagination, his plump dick pressing into the fabric, outlining his shaft and cut head.

"Where'd you go earlier?" I asked.

"Back to the boat to do some work on it" he said. "I finally got the part I'd been waiting on".

"So it's almost done?" I asked, unpacking the rest of the items.

"Yeah, it's done, just need to take it out for a test run" he said.

"Cool" I said.

"You want to come with me?" He asked. I recalled his talk about stripping down when he got out on the water and thought it would be a great way to get naked with him again.

"Sure, when?" I asked.

"We could go now, just need to clean up first." He said, looking down at his arms and chest.

"Sure, I didn't have any plans this afternoon besides the shopping" I said, giddy with excitement at the prospect of a naked boat ride. He headed to the stairs while I busied myself straightening up the kitchen.

"I could use someone to wash my back" He said as he started up the stairs.

I wasn't sure I heard him right, but I put down the rag and nearly ran up the stairs, pulling off my shirt as I went.

When I got to the bathroom, he was already undressed and the shower was running. He spotted me coming in and smiled. Guess I didn't need to wait for the boat to have some naked time with him.

"Are you sure?" I asked before a dropped my shorts. He nodded and I let them fall. He turned and faced the wall, letting the spray run sideways down his back. I stepped into the shower with him and shut the door. It was a tight fit, which only made me step in closer.

My dick had started growing when he came in and was now fully hard and aching for relief after the teasing it had gotten from Jake next door.

I grabbed some soap and began to lather up my hands before pressing them into his shoulders. He sighed as I worked my way down his strong back muscles while he worked at the grease on his hands. His pits were ripe from working out in the sun. I leaned in close and sniffed his soft skin. I wanted to lick them, like when he'd licked our cum from my side. I didn't know where we stood, though. Would he let me go further this time?

He let out a soft moan as my hands moved down his back and reached the top of his ass. I worked his lower back, massaging the soap into it with my thumbs on either side of his spine. He leaned forward and pushed out his ass, allowing me to better get at the tight muscles.

As he did, my cock grazed his left ass cheek. I felt him tense up, so I moved away, breaking the contact with his skin.

He pushed back further, deliberately restoring the connection. I pressed my dick onto his bare flesh, feeling his tight ass give and press back into me. I moved up his back to his shoulders and moved closer, so my dick slid into his crack. It slid up his crack toward his lower back as I focused on his shoulders. He pushed back his ass and let my fully hard cock rest in his ass cleft.

I couldn't help by press forward and feel the warmth of his skin and the soft hairs rub along the length of my shaft. If I wasn't careful, I could find myself slipping down and plowing this straight boy's ass raw. The thought made my heart pound in my chest and my dick pulse. I don't normally produce a lot of precum, but I could see some leaking into the middle of his lower back.

"This ok" I asked, humping his crack with more intensity.

"You remember in the video, when the guy did that to the other guy's ass" he said.

"Yeah" I said.

"I can't stop thinking about it, what's it like?" he asked.

His hand moved down and grasped his dick. I leaned forward and looked over his shoulder to see he was fully hard, with his right hand gently moving up and down his shaft.

"You want to find out?" I asked, stepping back and letting the water run down his back and hairy crack. He gave me a non-committal nod like he wanted it more than anything but didn't want to seem like he was asking.

I ran my hand over his crack, rinsing out the soap. I felt my finger glide across his pucker. I couldn't take it anymore, I stooped down behind him with the water spray hitting my face and buried my tongue between his ass cheeks.

He gasped as it came in contact with his hole. He pushed out his ass as I began to lick and suck and chew on his hole.

"Fuck!" he let out with a sigh.

I pulled his cheeks apart and let the water run over his ass ring. It was surrounded by soft dirty blond hair that waved back and forth as the current caught it. I marveled at how perfect and tight it looked. I longed to stretch it out and wreck it with my thick cock.

I dove in again, this time pressing the tip of my tongue into his opening, trying to pry open his vice-like grip. He whimpered as I invaded his hole. His stroked his cock furiously with his fist tight around his shaft. My tongue pressed in, maybe half an inch. He was so tight, I didn't stand a chance of getting my cock in there without a lot of prep work and a bucket of lube. I contented myself that I was making him squirm just with my tongue.

His balls hung down between his legs and bounced as he stroked himself. I licked down from his ass and tugged on his balls, being a little more rough with them than I would have with anyone else. He'd already demonstrated a high tolerance for pain in his testicles, so I manhandled them and pulled them back between his legs. I sucked one into my mouth, letting the other bounce on my chin. One ball was almost too much to fit in my mouth, so there was no way to get both in. I felt them tighten as he tugged on his dick like he was getting close, and they were getting ready to deliver their seed.

They tightened and pulled up against him as his body shook. I switched back to his hole and felt it quiver around my tongue as his load shot onto the wall. I thought it was a waste to not have his cum in my mouth, but I was also enjoying the way his ass was clenching each time he sprayed more cum on the wall.

"Fuck!" He grunted as cum dripped off his fingers and onto the shower floor to be swept away into the maelstrom of the drain. His legs were shaking and mine were crying out in pain from stooping for so long. I stood up and let them stretch out.

It only took a couple of strokes for my dick to unleash a torrent that hit the middle of his back. The globs of cum stuck in the hair above his ass and rolled down him. I leaned forward and licked up the cum, going back to his hole one last time. I pressed my cum soaked tongue into his hole as if I'd just fucked him raw and delivered my seed into him.

His hand went to the back of my head and I thought for a moment he was going to push me away. But instead, he held my head to keep my tongue in place as the last aftershocks of his orgasm rocked his body.

Finally, he let go, and I felt the spray run cold on my cheek. The rest of my load slowly made its way to the drain, circling his as if orbiting together like binary stars caught in the gravity of a black hole.

Chapter 8
Boat Trip

I heard the doorbell and a light knocking on the door. I scrambled to grab my clothes from where I'd dropped them as I raced to the door, leaving Evan in the bathroom toweling off. My hair was still dripping wet when I reached the door and peeked through the window.

On the other side stood Jake. He spotted me, flashed a glimmering white smile and held up a case of beer. I opened the door, nervously glancing back over my shoulder to make sure Evan wasn't coming down the stairs naked or something.

"I wanted to thank you for helping me out earlier." He said, holding up the beer.

"That wasn't necessary" I said. Later, I wished I had added, "happy to help out a neighbor". I would have helped him out of those shorts he was wearing and helped take care of that cock of his in a heartbeat.

"Nat is out with the kids the rest of the day, so I have some free time, wanted to see if you wanted to watch the game" he said. Jake had never invited me to watch a sporting event with him before. Apart from the polite greetings in the street, we'd hardly talked at all.

We'd hung out at a couple of the neighborhood block parties, but again it was just mostly friendly banter like "Where do you work?" and "Can you believe they are raising the water rates again?" But here he was out of the blue with beer in hand and ready to hang. Could it have anything to do with the tension I felt as we put the swing set together?

"Oh hey" said Evan, coming down the stairs. It was with great relief that I turned to see he at least had his shorts back on.

"We were just heading to take the boat I've been working on out on the water, wanna join us?" Evan asked. So much for my plans to get naked with Evan again.

"Sure, let me text my wife and let her know" Jake said, pulling his phone from his pocket and setting down the beer. I packed some sunscreen and towels into a backpack and grabbed my cooler, filling it with all the ice I had in the freezer. I added some beer I had in the fridge to what Jake had brought and we set off. Jake's wife and kids were using their SUV, so we took Evan's truck to the waterfront.

Though a maze of docks, Evan led us to the boat. There must have been hundreds of boats in all different shapes and sizes. He led us to a sleek looking, 25 foot motorboat with a navy hull and white interior.

"She's a beaut!" Jake said, stepping from the dock onto the deck as it rocked gently.

"Pity she isn't mine" Evan said wistfully.

I'd been on a few boats, but most of them had been cruise ships. I passed Jake the cooler, then hopped aboard myself. Evan busied himself untying lines and checking the engines before pushing us away from the dock.

He seemed in his element on the water like this. He moved about the boat like he was a ballet dancer, gliding from one place to the next. I could imagine him being a deckhand or captain of a ship in another life. As we left the harbor and headed into the channel, Jake stripped off his shirt and grabbed a beer from the cooler.

"I need to get me a boat" he said smiling as he relaxed into one of the two swivel deck chairs anchored to the deck. Evan stood at the helm, peering out at the open bay through mirrored sunglasses.

I was the only one still wearing a shirt. I felt a little self conscious about my shoulder but figured when in Rome and stripped off as well. I caught Jake getting a glimpse of my body as I took the seat next to him. Maybe my suspicion about the earlier tension wasn't just my imagination. With my sunglasses on, I could more easily stare at his crotch looking for signs of movement without the fear of getting caught.

"War wound?" Jake asked pointing to the red scar.

"Something like that, had a bad tumble off my bike during a race" I said.

"You raced bikes?" He asked.

"Yeah nothing serious, just some local races. This pit and end to that", I said.

"Sorry to hear that, does it hurt?" Jake asked.

"Sometimes, especially when it's cold or it rains" I said.

I looked up to watch Evan at the wheel, his lithe arms making adjustments at the throttle that rippled down his back. He was barefoot with only his thin shorts which I knew from experience were all that stood between us and his bare ass.

"This is the life" I said as we sped up, and the wind whipped through my hair. You couldn't ask for a more perfect day to go boating. The bay was calm as glass and the sky was a pure blue with only the wispiest clouds to mar its surface.

Evan ran the rebuilt engines through their paces, making wild turns and loops while shouting into the wind. It was exhilarating and more than a little frightening. I gripped the hand hold tightly until my knuckles turned white.

Evan slowed the boat and pulled into a quiet cove, then cut the engines. He made several more adjustments to the throttle and then turned to face us.

"That was a rush" Jake said, handing Evan a beer from the cooler.

"Nice, huh?" He said popping the tab on the beer.

"Very nice!" Jake said already finished his first beer and grabbing his next one from the cooler. I nursed mine, not wanting to get too hammered. That could be dangerous around these two.

The boat rocked softly with the wake of other boats well off in the distance. We had the small cove to ourselves. This would have been the perfect spot to strip down. We probably would have been naked already had it not been for Jake here with us.

The back part of the boat was an open flat deck perfect for sunbathing, so I decided to get up and lay out my towel to get just a touch of sun.

"That looks like a great idea, you mind?" Jake said, nodding to the extra towels I'd brought along.

"I brought extras for you" I said, applying lotion to my arms and face.

"Good idea," Jake said, taking the lotion bottle and dabbing some on his arms.

Evan joined us, taking the other towel, he laid it out on the other side of me. He looked at Jake, then at me, then, to my utter shock, dropped his shorts and laid down on the towel naked.

Jake spit out the mouthful of beer he'd just swigged and went into a coughing fit when he turned and saw Evan naked.

Chapter 9

Fun in the Sun

"**O**h, sorry," he said, grabbing his shirt to clean up the mess.

"Hope it's ok, this is what I like to do when I get out here" Evan said, beaming at us, his dick resting heavily across his thigh.

Jake eyed him and then me.

"Fine by me, I guess" he finally said, looking around sheepishly.

"When in Rome..." I said shucking my shorts as well. I was shaking with excitement and desperately hoping we could convince Jake to join us. Jake's eyes grew wide at the sight of us both naked on the deck below him.

"Come on, join us" Evan encouraged. Jake looked around one more time and his face grew red, as if he'd already started to burn.

"I don't know" he said. The lump in his shorts looked like it had doubled in size.

He turned away from us, slipped his thumbs under the waistband of his shorts then hunkered down as if someone might see him, then lowered them the rest of the way.

"I can't believe I'm doing this" he said, sitting down on his towel. His body blocked my view of his crotch from this angle, but I could see his bare ass where it met the towel and the stripe of dark hair leading down into his crack. He sat up for a while, seeming afraid to lay back and expose himself so completely.

I looked over and found Evan also eyeing Jake.

They'd known each other better than they knew me, being dads of young kids, they had a lot more in common with each other and a lot more opportunities to hang out, in the park or at the playground. If I hung out at the playground I'd get weird looks for sure.

"Relax dude, he's cool," Evan said, and to illustrate how it was done, he leaned back and put his hands behind his head. I wondered what he meant by the last part, but it seemed to relax Jake. He looked back at me then laid back.

"You won't say anything?" Evan said.

"What's there to say? I get naked with a bunch of guys at the gym all the time, no big deal" I said.

"Yeah, I guess you're right" Jake said, leaning back finally. I got a quick glimpse of his body before I laid back as well. The hair that gathered between his pecs funneled down to his navel in a cascade of dark brown before it melded with his trimmed pubes. I could only see the base of his cock, as the rest hung down between his legs. I wanted desperately an excuse to get up and see more.

"Oh shit, almost forgot to get down there, hand me the lotion" I asked Jake sitting back up. He sat up and grabbed the tube.

"Oh yeah, good point, I don't want to get a sunburned dick" he said.

"That wouldn't be pleasant" Evan said, sitting up.

Jake squeezed some lotion into his palm before handing the tube to me. I watched as his hand ran down his abs, spreading the white goo into his pubes and down his legs before grabbing his soft cock. As he worked it in, I got a clearer view of it. He was uncut, with a foreskin that hung over the head. The head was big and thick, giving the impression of a python that had eaten a large rodent. It was a shade darker than his skin. He pulled back the hood, revealing a wide head and paler skin on the top half of his cock. With the manipulation, his dick definitely looked like it was starting to swell.

I squeezed some out directly onto my dick, then held the bottle over Evan's crotch. He gave a nervous laugh and nodded. Air trapped in the tube came out with the lotion and made a spray across his dick and balls like he's just cum all over himself.

"A bit premature there" Jake laughed, looking down at the mess I'd made. Evan chuckled and made a show of slathering his dick and balls with it. Jake chuckled as well, shaking his head.

Satisfied we'd covered all the important bits, we laid back down on our towels. I tried desperately not to pop a boner. But the rocking of the waves and the cool breezes across my crotch, not to mention the mere fact that I had two incredibly hot daddies on either side, ate away at my resolve.

"Someone is enjoying this a bit too much" Jake said. I turned my head to see he'd sat up a little and was gazing down at my growing dick. I tried to hide it under my hand, though I couldn't adequately conceal it.

"Sorry, I can't help it," I said.

"When the boat's a rock'n" Evan said, also sitting up. He, too, looked like he was on his way to becoming fully hard.

"I'm glad I'm not the only one" he said, smacking his dick against his leg. I sat up, wanting to see what was producing the thud I could hear clearing emanating from his thigh.

"Damn, you two make me look like I've got a toddler's penis" he said looking down at his dick. It was maybe 3 inches soft but seemed to be growing. He looked over at our hard 8 and 9 inches respectively.

"Cassy always complains I'm too big, and it hurts," Evan said.

"I've never had a problem that a liberal application of lube and adjustment time didn't solve," I said.

"No complaints like that here" Jake said, idly pulling down his foreskin and then bunching it back up.

"You have that advantage over us" Evan said, indicating the Jake's foreskin.

"I bet you could stretch out that foreskin, so it's as long as us" I said. And Jake did just that, he had pulled it out as far as it would go, which was impressively far.

"Damn, I kinda wish they hadn't chopped me" Evan said.

"Yeah, it may not look as nice as this but, I bet it feels so much better" I said.

"I can't believe we're comparing dicks like school kids at sleep away camp." Jake said.

"Just that one time at band camp," Evan said, and we all cracked up. It was kinda surreal to be overtly watching each other play with our cocks like this out in the open. There was something thrilling about it. All I wanted to do was take Jake's cock in my mouth and Evan's cock in my ass under the bright blue sky.

"Time to flip over" Jake said.

"That's easier to do for some" Evan said, trying to roll over and finding his cock kept him from laying flat. I watched his hard cock pound the towel like he was fucking it a couple of times.

"Can someone do my back?" Jake asked.

"I'd be happy too" Evan said, swinging his fat cock in Jake's direction. Evan and I burst out laughing.

"Pervs! You know what I meant," Jake retorted.

I grabbed the tube and squirted a glob of lotion onto Jake's back, just above the hairy patch north of his ass crack.

"He spooged all over you," Evan shouted, bursting into a fit of giggles. It did kinda look like I'd left an impressive load in the small of his back.

"Ha ha, very funny" Jake said, wiggling his butt.

I reached down and spread the lotion up his back and over his shoulders and neck. Then moved down, pushing it along his back and sides. His ass was perfect, plump yet muscular and covered in a fine coating of soft dark brown hair. The hair above his ass crack looked like an arrow pointing to where to insert my cock.

I was conflicted, I had a perfectly legitimate reason for continuing down and over his ass, but I worried if he would think so. I massaged the lotion into his skin, inching closer and closer to his ass cheeks. Finally, I just went for it. My dick was hard and dripping as I slid my greasy hands down both hairy globes. I could feel the muscles clench as I moved over them. He didn't object, so I continued down his legs, applying more cream as his thick leg hair soaked it up. I moved back up his legs, seeing his heavy ball sack resting between his legs. I lightly grazed his balls as I moved up his inner thighs. I spread apart his ass cheeks to rub some lotion along his crack.

"Gettin in the danger zone there" Evan said, smiling. He and I both knew what I'd done to his danger zone earlier. He seemed to enjoy watching me work on Jake's most private areas.

I lingered as long as I could reasonably linger on his ass before sitting back.

"My turn," Evan said, trying to figure out a good place to put his still very hard cock, so I could rub his back. I straddled his legs, making it obvious my dick was resting on his leg just below his asshole. Jake turned his head to watch as I gave Evan the same treatment I'd given him.

He smiled and pumped his ass a few times, pressing his dick into his towel.

I leaned in and got Evan's shoulders, letting my dick slid up his crack. Jake's eyes grew wide as he watched what must have looked like my dick slipping into Evan's hole. Actually, it only slid down between his legs and grazed his balls. I got more daring with Evan, knowing what he'd already allowed me to do, and I ran my finger down his ass crack and pressed it to his opening. He sucked in a breath as I penetrated him with my finger, just barely half an inch.

I heard Jake mutter "fuck" under his breath as he watched. Evan's dick pressed painfully out the side of his pelvis as I pushed down on his ass.

"Damn, at least buy me dinner first" Evan said, pulling away when he looked over and realized Jake was watching.

"I already did, the steaks are in the fridge" I retorted.

"Haha good one. A bbq sounds really nice" Jake said.

"You got plans? I'm sure there's enough for the three of us" I offered.

"I'm on my own for dinner, my wife is going out with her mother." He said, scrunching up his face.

"You don't get along?" I asked.

"She is not my favorite person in the world. I think the feeling is mutual. So I try to avoid her as much as I can" Jake said.

"Cassy's mom is the devil! I swear, she's always hated me, never thought I was good enough for her daughter" Evan said.

"Amen to that, brother!" Jake said. "Be glad you are single".

"I'm happy to be single for now, but I'd settle down for the right guy" I said.

"And what's the right guy to you?" Jake asked.

"Kind, a good sense of humor ..." I started.

"And an enormous dick, so I guess that eliminates you" Evan said to Jake.

"Oh haha. And I guess having a good sense of humor eliminates you" he jabbed back.

"He's got you there" I said, "but seriously, as I get older, I've become less concerned about him having a big dick. I'm looking for someone with more intangible qualities ... you know, like having a cute butt!" I said, smacking both their asses and laughing. They both laughed at my little joke.

It got quieter after that, like we were all thinking about something but no one wanted to be the first to say anything. We lay baking in the sun for a while as it slowly grew lower in the sky.

"Don't know about you, but I could use some relief" Evan said, rolling into his back. His dick was hard again, or maybe it had never stopped being hard. He began to stroke it while fondling his balls. Was I dreaming again, or was this really happening?

Chapter 10
A Secret Revealed

I looked to Jake for his reaction. He rolled over and grinned at Evan. His dick was hard and pulsing as It hovered over his abs. It was maybe 6 inches hard, the foreskin pulled back a little from the head. It had thickened a bit in addition to growing longer.

"I hardly ever get time like this alone anymore" he said, moving his hand to his dick. What was going on here? They were teasing me, right?

"You serious?" I said rolling over as well. I was instantly hard and having a difficult time deciding which way I wanted to look. Both views were equality appealing. Jake looked over at me and Evan pumping out dicks and smiled.

"Too bad this thing doesn't have a tv, we could put on some porn." He said, winking at Evan.

"Damn I've missed our game nights" Evan replied. I felt like they were speaking in code. Evan seemed to sense my confusion.

"Ok to tell him?" He asked Jake.

"Sure, it's pretty obvious now anyway" Jake said. I was still puzzled, or maybe a little out of it from the sun and beer.

"You remember I told you a buddy and I used to jack off to porn together?" Evan asked.

"Sure," I said, then looked at Jake smirking at me. Realization dawned on me all at once. My mouth hung open wide in surprise.

It made perfect sense now, I hadn't imagined the sexual tension between us.

"We got drunk one night watching the game at my place, it ran into overtime and got late. I think I passed out at one point and when I woke up this one had his dick out" Jake said.

"I thought you were asleep. Cassy frowns on me jerking off, so I figured I'd rub one out quick before I headed home." Evan said.

"She doesn't let you jerk off?" I asked in shock.

"If she catches me, she gets kinda mad, thinks it's like cheating" Evan said.

"'That's a little nuts" I said.

"My wife doesn't care if I do it, she's caught me loads of times, if she's in the mood, she joins me, otherwise she just rolls her eyes and leaves me to it" Jake said.

"Must be nice. So I'm jerking off, and he catches me and says mind if I join you" Evan said.

"No, I said, 'you enjoying yourself?'" Jake corrected, "then you got all embarrassed, then I said 'I could use some relief too'. Then you said 'join me'"

"So you started it?" I asked Evan. He got red in the face.

"I guess I did," he admitted, "but you were the one that put on the porn".

"Guilty" Jake said as he tugged on his foreskin over his head then let it roll back exposing the head like a turtle coming out of its shell. The head was wet and shimmered in the afternoon sun.

I couldn't believe what I was hearing. My two straight neighbors had been jerking off together.

"How long ago was this?" I asked.

"Been a couple years, then the pandemic happened, and we couldn't get together anymore, and then we just never got back into it" Jake's said.

Evan was holding his hand over his hard cock, rubbing his frenulum subtly. I shinny pearl of clear liquid formed at the tip of Evan's cock, caught the sunlight and shone like a diamond. I watched them both like I was watching a tennis match. My dick was impossibly hard and could have exploded at the slightest touch. They were both looking at me and each other as well. It seemed like they hesitated just playing a little, not wanting to be the first to cross a line into full on jacking off.

Since I was the most comfortable with other's guy's dicks, I broke the ice by confidently stroking my dick for both of them to see. I'd be an elite competitor if jerking off was an Olympic sport. I was dying to know how it all went down between them after that. Did they just pull out their dicks and start stroking in the open, or did they hide them inside their shorts? Did they watch each other or just look straight ahead at whatever porn was playing? Had they helped each other out? So many questions, but I tried to restrain myself. I wanted to reach out and touch them so badly.

"So you would get together and just like whip it out?" I finally asked, still trying to get my head around it.

"This one isn't shy, plenty of times we'd be watching the game, and I'd look over to see he had his dick out." Jake said.

"You insist on watching Baseball, what else is there to do between innings?" Evan laughed. He was now stroking himself more casually.

"And all you've done is jerk off to porn?" I asked.

"Well ... I did ask if he would help a brother out, but he wouldn't," Jake said, smirking.

"Maybe if you had done it first ... I might have returned the favor," Evan admitted.

"Oh yeah? And I'm just learning this now." Jake said with mock outrage then added, "Of course, knowing you, you'd have left me with blue balls after I finished you off".

"I've missed game night" Evan said, looking directly at Jake's dick.

"Yeah me too" Jake said watching Evan move his hand up and down his enormous member.

"Get a room you two" I said jokingly.

"That offer still stands?" Jake asked.

"Sure, I guess" Evan said. I was feeling a bit like a third wheel.

"You've got a gay guy here that would be more than happy to help you both out" I said.

"You've got a point there" Jake said and Evan nodded.

"Seriously?" I asked. Not in a million years would I have imagined I'd be given such an opportunity.

I let go of my cock, which hovered and drooled over my abs, and reached toward Jake first. He let go of his grip as I moved closer. I felt along his pelvis and his neatly trimmed bush until I held my prize. His cock was thinner than mine, but that wasn't to say it was thin, rather maybe a little above average. The extra skin made it look thicker. I pulled up on it, feeling the skin gather around the head and slip over it. I love to jerk an uncut cock, something about the way the skin moves up and down the shaft is so exciting to me. Maybe, because I'm cut, it feels so different from my own.

"Mmm, that feels good" Jake said as I got into a good rhythm.

Evan coughed as if to say, "What about me?" I was so focused on Jake, I'd neglected the massive cock to my right.

I switched hands and held Jake in my left and reached over and held Evan in my right. I attempted to stroked them in unison, though Evan took a slightly longer stroke to get the full length.

"Damn, why didn't we do this sooner" Jake said, leaning back and letting me do all the work. Evan just nodded, he seemed a little nervous.

My dick pulsed and leaked more precum than I ever normally make, but I couldn't offer it any relief, since I had my hands full.

"You want some help?" Jake asked, holding out his hand.

"You don't have to ..." I started to say.

"... but you wouldn't turn down an offer" Jake said, completing my thought. He reached over and took hold of me. He was a little awkward at first.

"See, I'm true to my word" he added, directed at Evan. He just shook his head. I'm sure he must have been as shocked as I was at how relaxed Jake was about all this. Soon, Jake was stroking me at the same steady rhythm I was stroking him and Evan. When I felt I was getting close. I slowed my pace on his cock, and he seemed to take the hint and slow his strokes. Something like this rarely happened, so I wanted it to last as long as possible.

I could feel streams of precum flowing over my fingers as I grasped each of them. I wanted to bend down and lick it off their shiny heads and take them both in my mouth. The thought almost sent me over the edge.

"Would you ever consider getting a blowjob from a guy?" I asked. Evan shook his head no, but not emphatically, like it was the expected response.

"I have, actually," Jake confessed.

"You cheated on Natalie?" Evan said, in shock.

"No, it was her idea" Jake said. My mouth opened and shut like a trout finding itself suddenly in the middle of the Mojave.

"No fucking way!" Evan said.

"Now you have to tell us everything," I said.

"When we were still dating, we got to talking about crazy things we'd done. She told me she's kissed a girl in college. I told her I could top that." He said, then continued. "I knew this guy in college, we'd hang out together all the time. After this party, we were both pretty high at the time" he said miming like he was inhaling a joint.

"Anyway, he tells me he's gay and thinks I'm hot. He's all afraid I'm going to freak out about it. I tell him I'm cool with it. Then he flat out asks if he could suck my dick."

"What the fuck? Really, he just came out and asked you?" Evan said.

"Yup, and I was like, I don't know, but then again, I was a horny college student who hadn't gotten any in a while." Jake continued. While he told the story, I could feel his dick getting harder as he thought back on it.

"So you let him?" I asked.

"Yeah, I was curious what it would be like" Jake said.

"And did you enjoy it?" I asked. His dick jumped in my hand and leaked precum down my fingers. He didn't need to say more, I had my answer right there.

"I loved it, he was amazing at it. Not that I had a great deal of experience, but it was way better than any of my girlfriends up to that point. " Jake replied.

"So, what did Natalie think?" Evan asked.

"She said she wished she's seen that. It definitely got her wet talking about it" Jake said.

"I can't believe you told her that" Evan said.

"We don't keep anything from each other." Jake said.

"So how did you end up with her watching" I asked, still stroking both of them. They seemed to get harder the more Jake told the story.

"Yeah, so I guess she told this gay friend of hers. He told her he wished it had been him. I guess he'd been crushing on me for a while" he said.

"So you let him suck your dick?" Evan asked.

"She told me about the exchange, then asked what I thought. I could tell she was really turned on by the idea, so I said yeah why not".

"Fuck!" Evan said what I was thinking.

"She arranged for the three of us to go out one evening, we all got a little plastered. This was before we had kids. Anyway, we ended up back at our place and then one thing led to another, and we got naked." Jake said, cracking open another beer and handing one to Evan, all without me losing a beat on their dicks.

"So, what was it like?" Evan asked.

"One of the best, if not the best blowjobs I've ever had, even better than in college," Jake said grinning.

"Guys know what guys like," I offered.

"You got that right" Jake said, returning his beer chilled hand to my shaft.

"But that's not the end of it. She wanted to see me try" Jake admitted.

"You sucked dick!" Evan exclaimed. Jake got a bit embarrassed.

"Yeah, it wasn't bad" he said. I pictured a dick slipping between Jake's wet lips and nearly lost it.

"You'd do it again?" I asked.

"I did, we hooked up a few more times after that with and without Nat there until he moved away." Jake said.

"She was cool with it?" Evan asked.

"Yeah, she brings up how hot it was to watch me go down on him every now and then, but we've never had another opportunity to do more. And now with the kids, it's become a lot less likely to happen" Jake said, lamenting the fact.

"Cassy would shit a brick if she ever saw me do anything like that. She's always thinking I'm cheating on her when I'm not," Evan said.

"You've got to have open communication. It's why Nat and I have stayed together so long" Jake said.

"You gonna tell her about this?" Evan asked.

"I know it's complicated for you right now, if you don't want me to I won't" Jake offered.

"I don't want you to lie on my account." Evan said.

"Ok, besides nothing has really happened, despite what Cassie says, jerking off doesn't count" Jake said.

Evan looked down at my hand moving up and down his shaft, as if just now contemplating the ramifications of what was happening.

"I just wish I could find someone like him again" Jake said, looking directly at me. His piercing slate blue eyes seemed to see right through me.

"Do you want it to?" I asked weakly, I was surprised I'd had the courage to ask.

"I've been waiting all day for you to ask," he said, beaming brightly. Evan looked a little taken aback. Jake twisted around and grabbed hold of my cock while still allowing me to continue to stroke him. I wasn't sure what was happening when suddenly he leaned forward and put my dick in his mouth.

"Oh Shit!" Evan said watching his friend suck my dick. I had intended to suck him, but he seemed eager to get down to business. I wondered if he'd really needed any help with the swing set at all, or if he was trying to find an excuse to suck my dick. He licked and sucked my shaft like a practiced cocksucker.

"Damn, I've missed this," he said, holding up my wet cock in the gleaming light. "When I saw you getting hard in your shorts this morning I knew I had to find a way to get it" Jake said before going back to expertly sucking me while Evan looked on in astonishment. If I wasn't careful, I knew I wouldn't last long.

The image of my straight hunky neighbor, father of two, going down on me was now permanently etched in my memory. The way his stubbled cheeks rubbed my thighs as he licked my balls, or the way his tongue felt sliding over my head, was sending me over the edge. The ravenous look in his steel-blue eyes when they met mine was all it took to push me over.

"Oh shit! I'm gonna cum" I said, expecting Jake to pull away. He didn't, if anything it lit a fire under him. He stroked and sucked until I exploded in his mouth. He deep throated me and took some of my load straight down his throat. He pulled back and savored the hot cum filling his mouth. He made an effort to swallow every drop.

"Oh shit" I heard Evan say. I'd been automatically stroking him as I blew my load in Jake's mouth, and he'd been bucking his hips into my hand. Now a flood of cum was erupting from his dick all over his abs and down my hand.

"Fuck fuck fuck fuck" he yelled as a load just as massive as earlier today spilled out of his enormous nuts.

Jake cleaned up the last of my cum, not missing a single drop, and sat back licking his lips. He eyed Evan's dick with a look in his eyes like he would love to clean that one up too.

"Your turn" I said, pushing Jake back and leaning into his crotch. I switched hands and brought my cum covered right hand to his shaft, slicking it up with his buddy's cum. Then I took him deep in my mouth, tasting Evan's sweet and salty cum on Jake's dick. I ran my tongue over and around his foreskin covered head, eliciting a whimper from Jake. I could tell sucking my dick had gotten him extremely excited, and he wouldn't last long, no matter what I did.

I quickly memorized every bump, ridge and pocket of skin with my tongue before I felt a warm spray eject from the tube of his foreskin.

"Oh fuck" he said, holding my head as load after load filled my mouth. I swallowed the light, buttery cum with relish.

"Shit!" He said through clenched teeth as I scooped the last of his cum from inside his foreskin with my tongue. Reluctantly, I let him push my head away from his overly stimulated cock.

"Fuck, I think I have a new first place. That was amazing," he said, grinning from ear to ear.

Evan, who had been watching until this point, turned and looked out onto the sparkling water. The sun was nearly at the horizon now, and the boat had drifted into the shade of the trees on the bank.

"What time is it?" Jake asked, looking around for his shorts to find his phone.

"7:30" Evan said, looking at his watch as got up and cleaned himself up with a towel.

"Wanna head back? I'm starving" Jake said.

"You just ate" I said to him as an aside with a wink.

"That was just an appetizer, I'm ready for the main course" Jake said, turning his shorts right side out in preparation to put them back on. My dick jumped, was Jake implying he wanted something more than a bro job? Jake seemed much more open than I expected from a straight guy that had just cum. Evan, however, seemed much more introspective. Was he feeling guilty for getting a hand job from me in front of Jake.

I was sad to see our naked time coming to an end. I reluctantly slipped my clothes back on. At least we all left our shirts off, Jake especially since his smelled strongly of spilled beer.

Evan slipped his shorts back on, though it looked for a minute like he was just going to take us back naked. He gunned the engines and headed back out into the main channel and toward the harbor.

Chapter 11

Morning Run

The smell of charcoal and searing meat filled the air. We were hanging around in my backyard with the grill fired up and the steaks cooking. It was like earlier never happened. They were talking about sports, which I didn't follow while we waited for dinner to be ready. The sun had already set, but it was a warm evening. We remained shirtless, though I threw in an apron when I was working the grill. There was no mention of what had happened on the boat. No innuendo or flirting, just regular neighborly banter.

I could still taste Jakes cum every now and then, so I knew it happened. To them, it was as if it happened in some other dimension.

The steaks turned out perfect, and we relished them with more beers and sweet corn.

"I'd better head in, Nat just got back." Jake said, checking his phone. I was a bit disappointed we hadn't continued where we left off. He put out his hand for me to shake it, then he pulled be in toward him, so he could pat my back. "Thanks again for earlier, we'll have to do it again soon" he whispered in my ear. After zero acknowledgment of what happened earlier, this was finally some indication that it did happen, and it may continue in the future. I smiled broadly in response.

"Good night man," Evan said, giving Jake a fist bump.

"I should probably turn in as well, I've got to take the boat to the owner in the morning and get paid" he said.

"Too bad you have to take it back, wouldn't mind doing that again" I said.

"Yeah, I love being out on the water" he said. I wasn't really referring to being on the water as much as the naked fun had. I could sense some awkwardness around that topic, so I let it go.

I went up to take a shower and get ready for bed. I left the bathroom door open, but Evan didn't come in. As I was leaving to head to my bedroom, he came up the stairs. I was naked while he was still in his shorts.

"Good night" he said before ducking into the bathroom and closing the door tightly behind him. I felt the same weird vibes from him. Did things go too far earlier? Seeing Jake suck my dick may have been too much for him. I fell into a restless sleep.

In the morning, once again, I found the sofa empty and Evan gone. He'd left his tools, though, so I knew he'd be back this time.

I got dressed and headed out to go for a run, something I'd been neglecting for a while. With ear buds in and just my yellow running shorts on, I set out into the park.

I stopped around the middle point in my run to admire the sun gleaming off the water and to catch my breath.

"Hey" I heard a familiar voice behind me. I looked back to see Jake standing there also in his running gear. It consisted of just a pair of very short running shorts with slits up the sides, so his entire leg was exposed. His chest was bare, but he wore a camel back strapped to his back, so the straps framed his hairy chest nicely.

"Hey" I said, taking in his sweat soaked hairy chest. Toying with me, he ran his hand down his chest then reached under the waistband of his shorts to adjust his bulge. I would have dropped to me knees in an instant had it not been for the fact that the path was quite busy with other joggers and people walking their dogs.

"You always take this route? I never see you" Jake asked.

"I'm just getting back into running. This is the first time I've gone this way. I love that we live so close to the water." I said.

"Yeah, it's great. I usually take the path going that way, it heads into a more industrial area, but it's less busy." He said, nodding to another path.

"I've never taken that way," I said.

"You want to join me?" He asked.

"If I can keep up, I'm not the fastest runner" I said.

"I'll take it easy" he said and started off toward the path.

He was right about it being more industrial. Large tanks soon loomed overhead, and the path was littered with trash in places. It was probably why most people didn't come this way. It was less busy, in fact, after 10 minutes along the path I'd not seen another soul. At one point, the path grew more narrow so that we couldn't jog side by side anymore. I let him go first and followed, getting a great view of his back. Below the camelback, the muscles shifted along his spine with each step. A patch of dark hair grew just above the waistband of his shorts. His ass filled out the shorts to the point where I was afraid they couldn't contain it. I was struggling to keep up with him, as I gulped the humid air. The path veered off into some kudzu vines covering the nearby trees. It was hardly a path anymore. It screamed a place to hide bodies or get mugged, but Jake seemed unperturbed. I noticed a gold condom wrapper on the ground, thinking who would be having sex here?

Jake stopped abruptly, and I nearly ran right into him. I reached out a hand and caught his right shoulder, steadying myself from falling forward as I caught my breath.

He took a sip of water from the tube by his left shoulder.

"Can I have some?" I asked, my lips parched and my tongue sticking to the roof of my mouth.

"Sure, as long as I can have a drink from your hose" He said, offering me the tube and looking down at the outline of my soft cock against the light fabric.

"What right here?" I asked before I took a sip of the tepid, slightly plastic tasting water. It quenched my thirst nonetheless.

"Why not?" He said, our eyes met, and he smiled that wide toothy grin that makes me melt. He looked around cautiously, then reached down and grabbed my cock through the thin joggers.

"I can't stop thinking about this dick" he said in a low voice even though there wasn't anyone around. I was still catching my breath as he fondled me. I felt cool air rush over my sweaty cock as he pulled down the waistband and brought it and my balls out into the open. I could tell his cock was already hard, pressing into the shorts, making a circus tent in the front.

I reached out and brushed the slick fabric over his head and felt wetness. Suddenly, it slipped from my grasp as he stooped down in front of me. I felt my dick slip into his warm mouth. He moaned as his nose nestled in my sweaty pubes.

I grew inside his mouth so that when he pulled back it was like a magic trick, my small soft cock was replaced by a fully grown python. It stretched his lips as he pulled it from his mouth and admired the slick steel. He stroked it and licked at the head, coxing out a bead of precum, which he greedily lapped up. The fear of getting caught and the fact that for the second time in as many days, my hunky next door neighbor had my cock in his mouth had me rushing toward orgasm.

"Why didn't we do this sooner?" he said between slurps.

"You know I'm literally right next door, you could come over any time" I said.

"This way is more fun" he said. I couldn't argue, it was much more thrilling to do this outdoors where we could get caught at any moment. There was something savage and wild about the surroundings as well that added to its primal nature, that a well decorated bedroom and comfy sheets couldn't replace.

He'd pulled his dick out the leg hole of his shorts and stroked it as he lavished my cock. I was getting close already, but didn't want it to be over too quickly. I pulled up from his arm pit, prompting him to stand.

We lined our cocks up stacked one on top of the other, his only reaching part way down my shaft.

"Fuck, I don't even come close" he said.

"You've got a beautiful cock," I said, pulling back the foreskin and lining up our heads. I pulled the skin over my head and down my shaft.

"Oh fuck, I've never tried that before" he said, while his foreskin stretched over my thick shaft.

"You like that?" I said, stroking the two of us with his foreskin.

"Feels so good" he said, his eyes rolling back as I squeezed them together tightly.

We stood there playing with each other's cocks until I couldn't resist stooping down to lick the growing amount of precum gathering inside his tube. I slurped and sucked his sensitive skin, still he had to pull me away before he exploded too soon inside my mouth. I licked his balls while his dick pulsed and bounced, leaking a steady stream of clear liquid. I could taste the salty funk on his balls. It was intoxicating. I licked lower until I found myself clawing my way toward his ass from under his balls.

I smacked his ass and yanked down his shorts below his knees, urging him to turn around. He reluctantly obliged, leaning forward and grabbing a tree branch to lean on.

I licked up his hairy crack, finding the pungent odor coming off his ass made my dick so hard it ached. I licked the wet hair and skin, tasting salty sweat and earthy funk, until I found his soft hole.

"Oh fuck" he whimpered as I plunged my tongue into his hole. I was surprised to find my tongue was able to slip inside his trench more deeply than with Evan. He whimpered and pushed back against my tongue, splaying his ass open on it and my spit soaked beard. I drilled his hole, feeling it clamp down hard as he stroked himself.

He reached back at one point and shoved my head against his ass so hard I was afraid he might break my nose in the process. He fucked himself on my tongue, moaning and grunting like a wild animal.

"Fuck me" he finally said. I wasn't sure he actually meant it, or if he was just caught up in the moment.

I slicked up my finger and slipped it into his hole. I could feel his tight ring press down on it as he wiggled his ass around it. I could feel the hard ridge of his prostate and poked at it a few times. He whimpered and drooled more precum from his hooded cock. I replaced my single finger with two, then three as he pushed back on them willingly.

"Give me that dick!" He finally said, fitfully pulling my fingers from his hole.

I stood behind him, lining my cock up with his hairy crack. He looked back in anticipation, gripping the tree branch so tightly his knuckles looked white. I spat and let a long string fall from my mouth onto his already wet crack. I pressed the glob into his hole, then spit again. This time on my cock, slicking it up a few times before pressing the shiny head into the mat of fur lining the ring of his hole.

"You sure you can take this?" I asked, smacking my dick against his hole a couple of times.

"Fuck yes! It's all I can think about" he replied. I'd never encountered a straight guy so eager to impale himself on my cock. Though he was eager, his ass was not so cooperative.

I pressed in and felt like I hit a brick wall. I could feel his opening clamp down, refusing me entry. I tried more spit and another finger.

"Relax and push out" I said softly in his ear as I nuzzled his neck.

"Sorry, you are a great deal bigger than Nat's strap on" he said. So he's been fucked before? And with a strap on, no less. This man is full of surprises.

"She's fucked you with a strap on?" I asked, dying to hear the details, but also as a way to distract him and alleviate his anxiety.

"Over the years, we've explored a lot of things. She is pretty open-minded" he said. "I used a dildo on her, and she said I should try it. So she shoved it up my ass. I have to say, it felt really good once I got used to it. I don't think many guys realize just good it feels to play with your ass."

"Oh, I know, if god didn't want us to play with our asses, why did she make it feel so good?" I said. He laughed and then reached back to feel my dick pressed into his hole. While we were talking, I'd managed to slip inside him an inch or so.

"Holy shit! You're actually inside," he said, catching his breath and feeling my dick slip into him through his fingers.

"Is this your first time with a real dick?" I asked.

He grunted but didn't answer my question, I let it go for now. I moved in and out, just a millimeter at a time. I tried going a little deeper. His eyes grew wide, and he looked back at me with a clenched jaw.

I knew I was hurting him. I was about to give up and pull out when he reached back and held me in place. I felt him clamp down on me hard a couple of times, then loosen up.

"It's been a while" he said. "Not exactly something you want your kids accidentally catching you doing".

I patiently waited until I felt something give, and I slipped back in. This time I sank inside until my pubes mingled with his ass hair.

"Oh fuck!" He exclaimed as I let him get accustomed to the thickness of my dick. While I waited, I became more and more aware of just how exposed we were here, him with his shorts around his ankles and mine down on my thighs.

"Fuck me" he insisted, drawing me back from inspecting our surroundings to his warm wet ass.

I took a tentative stroke to gage his reaction. He grunted and pushed back. Clearly I wasn't being aggressive enough for him. He began to fuck himself on my dick, pushing back hard and grunting loudly as he did.

"Oh fuck, that feels incredible!" He said, finally letting me take over as I grabbed his hips and slammed into his hole hard. He whimpered, and his eyes rolled back in his head, so I could just see the whites of his eyes.

He'd stopped stroking himself, but his dick was still producing a stream of precum. It looked like spider silk as it stretched out into a long strand below him and gently swayed with the motion of our fucking.

I leaned in close, pressing our sweat drenched backs together, and reached for his tit across his hairy chest. I felt his ass clench as I twisted his nipple. Our faces were inches apart now as I pounded his hole close to completion.

He twisted his head and kissed me. I wasn't sure he'd be into kissing a guy, but sure enough, we started to make out with sloppy wet kisses. His scruff and my beard rubbed against each other as we wrestled tongues. I couldn't hold back any longer.

"I'm gonna cum," I warned him.

"Go for it! Breed my hole" he said. That was all I needed to let loose and fill his hole with my cum.

"Fuck!" I yelled a bit too loudly as my balls drained into him. With my shaft still buried inside him, he grabbed his dick and stroked it furiously. I could feel him clamp down on me hard as he grunted and shot a massive load into the trunk of the tree. I nearly came a second time as his ass milked my cock and his strokes slowed.

"Fuck, that was ..." he started to say, but looked as if lost for words.

"I know, that was amazing" I said, holding him close, so I could keep my softening dick inside him for as long as possible. I reached down and felt his wet cock, getting some of his juice on my fingers.

I brought them to his lips and he sucked the cum from then before leaning in and kissing me once again, sharing his seed with me.

Finally, he pulled off my cock with a loud slurping sound and pulled up his shorts. I reluctantly pulled my shorts back up, tucking my still semi hard dick in to the side.

"Any time you want to come over and do that again, you are more than welcome." I told him.

"I will definitely take you up on that." He said with a bright smile. I couldn't believe my cum was now inside this stud. I'd bred his hole and he loved it. If you had told me this was where I'd be and what I'd be doing less than a week ago, I would have laughed in your face. But here we were recovering from one of my now top ten experiences in fucking.

I looked around again and found more used condoms along the side. I guess now I understand the appeal. I also noticed a patch of poison ivy and realized just how close we came to brushing up against it. Getting a poison ivy rash would have been worth it, though.

We headed back to the main path. It was easy to get lost in the side paths, which I guess was the point. Once back on the main path, Jake said. "I can't wait to tell Nat!"

He started to run at a regular pace ahead of me. I followed, watching his ass bounce up and down in front of me, knowing my dick had just been inside that. Further evidence of the encounter began to seep through the thin fabric. Hopefully, for Jake's sake, everyone would just assume it was sweat pooling in his ass crack. I would know it was my load leaking down his leg.

"Did you tell her about yesterday?" I asked.

"I left out Evan, but I did say we'd sucked each other's dicks. She loved it, best sex we've had together in months" he said.

"What should I say when I see her?" I asked. I wasn't sure how I would act the next time I ran into her on the street. It felt weird to know she knew and in fact was encouraging her husband to pursue his bisexual side.

"I don't know, you don't have to mention it. I don't want you to feel weird about it" he said.

"It's ok, I've just never met a couple that was so open like that" I said. We made our way back toward our neighborhood.

We headed to our respective steps to stretch out and recover.

"Hey, can you do me a favor?" He asked.

"Sure, anything" I said, wondering what more I could do.

"Can you send me a picture?" he asked, glancing down as my still fluffed up cock tucked into my shorts.

"Ah ... sure" I said and thumbed through my photo's, a large percentage of the storage space on the device was devoted to dicks, many were my own.

I found one I liked with good lighting and sent it to his phone.

"Nice! But it doesn't do it justice" he said looking down at the picture and then over at the lump in my shorts.

"I know," I said.

"Return the favor?" I asked.

"Sure, I'll find one for you" he said. "Damn, should have had you record it"

I rolled my eyes. Why didn't I think of that? I imagined all of the loads I would have for years to come, watching and rewatching my dick sliding into his ass.

"Guess that means we have to go do it again" I said

"Sounds like a plan" he said.

"I'm gonna head in to shower, it was great running into you" I said.

"Yeah, we should plan on running together again soon." He said, heading inside his house. He stuck his head back out once more before I headed inside, "Hey, can you not tell Evan about this? I don't think he's as open-minded about it all".

"Sure, I kinda sense that he's got more hang-ups than you" I said, giving him a wink then heading inside.

Chapter 12
The Splits

I didn't see Evan until later that evening when he came in. He immediately slumped down on the sofa, looking a bit like a lost puppy that had just been kicked in the face. He was staring off into the corner of the room where the wall meets the ceiling, like there was something extremely interesting in that corner.

"You ok?" I asked.

"Yeah" he said in a tone that would convince no jury in the country. I wanted to talk it out with him some more but thought he needed some space. We'd not really talked about what had happened on the boat between me and Jake. I figured it was a lot to take in.

"Ok, if you need anything you know where to find me" I offered, heading toward the stairs to get ready for bed.

That's when I heard him whimper like he was in excruciating pain. I turned to find him with his head in his hands and his body shaking as he cried.

I went back to the sofa and sat down beside him. I rested my hand on his back and gently rubbed between his shoulder blades, trying to comprehend what he was blubbering between sobs.

"She wants a divorce" he said, gulping back tears. I continued to stroke his back and held him in my arms as his body convulsed with each sob. I didn't really know what to say. I wished I could take away his pain. I held him until he began to relax and sniffed back tears and snot. I handed him a tissue from the box to blow his nose.

He looked like a small child who'd lost his parents and was completely inconsolable.

I pulled him into a hug, letting his head rest on my bad shoulder despite the discomfort it caused. Through it, I shared in his pain.

Once he let it all out, he seemed to calm down and relax into my embrace.

"It's going to be ok" I said softly.

He pulled back from the embrace, then leaned in and kissed my lips. My eyes grew wide in shock. I opened my mouth and I felt his tongue slip inside tentatively.

I tasted his salty tears on his lips as our kiss extended. It was like a floodgate was opened by the intimacy and pent-up desire flooded out. We kissed as only two men can, beards rubbing and tongues wrestling. He pressed into me and I submitted, rolling on to my back as he climbed on top of me. Our bodies writhed as we continued to kiss with deep wet kisses.

I was instantly hard inside my shorts as I felt his hardening dick rub up against mine, sandwiched between us under our clothing. His bare chest rubbed against my light linen shirt. He tugged at my shirt violently, and in the process he tore off some of the buttons. I didn't care about my shirt, he could have ripped it to shreds if he wanted to.

With my chest now exposed, he leaned down and licked until he found my nipple and sucked it into his mouth. His beard tickled as it rubbed around my chest, tangling with my chest hair. I pulled him closer, grabbing his ass and tugging down the back of his shorts. He moved up my body until the distended front of his shorts was inches from my face. I took a deep inhale of the heady scent of his crotch before leaning forward and licking the material covering his cock head. He grabbed the back of my head and pressed my face to his crotch. I purred in contentment as my dick lurched in my shorts. I could taste his precum, seeping through the thin material. I had to taste his bare skin. I pulled down the waistband and tucked it under his ample balls.

There it was, my prize, all nine plus inches of it, looming over me. A drop of precum appeared at the tip, and I stuck out my tongue, collecting the dew. It was warm and sweet. I parted my lips and let his cock sink into my mouth. I ran my tongue along his wide helmet head and up his piss slit. I tasted more nectar flowing from the source. I ran my tongue along the underside, feeling the sensitive place where his circumcision scar was. I looked up trying to catch his eye, but he was looking at the ceiling, holding my head in his hands.

He slowly began to fuck my face, feeding his long tube down my throat. I tried my hardest not to gag on it. I held on to his ass, feeling it clench with each stroke as his pace grew more urgent. This was not a tender shared moment. It was him using my throat to hammer out his anger, pain, and frustration. I was happy to be his vessel. Happy to take the pounding if I could help him forget for a moment and find relief.

He jackhammered my mouth until my jaw cried out in pain as it became unhinged trying to accommodate his girth. Just when I couldn't take it anymore, he grunted and grasped the back of my head, thrusting his dick deep into my throat. I couldn't breathe, I couldn't even gag, he was so deep. I felt the warm spray drip down my throat like mucus. It burned as it managed to go up my nose. When he finally let go, and I could breathe again, I could taste it on my lip as it dripped out of my nostril.

I was in tears and soon found that he was too, but for very different reasons. Warm drops fell on my shoulder as he held my head on his cock. His body shook as waves of emotion seized him. I felt his dick deflate inside my mouth. He didn't let go of my head for minutes, even after he was completely soft.

Finally, he looked down and met my eyes, seeming surprised to find me still impaled on his dick.

He pulled back and slipped from me, leaving a trail of drool and cum running down my chin.

He leaned down and kissed me while dragging his heavy cock over my chest. He pushed back, and I felt my dick press into his ass crack. I humped his crack while we made out with sloppy wet kisses.

Then he kissed down my neck and over my chest, stopping at my nipple to give it a brief lick. He scooted back, stepping over my dick as he moved down my body, kissing and licking the skin as he went. I looked down and caught his eye as he held my dick in his hand by the base.

He looked up at me, locking eyes with mine as he tasted the wet head. He leaned back, contemplating his next move like a chess master. He stroked my dick a few times, feeling the thickness and heft of it. I nodded encouragement, not really expecting him to go down on me.

Then, holding his breath, he leaned forward and slipped it in his mouth. I gasped at the sudden movement as his warm mouth enveloped me and his tongue flicked along the sensitive underside.

He proceeded to lick and suck like it was his first meal in days. What he lacked in skill, he made up for in enthusiasm. Unlike Jake who'd had some previous experience, Evan was a bit too many teeth, which made me cringe, but I didn't correct him. I didn't want to scare him off. This was less about my pleasure as it was about his curiosity. He stroked my slick cock as he climbed between my legs and licked my balls.

I pulled my legs back to give him easier access to my balls. He sat back and looked at my tight ass, and for the briefest moment I thought he might lean in and lick me hole. His face scrunched up in a look of disgust. I let my legs go back down. I knew he wasn't ready for that. Hell, it had taken me years before I realized how much I enjoyed rimming someone.

Thankfully, I'd not broken the spell completely. He stroked me, holding my cock tightly as I fucked his hand. He leaned in and licked my head a few more times. It was nearly enough to send me over the edge.

"I'm close," I warned him. He surprised me again by licking up my balls and along my shaft. He sunk his mouth around the top half of my cock while he stroked the bottom half. I panted and groaned as my balls tensed.

"Oh fuck! I'm gonna cum!" I screamed, in case he missed all the other clues. He pulled me out of his mouth and stroked me, watching the first shot sail through the air and land on my chest. I was a little disappointed he didn't take my cum, but I never really expected him to. He continued to stroke me as my abs tightened, and my balls drained their reserves onto my belly, then dribbled down his fingers.

As my orgasm subsided, he held my cock in his tight fist, inspecting the whitish goo pouring out like lava. For a moment, it looked like he was about to lean forward and lick some up, but instead he turned away, looking for something to wipe his hand off with.

I tossed him my shirt, having nothing else handy. He sat back, wiping the remnants from his fingers, then wiped the little bit of cum that had oozed out of his dick on my shirt. Now, of course, I could never wash that shirt again.

He sat back, his still impressive, soft member lounging against his thigh. I twisted around, so I was sitting up next to him. I wondered what was going through his head. Did he feel guilty or weirded out by what just happened? Did he still have that nagging feeling he was cheating even though he knew it was over between them?

I wanted to fill the empty void between us with something, but fear kept me from speaking.

Without saying a word, he stood and headed to the stairs. I little while later, I heard the shower go on.

I went to the kitchen and got a drink of water to wash down the funky cum gathered in the back of my throat and to clean up my chest. I was at the sink, so focused on getting the little bits of cum out of my chest hair that I didn't hear the wet footfalls behind me.

"Here, let me" he said, reaching around from behind me to take the wet paper towel from my hand. He pressed his wet body to mine, the water dripping down his body between us. As he rubbed the cum around on my chest, he leaned in and kissed my bad shoulder lightly, then kissed my neck. I turned, and he kissed me softly on the lips.

"Thank you" he said after our lips parted.

"For what?" I asked.

"For being patient with me and for opening your home to me. You were there when no one else was. You took me in and a cared for me. No one has ever been so kind to me before" he said. His eyes were glassy with held back tears.

I couldn't hold my tears back, they streamed down my face as a mix of his leftover cum and snot dripped from my nose. I hugged him close, so he couldn't see what a blubbering mess he'd made of me.

"You will always be welcome here," I whispered in his ear. We held each other standing naked and wet in the middle of the kitchen for what seemed like hours before he finally let me go. I cleaned up my face and handed him a tissue as well.

"Guess I'll turn in for the night, I've got work in the morning" I said.

"Oh ... ok" he said, looking to the sofa.

"Good night" I said, heading to the stairs before pausing and leaning in to kiss him once more. He smiled awkwardly and kissed me back before turning to the sofa.

When I got to the top of the stairs, I kicked myself for not asking if he wanted to join me in my bed. The moment had passed, and I felt weird about going back downstairs.

I got ready for bed and turned out the lights. Thoughts were spinning in my head about what it all meant when I heard a faint knock at my door. It was so soft I wasn't sure I'd actually heard it at first. Then it came again.

"Come in" I whispered. A figure made his way across the room and slipped into the bed next to me.

"I couldn't sleep another night alone on the sofa" he said softly.

I rolled onto my side, letting my leg drape over his hairy leg and my hand run through his hairy chest. He sighed and relaxed in my arms as we both drifted off to sleep.

Chapter 13

Food Fight

When I woke the next morning, I was sad to find the bed empty. That was until the rich aroma of coffee brewing and bacon cooking wafted into the bedroom. I got up and headed downstairs, not bothering to get dressed, following the smells and the sounds of sizzling bacon.

"Morning" came a greeting I'd not expected. There at the kitchen counter was Jake in running shorts and no shirt. Evan was wearing shorts and had an apron over his bare chest as he worked the stove. He turned to see me enter the kitchen. Jake looked down at my half hard dick and gave me a wink. I wasn't expecting him to be there and thought for a minute I should retreat upstairs to dress.

"Morning, hope you don't mind that I invited Jake in for breakfast" Evan said, smiling wryly at my state of undress.

"No, not at all, let me go get dressed, I didn't realize ..." I said, turning to head back upstairs.

"Don't do it on my account," Jake said, beaming at me. "I stopped by to see if you wanted to join me for a run, but you were still asleep".

"I overslept, I've got to start work in a little while" I said, checking the clock on the microwave which was perpetually off by an hour.

I took a seat at the counter next to Jake while we waited for Evan as short order cook to finish his preparations.

I grabbed a mug and Jake poured me some coffee. He sat the pot down, then reached over into my lap and tugged on my dick. I quickly looked up at Evan, whose back was turned from us as he flipped the bacon sizzling and sputtering in the pan.

My cock grew as Jake stroked it covertly under the counter. If he only knew what had happened last night with Evan, he may not have been so concerned about hiding what he was doing. Then again, I wasn't sure Evan was ready for it to be common knowledge either, so I played along with the charade. I reached over and felt Jake's already hard cock through the slick material. He smiled and leaned his head back as I rubbed his foreskin covered shaft. Evan turned and faced us, depositing the bacon on plates in front of us, seeming not to notice what was going on under the counter.

"Help yourself" He said, uncovering a plate of blueberry pancakes. Or "help your neighbor" I thought, holding Jakes rigid cock tight before letting go.

"Oh, better yet, let's take these up onto the deck" Evan said, grabbing a tray I had on the side and staking the plates and mugs on it.

"Uh ok" Jake looking guiltily at my hard dick and his tented short.

"Right behind you" I said, busying myself with adding sugar and cream to my coffee. Evan grabbed the tray and headed to the stairs.

"Oh shit" Jake whispered.

"Relax, I think Evan will be cool," I said, not at all sure of that fact.

"Oh yeah, did something happen?" Jake asked as he got up from the stool.

"You could say that. I'll explain later" I said, grabbing my coffee and the forgotten syrup from the counter. Evan was already outside before Jake and I reached the top of the stairs.

I put my coffee down and grabbed a pair of shorts to slip on to go outside.

"That's a pity" Jake said, smirking as I stuffed my hard cock down the leg of the shorts. There was little Jake could do to hide his still hard member, but he did his best to tuck it in the corner of his shorts under the waistband.

We headed out into the bright morning sun, a cool breeze was all that remained of the night, as the temperatures were expected to soar later in the day.

When we got to the top of the winding spiral staircase, I nearly spilled my coffee all down the front of myself when I looked up. There was Evan sitting on the outdoor sofa, completely naked. His discarded shorts sat in a crumpled pile at his feet. His dick looked solid, but not fully hard yet.

"Oh" Jake said, nearing knocking into me when I stopped. He looked down to see Evan's naked body on display for us.

"I figured it would be a nice day to get some sun" he said, stretching out his arms across the back of the sofa.

"Didn't you get enough sun the other day?" Jake said, looking around to see if we could be seen from up here.

"Never" Evan said, smiling brightly. Gone was the melancholy of the previous evening. Maybe he had accepted his fate, or more likely, he was in complete denial. Either way, he seemed to be in an exceptionally good mood this morning.

I set my coffee and the syrup down on the tray and tugged at my shorts, letting them fall to my ankles. My still semi-hard cock dangled in front of me. I took the chair next to Evan and spread out nude, feeling the warm sun kiss my body.

Jake stood for a moment holding his coffee mug in front of his distended shorts, looking furtively around.

"Come on, lose the shorts and let's eat" Evan said. Eating breakfast was the last thing on my mind at the moment, at least not the breakfast on my plate in any rate. I wanted to eat both sausages in front of me instead. The question was, were they on the menu?

"Oh alright" Jake said, fumbling with his shorts and letting them drop. His hard dick jumped up and smacked his abs before settling itself out in front of him. He blushed and attempted to hide it behind his coffee mug.

"Somebody's a bit excited this morning" Evan said, laughing and pointing to Jake's crotch.

"Oh ha ha, from the look of it, I'm not the only one" he said nodding at my crotch. He was right, this was too much for my dick to handle without filling completely with blood. Evan looked over at my dick getting hard, and his also began to thicken and stir along his leg.

"Let's eat before it gets cold" he said, digging into the mound of pancakes.

"Missing my run and now loading up on carbs, ugh" Jake said, sitting down on the sofa next to Evan. "How do you manage to stay so thin eating like this?"

"I've always been like this" Evan said. Given how active he was, it was no surprise he managed to stay thin. He was like a hummingbird, never resting too long in one spot.

"Just wait, it may catch up with you when you get older" I said, looking down at my growing belly. A run with Jake this morning would have done me good, but I wouldn't trade that for the sight of the two across from me.

We got down to eating, as if it wasn't odd to be naked as we were. I remained hard, but Jake's erection relaxed a bit, while Evan's remained in a half hard state. We ate and talked about mundane things while my mind raced at the possibilities forming.

"Oh shit" Jake said, looking down at his bush where a sticky syrup covered bit of pancake had fallen off his fork into his lap. His pubes were covered in the sticky substance where it had landed.

"See, if you'd been wearing your shorts that would have made a mess" Evan said, laughing.

"It still made a mess" he said, picking the bits of crumbled pancake from his pubes.

"He'll clean that up for you" Evan said, nodding in my direction.

"I bet" Jake said, laughing it off as a joke. I was sorely tempted to offer to do it. Was Evan prompting me to do it? The tension hung in the air between us.

"Oops" Evan said, dropping some of his pancake in his lap.

"You did that on purpose" Jake said.

"And you didn't?" Evan said.

"I didn't, it was an accident" Jake said.

"Sure" Evan said, rubbing the syrup into his pubes and down his shaft. I couldn't believe what I was watching. He quickly grabbed the bottle of syrup and poured it on Jake's dick.

"What the hell!" Jake said, jumping away. Evan bent over laughing. Jake stood over him, syrup dripping down his cock and into the deck in long strands, while Evan tried to back away. Some dripped onto Evan's leg and some on the sofa. Good thing it was outdoor furniture and easily washed.

"Now you're going to pay for that!" Jake said, grabbing hold of Evan's neck.

Evan struggled to pull away, but Jake held on tightly with both hands. The muscles on his arm flexed and strained to pull Evan toward his sticky crotch. Evan squirmed and struggled against Jake's grip. Jake pushed Evan down and held his head in front of his crotch. Evan struggled, but only half-heartedly, as Jake forced his face into the sticky mess that was his mound of pubes.

"Go on, clean it up!" Jake said. Evan closed his mouth tightly as Jake rubbed his nose in his crotch, spreading the syrup in his beard.

"Mmmf" Evan said, trying to move his head from side to side away from the Jake's dick. I was hard as rock watching them struggle.

"Come on, lick up the mess you made!" Jake demanded, smacking his sweet dick against Evan's closed lips. He smacked Evan's cheek with an open palm, causing Evan to open his mouth in shock. That's when Jake's dick slipped in to his mouth, stifling his protest. Something shifted in Evan. No longer was he pretending to protest.

He opened his mouth and sunk down on Jake's cock, lapping at the syrupy skin.

I audibly gasped as I watched. Jake pushed him down so that his entire cock disappeared into Evan's mouth and throat, his nose buried in his pubes.

I couldn't hold back any longer. I got up and sunk down next to Evan. I leaned in and licked Jake's sticky balls while Evan licked the head and shaft.

"Oh fuck" Jake said, looking down at both of us lapping up his maple flavored skin. Evan seemed fascinated by Jake's hooded member. He pulled down the loose skin and let out a half laugh as he pulled it back up over Jake's engorged head.

I licked under his balls, then shifted around, so I was behind him. Jake bent forward slightly, pushing out his bubble butt. I moved under him, licking his low-hanging balls while Evan sucked his dick. I moved back and licked behind his balls and up this taint. The syrupy taste dissipated, replaced by a raw taste of sweat man cunt.

"Dude!" Evan said, sitting back and watching me lick Jake's hole. Jake was too far gone to care what Evan thought of the situation. He grabbed my head and pressed my tongue into his opening.

"Don't knock it till you've tried it" Jake said, then his voice slurred into an extended "fuuuuckkk"

Evan sat back and watched, I caught glimpses of him stroking his cock as I went to town on Jake's ass. I managed to get maybe an inch of my tongue inside his hole.

I wanted to fuck Jake again so badly. His ass was so perfect and took my cock so well the other day that it was all I could think about. Jake seemed to have the same thing in mind. I'm sure our run would have taken us back to that grotto with the used condoms, where I would have fucked him again without hesitation.

Now I paused, knowing Evan was watching and how that complicated things. What would he think of his friend taking a dick?

I was worried it would freak him out, but my fear was overtaken by my desire to fuck his sweet hole.

Jake knelt down on the sofa next to Evan, his ass sticking out prominently. He leaned forward over the back of the sofa, pushing his ass out so that his hole was clearly visible to both of us. I pressed two fingers into his opening. Evan gasped as he watched Jake take them. Jake clamped down his hole on my fingers, preparing himself to take me.

"You're not going to let him fuck you, are you?" Evan asked.

"He did," Jake confessed in his typical nonchalant manner that took Evan aback.

"Really? The fuck? When?" Evan said, punching Jake in the arm.

"Yesterday" I said, jamming a third finger into his stretched hole.

"Dude!" Evan said, seeming unable to tear his eyes away, while at the same time scrunching up his face in disgust.

"You sure you want this?" I asked, smacking his ass with my heavy cock.

Jake nodded enthusiastically. Evan looked like a trapped animal.

"I'm not sure I wanna see this" he said without looking away.

I positioned myself behind Jake, sliding my dick along his hairy crack a few times before tapping his hole.

I pressed my hard dick into Jake's crack, but the head struggled to go in.

"No way that's going in there" Evan said. He had stopped stroking himself, but was still impossibly hard and leaking.

"Give it a minute" I said.

"Grab my shorts" Jake said to Evan since they were at his feet. Evan picked them up, holding them out like they were radioactive. I took them from him.

"In the pocket" he said. I felt a lump and reached in the pocket to find a small packet of lube. I guess he was prepared to take me again, like I speculated.

I tore it open and squeezed the contents on my cock and let it drip down his crack. I pressed two fingers back inside him, this time aided by the lube. I slicked up my cock once more and then pressed the head to his opening. He gritted his teeth as my head popped inside.

"Holy shit!" Evan exclaimed as my lubed shaft slipped in.

"Oh fuck" Jake said. His ass gripped me as he watched Evan's dick jump and leak more precum. I knew he wanted Evan's thick member inside him. He may have been craving it for a while now.

He grunted when I finally bottomed out inside him, my pubes pressing into his. Evan leaned forward to get a look at the base of my cock, ringed by Jake's hairy ass.

"That's so weird" he said.

"Feels so good" I said, taking a short stroke. Jake put his hand up to pause my strokes while he grew accustomed to my girth.

"Doesn't it hurt?" Evan asked, a look of curiosity rather than disgusted on his face.

"No" he said, though I could hear the discomfort in his voice.

"Sure look's like it does," Evan said.

"Ok it takes some getting used to, but once you get past that it's worth it" Jake said.

"I don't plan on finding out" Evan said.

"You don't know what you're missing" Jake said as his ass loosened up, and I slipped in and out of him. His eyes rolled back in his head and I knew he was starting to really enjoy it. I started to truly fuck him as Evan looked on in fascination. I pulled my dick nearly all the way out, then jammed it into Jake hard. He whimpered in delight. I fucked him with long strokes, putting on a show for Evan.

I was getting dangerously close to cumming. His ass felt too good, and the fact that we had an audience only heightened my excitement. I pulled back and slipped out. Jake reached back to pull his creeks apart. His ass was wide open, a dark cave surrounded by black hair.

"You wanna give it a try?" I asked Evan. He'd been stroking his cock, staring into that inviting void. He looked up as if he hadn't heard what I said. Then he looked as if he was considering it for a minute, then caught sight of Jake looking over at him. Jake nodded his encouragement.

Evan looked between his face and ass, then shook his head. Jake looked a bit disappointed. If he was loving my big, thick cock, I'm sure he would have gone nuts over Evan's bigger and thicker cock.

"Flip over" I commanded and Jake got up and sat back down on the sofa. He leaned back and pulled his legs up. He was rock hard and leaking a steady stream of precum from the funnel of his foreskin.

I leaned forward and licked a drop from his head, and Jake swooned in delight. I sucked the foreskin into my mouth, pulling his shaft in with it. I licked around and found the opening, sticking my tongue under the skin folds. I knelt down, though my knees protested, and aimed my cock at Jake's open and lubed hole. I sunk into him while keeping his foreskin between my teeth. I began to fuck his ass hard while sucking and slurping his cock.

"Damn!" Evan said watching me fuck and suck his friend. I felt Jake's ass clench and knew he must be close with the combined sensations on his dick and ass. I let his cock fall from my mouth with a wet slap and nodded for Evan to get up. He hesitated in front of Jake, but then seemed to let go of his inhibitions and stood. His dick loomed between us, hanging over Jake's chest. I leaned forward and licked his shiny head. Jake reached up and grabbed his dick, holding it in place for me to stick in my mouth. Evan pulled back briefly, like a line had been crossed between them. Jake held on tightly, not letting Evan back away. I leaned in again and sucked him into my mouth as I continued to pound Jake's hole. Evan looked down and must have seen it all from his angle. His dick being sucked, Jake's dick wildly jumping and releasing precum all over his belly, and my dick sinking in and out of Jake's ass.

"Oh fuck!" Jake screamed loud enough to be heard from the street below. His ass quivered, and his dick began to erupt untouched. My cock poked his prostate, sending geysers of cum onto his chest and belly.

Evan was mesmerized, watching his fiend cum without being touched.

Jakes ass tightened around my cock with each spasm. I knew I wouldn't last too much longer. I grabbed Evan's ass, pulling him into me to jab his dick down my throat. In the process, I pulled apart his ass cheeks. As he fucked my face, I moved my hand closer to his crack. I ran my finger down the hairy trough until I found the soft, puckered opening. As soon as I pressed a finger to the opening, I felt a shot of warmth fill my mouth and throat.

"Oh shit!" Evan grunted as he unloaded in my mouth. The taste was all I needed to send me over the edge. I shot my load deep in Jake's ass. He moaned when he felt the warmth spread inside him.

Evan grabbed my head and held me still as the last of his load trickled out and his body shook. I waited holding his cock in my mouth as my dick softened inside Jake before it slipped out along with a gusher of cum onto the cushion. Evan stumbled back, pulling his still hard cock from my mouth, and fell back into the chair. He watched as my dick pulled from Jake's stretched hole.

"That was so fucking hot!" Jake said, reaching down to rub his cum over his abs. "I've never cum hands free like that before".

I stood and held on to the railing. My legs felt like jelly and my knees stung with pain, but it was totally worth it. I leaned in and kissed Jake, sharing Evan's cum with him. He moaned when he tasted it, knowing it came from his friend.

I sat down next to Jake and basked in the glow of orgasm and the bright morning sun. It was then I realized it must be late, and I was probably missing a work meeting. I didn't care, I'd apologize to my boss later, telling him I had an appointment I'd forgotten to put on the calendar.

Evan sat in quiet contemplation with his eyes closed and leaned back against the head rest of the chair. His dick still looked just as thick as it had when it left my mouth. A smudge of cum glowed in the sun on his leg. I bent over a licked some cum from Jake's chest, comparing it to Evan's. Jake's was milder with a buttery flavor, while Evan's was a little more bitter. Both tasted amazing to me. Jake squirmed as I ran my tongue over his lightly haired abs, lapping up his load.

"I'd better head home and grab a shower before work" he said sitting up.

"Feel free to use my bathroom to clean up before you go" I said.

"Nah, Nat will get a kick out of the fact that I'm coming home covered in cum." He said with a wink.

"I still can't believe she's so cool with it" Evan said.

"I know, I'm a very lucky man" he said. "See you boys later". He got up and headed down the spiral staircase, leaving me alone with Evan. We sat in silence for a while, enjoying the light breeze licking at our skin.

"I can't believe you fucked Jake" Evan finally said, shaking his head.

"I can't believe it myself" I said.

"He looked like he really enjoyed it" he said.

"I've only ever made a guy cum while fucking him once before" I said.

"That shit's crazy. Never knew Jake was into all that," he said, shaking his head. He got quiet after that. I wasn't sure what he thought about what had just happened. He seemed to be taking it all in stride. After a long pause in which his cock still didn't seem to shrink, I went to get up and head in.

"I'd better get to work" I said.

"Yeah, I have to start on my next boat today" Evan said.

"Oh nice!" I replied. What followed was a detailed description of the boat down to what horsepower engines it had and numerous specs I couldn't guess at figuring out. He was most animated when he was talking about boats, it was really his passion. His enthusiasm was infectious. I finally had to stop him and remind him I had work today. We gathered the dishes, put our shorts back on, and went inside.

Chapter 14

Confrontation

"**A**re you sleeping with him!?" Casie asked accusingly. She'd spotted me leaving and had come up to my car before I had a chance to leave. She must have seen Evan leaving this morning. At this point, it seemed like it was common knowledge that he was staying at the home of the neighborhood queer. Rumors and gossip didn't take long to reach every corner of our neighborhood.

"I ... " I started to say, not wanting to lie but desperately trying to evade the question.

"He is staying at your house, right?" She said.

"Yeah, but ...," I tried to come up with something to say. It was no use, she could read my face.

"You are, I knew it, you should see the filth I found on our computer. Disgusting!" she said.

"Listen, it isn't like that" I started to say.

"You can fucking have him" she yelled, storming off across the street. She got in her car and drove off, nearly hitting several cars in the process. I stood there shaking from our encounter for minutes afterward.

"What was that all about?" I heard Jake say from behind. I found myself standing there, immobilized.

"She found out about Evan and me" I told him.

"Oh shit!" Jake said.

"Yeah, you knew she already wanted a divorce, right?" I said.

"Yeah, I heard it from Nat. She knows everything that goes on around here" Jake said smiling.

"You didn't tell her, did you?" I asked.

"No, I swear" Jake said, crossing his heart.

"She said something about finding gay porn on their computer" I said.

"Wow, really?! She said that?" Jake said.

"Well, she didn't say gay porn, but she implied it. Said she knew I was sleeping with him" I told him.

"You are?" He asked with great interest.

"It wasn't till last night. He was a mess. I guess she's confronted him, and told him she wanted a divorce." I said.

"Fuck! He seemed so happy this morning" Jake said with a wink.

"I know, it might have something to do with the fact that we slept together" I said.

"Damn! Did he fuck you?" Jake asked with a tinge of jealousy.

"No. He slept in my room last night instead of the sofa, but we didn't do anything." I said.

"You slept in the same bed, but didn't do anything?" Jake said incredulously.

"Ok, we did do something earlier," I blushed.

"Ah, so that explains his more open attitude this morning. I was a bit shocked" Jake said.

"He still managed to shock me this morning, but yeah, he told me about the divorce and broke down. That's when it just kinda happened" I said.

"Come on, I want details!" He said punching my arm.

I filled him in on what had happened, in graphic detail, while looking around to make sure no one was eavesdropping. Jake's dick pressed out the front of his shorts as I got more explicit in my descriptions.

"We haven't done anything more than what we did on the roof this morning." I confessed.

"Well, he's free to do whatever he wants to now. Don't tell Nat but screw Cassie, I never cared for her," he said. I knew Nat and Cassie were friends, so the situation was a bit awkward all around.

"It's gonna make living here and getting along a little strained." I said.

"Let me see if Nat can talk to her, maybe she can smooth things over" Jake said.

"How did Evan react to you fucking me?" Jake asked.

"He didn't seem too freaked out" I said.

"You think he'd ever fuck me?" Jake asked. I wasn't prepared for him to be so blunt and come right out like that.

"I don't know. He seemed both curious and disgusted" I said.

"I've wanted his thick dick ever since we watched porn and jerked off together" he said.

"I still can't believe you two did that. I wish I had known back then. I would have taken a much greater interest in sports" I said wryly.

"I wish I'd told you sooner, but honestly, I didn't know you that well, and I knew he didn't want anyone else knowing," Jake said.

"Now that he's free, I wonder if he'd been open to it" Jake pondered.

"We should try to make it happen" I said.

"I wish" Jake said.

"You never know. I never expected to do anything with him or you for that matter and look out that's turned out" I said.

"True" he replied.

"I'd better go, I was on my way to the store when she accosted me" I said.

"Ok, see you around, stud," Jake said, flashing me that heart melting smile and a wink. He adjusted his shorts and headed up the block toward the park. I watched his bubble butt shift with each step, knowing my dick had been between those cheeks only hours before. Some of my cum might still be inside him. The thought made my dick jump as I got in the car.

I didn't see Evan at all that evening. Once again, he was either totally engrossed in his work or he was avoiding me. I hoped it wasn't the latter. I knew when he had a project in front of him, he was unrelenting in his pursuit of it. Sometimes without stopping to eat or sleep.

I stayed up as late as I could, but my eyes wouldn't stay open a moment longer. I went to bed disappointed that Evan wasn't there to slip in behind me like last night. I longed to feel his dick press into my crack. My dick was hard, so I stroked it a few times, but it was inadequate, I needed him with me. I drifted off with my hand still wrapped around my cock.

I felt something pressing against my ass. I woke to find I'd rolled into my side during the night. Evan was pressed in behind me, his hard dick resting in my crack. He was steadily breathing, so I assumed he was asleep. He must have come in during the night and slipped in behind me. I stretched and pushed back, feeling his dick pulse and press against my hole.

I felt his hips roll toward as his dick tried to jab into my hole. I still wasn't sure if he was awake or asleep. If he was asleep, there was no question he was trying to fuck someone. His dick poked and prodded me without finding my hole.

Given that it has been a while since I'd been fucked, I was extremely skeptical he'd be able to penetrate me if that was his intention. I met his thrusts, attempting to align my hole with his enormous head. Something caught, and I felt it press on my tight pucker. He paused, and I felt warm liquid drip onto my hole from his leaking head. He mumbled something unintelligible. Did he just say "Cassie"? I couldn't be sure. I imagined he was dreaming about fucking his wife, well soon to be ex-wife. I felt jealous that he still wanted her more than me. I know it was completely irrational, it was just a dream, nothing he could control.

I felt dirty letting him hump me like this. Like some substitute pussy. I wasn't sure how he would react if he woke up to find his dick pressed into my ass cleft. At least he hadn't officially penetrated me yet.

I felt his dick flex and more warm drool seeped into my crack. He let out a sigh and grunted. He reached around and pulled me close to him. His cock pressed in and out of my ass, each time making my opening more and more slick with his precum.

Then, without warning, his head caught and popped inside. I stifled a gasp as a rush of pain shot through me. I tried to pull away, but he held me tight. His cock pushed in further. He grunted loudly. I held my breath, biting the inside of my cheek to distract myself from the literal pain in my ass. His was by far the largest cock that had ever entered me. I'm not much of a bottom, but I could tolerate getting fucked under certain circumstances, and this was one time I endured.

"Oh fuck!" He yelled as his dick wrenched from my aching hole. I rolled over to find he'd gotten out of the bed and was standing naked in the dim light from the street. He looked frightened, like a small child in a thunderstorm.

"Oh shit! I'm sorry" I said, sitting up in bed.

"Why?" He looked at me with a puzzled expression.

"I don't know, I didn't want to wake you and ..." I trailed off. He'd attempted to fuck me in his sleep. I should have tried to wake him as soon as I realized something was going on.

"I ... I'm ... sorry" he said with panic in his voice. He looked down at his still hard cock pulsing in front of him.

"It's ok, no one is to blame. I went along with it" I said.

"But I didn't mean to ..." he said.

"I could have stopped you if I wanted" I said.

"You're not upset?" He asked.

"No, not at all. Come back to bed" I said.

"I've got to pee" he said, turning and heading out into the hall.

Fuck! I said, inside my scull. I shouldn't have let him do it. I should have stopped it before it got out of hand. I beat the mattress in frustration. He took a while in the bathroom. Too long to only be peeing. I slipped off the sheet and got out of bed. The bathroom was dark, but there was a light in the kitchen downstairs. I headed down, my still hard dick bouncing with each step.

Evan was standing in front of the refrigerator, its glow illuminating his body. His dick had softened but still looked impressive, especially in the stark glow of the refrigerator light.

"You ok?" I asked.

He turned, looking startled to find me there.

"I can't believe I did that" he said, looking away.

"Don't worry about it, I was actually enjoying it" I said looking down at my still rigid member. His eyes followed my glance and came to rest on my dick.

"I didn't hurt you?" He asked.

"I've been fucked before, I know what I'm doing," I said. He did hurt, but I wasn't going to tell him that. I wanted it to hurt more because I knew after that it would feel amazing. He didn't say anything, but his dick began to rise. He must have been thinking about it. I took a deep breath, trying to relax. I wanted to tell him to bend me over the counter and fuck me for dear life. I picked my words carefully, like pulling on a fishing line to lure a fish to the hook without scaring it off.

"You can continue where you left off if you want" I said as causally as I could. He looked at me for a moment, clearly contemplating it. His dick got harder, perhaps swaying his decision in my favor. He stood inert as all the cold poured out of my fridge behind him.

I took another step into the kitchen and leaned into the counter, pushing my ass out ever so slightly. The bit of weight I'd gained recently had helped my ass fill in some. He followed the line of my back to the top of my ass and down the supple curves.

"Go on" I said softly.

He stepped away from the fridge, letting the door shut behind him, plunging the room back into darkness. I heard him shuffling around behind me and felt some part of him brush against me. His hand moved down my back and grabbed onto my ass. Then it slid into my crack. I felt a finger touch my pucker. I pushed out my ass, feeling my legs make contact with his. His dick thrust up against my ass, pressing into my right cheek.

I wish we'd been in the bedroom because I had a bottle of lube within reach. I could have grabbed it and slicked up his cock and my ass with it. I was prepared to take him dry, but for both our sakes, lubed would be preferable.

I reached forward and found a bottle of olive oil. I didn't care, I would make due with anything. I tilted the spout toward my hand and felt the cool oil drizzle over my fingers and a pool form in my palm. I reached back and pressed the oil into my hole and groped in the darkness until I found his heavy cock still near my upper thigh. I slathered it in oil as I would prepare a thick cut of meat for the grill.

I held his dick and guided it to my opening. It was now or never, I thought, breathing out all the air in my lungs to relax. The head pressed against my hole as I drew in my breath sharply.

God damn! I thought, this will be harder than I thought. Though he'd been an inch inside me a few minutes ago, my ass was still reeling from the invasion and refused him entry. I tried again but made little progress. I was desperate now, I knew each moment he was delayed from entering me was a moment he could second guess the situation and end it there. I pushed out with all I could muster. Suddenly, I was full.

"Oh fuck" I heard him gasp as his dick slipped inside me. I struggled to remember to breathe as pain shot through me and my legs threatened to give way. I held on to the far side of the countertop, white knuckled, willing myself to open up for all nine thick inches. In delicious agony, I felt his huge bush press against my crack and realized with stunned surprise he was all the way inside me.

I reached back to confirm that it was the case and felt him retreat. I grabbed the base of his dick with slick fingers and tried to keep him from slipping out.

"No, I'm good" I said unconvincingly through gritted teeth.

He waited a moment and I felt his hands grab hold of my hips. I pushed back, impaling myself on him to prove it was ok. He grunted as once again he slipped into my tight hole. I felt his balls swing between my legs and land on the underside of my balls. I felt his dick pulse deep inside me, stretching me to my limit. I nodded, though I wasn't sure he could see the gesture.

He moved inside me again, first with tentative strokes of mere millimeters. I felt more full than I've ever felt before. I pictured his cock deep inside me, displacing my colon and reforming my intestines. Then he shifted, and the stars came out in my kitchen like it was a planetarium. Colors swam before my tightly closed eyes that seemed to linger when I opened them again in awe. He began to fuck me harder, and I became aware of the puddle of drool forming below my mouth on the cool granite. My dick pressed against the cabinet drawer, leaking precum down the wood. With each thrust inside me, my dick pressed into the hard wood, stretching the skin and sending a wave of pleasure up my spine.

I lost all sense of myself as the air filed with the sounds and smells of his dick probing the deepest recesses of my bowels. I heard someone saying "fuck" over and over again, but I wasn't sure it was him or me. It seemed to echo around inside my head.

I was sweating. I could hear the wet slapping of his pelvis slamming into my ass. His raw dick felt like it would catch fire at any moment from the friction of his rapid strokes. He used me like a sex toy, working out his frustration on my poor ass. I wanted him to use me. I delighted in giving him pleasure like this.

"Take it bitch" he said, perhaps imagining I was his ex and he was taking her pussy. He let out a bellowing cry that quite possibly woke up half the neighborhood. I could feel the warm spray deep inside me. My sphincter clenched as he pushed forward and pressed my dick into the cabinet. My cum cascaded down the front of the cabinet like a waterfall over the bumps and ridges of the woodwork.

He leaned forward and pressed our sweaty bodies together. I felt his heart beat through my back and inside me through his still hard cock. His weight rested across my back as his heavy breathing began to subside.

His dick remained hard inside me, pulsing. Post orgasm, I felt the pain returning to my ass. I wasn't sure how much more I could take. I breathed shallowly with his small but muscular frame pressed down on me.

I felt him moving inside me again, this time slowly, cautiously stirring. He pressed in an inch, then pulled out an inch. I wasn't sure my ass would take anymore. I certainly wouldn't be sitting down without feeling it for days to come. I didn't protest, though. I knew he was probably good for multiple loads one after the other. My dick began to harden again as he took up a steady, slow pace inside my loaded ass.

He pulled out and rolled me over with more strength than I thought possible from his smaller frame. He pulled my legs up to his shoulders and leaned forward. I felt his cock slip back inside my used and leaking hole.

My eyes opened wide when I felt his lips touch mine. I reached up and pulled in closer, running my hands over his rippling back muscles. He explored my mouth with his tongue as we kissed deeply.

His rhythmic pounding continued, building to another crescendo over the next what seemed like hours. I lay there, with my legs pressed into his shoulders, as he worked himself up into a frenzy once again. My hole burned as he jackhammered it, lubed by his previous load and the remaining olive oil. I knew my hole was a mess, but I didn't care. It was raw and powerful and all I could think about was getting another load from him.

Sweat dripped onto my face from his brow. He took his time fucking me on the cool granite while we kissed. My dick jabbed into his abs with each stroke, leaking precum onto his hairy skin. It took him a good deal longer this time, but soon I heard him grunting and pounding me hard.

He pulled out suddenly and stroked his cock a few times. I grabbed my cock and frantically stroked myself to the edge. I felt warm wetness fall on my chest and abdomen.

"Oh fuck!" I cried, and another volley landed on my dick. The additional lube of his cum sent me over the edge. My ass quivered and forced out some of his previously load as I shot my load into the air. Some of it must have hit him in the chest, while the rest fell onto me, mixing with his cum.

The last of his load leaked out onto my balls, dripped off onto the counter. I was completely and utterly spent. I could have just fallen asleep on the cold countertop, and perhaps I did for a moment. I felt I light prodding on my chest. It was a dish towel rubbing across my splattered chest, soaking up his seed.

He pulled me up to face him. I stood weak in the knees like I might fall over at any moment. He seemed to sense it and grabbed hold of me, strong yet tender in his arms.

"You ok?" he asked as I swayed.

"Yeah" I said but though, better than ok. That was fucking amazing.

I could just barely make out his face in the dim light. I wanted to gage his reaction to having fucked me twice in a row. He smiled and leaned forward, kissing me once again.

"Bed?" He asked. I nodded as he helped me to the stairs. I felt his cum still dripping from my ass, but I didn't care if it ruined the carpet. I needed my bed more than anything. He left me to feel my way to the bed while I heard the water turn on in the bathroom.

I didn't so much as get into bed as fall face-first into it. I was out before my head hit the pillow.

I woke disoriented, not sure where I was for a moment. My legs ached like I'd run miles, and my back spasmed. My ass was the real complaint though, it throbbed painfully. It all came back to me like a dream. He'd actually fucked me. I'd had that thick cock inside me.

Fuck! I thought, becoming aware that I was pressed up against someone. My arm was draped over his side and my chin was resting in the stirrup of his shoulder and neck. The soft hairs of his nape pressed into my cheek. My chest was pressed against his back. I could feel my abdomen come in contact with his lower back with each inhale and separate with each exhale.

My dick was resting comfortably in his hairy crack, with the tip pointing to the little pocket of hair directly above it. My left leg was sandwiched between his legs, while my right was tucked up against his right leg. I felt each contact point in turn without opening my eyes. He stirred and pulled my arm around him like I was a blanket pulled over him to for warmth. I felt my fingers slip along his chest hair, like running my hand through a field of summer wheat.

"Mmmm" he sighed and wiggled his body under me. I pressed in close, feeling my cock harden as it rubbed against the corse hair and warm skin of his ass.

"Morning" he said, craning his head backward to see my face. I opened my eyes and looked into his face. He was smiling a warm smile. His face was half lit by the bright sun gleaming through the window.

The perfect moment came cashing down when my alarm began to sound, and I had to sit up quickly to find my phone on the nightstand and mash the stop button.

He rolled onto his back to my annoyance. I wanted to press my cock back into his ass cleft, but couldn't any longer. I settled for rolling onto my side and pressing it into his side instead. I looked down and found the sheet that was draped over his lower half was floating over him, as if a small ghost had taken to haunting his crotch. I went to pull the sheet away but found resistance. It was tucked under his side and wouldn't budge. I reached down and gathered the cloth around the base of his cock, forming folds like a closed umbrella. He was fully hard, all nine inches of it. He folded his hands behind his head with his elbows akimbo and watched as I played circus with his cock. I pulled up a flap from my side and entered the big top, searching for the giant under the warm yellow spotlight of the sun.

My nose filled with his heady aroma as I moved closer to his cock. I licked his balls first, tasting his salty sack and smelling his rich pheromones. My tongue raked over the wiry hairs covering his scrotum. I moved up and licked his bush where his pelvis met his legs. He squirmed in delight as I licked and sucked the sensitive skin.

I licked the base of his cock before changing my mind and going back to his balls. I shifted under the sheet and crawled between his legs. I kissed up the inside of each thigh until I reached his taint. I looked down at the hairy strip running under him to his ass. I licked and sucked it, getting as low as I could, moving slowly toward his pucker. I expected him to stop me at any moment as I approached his no-man's-land. What I didn't expect was that he'd pull his legs back and expose his hole to me. But there it was, the soft folded skin and muscle surrounded by a ring of dirty blond hair.

I licked it tentatively, tasting the earthiness of it. I blew softly on it, cooling the skin. It flexed and tightened. I teased it some more with my tongue, before diving in and putting my whole mouth on it. He gasped as I licked his hole and probed it with my rigid tongue.

"Oh fuck" he said, perhaps feeling this sensation for the first time in his life. I ate his ass, my beard wet with spit as my tongue probed inches inside him. I fucked him with my tongue until the muscles in my tongue and jaw ached with a dull pain.

I placed one finger alongside my tongue and probed him with it as I licked around it, adding lube. The finger moved around the rim of his tight ring, barely penetrating him. He whimpered as I fingered his virgin hole. I felt around inside him until I found the hard lump of his prostate. I ran my finger along it.

"Oh fuck!" I heard him grunt as I pressed on it. His dick spasmed and released a flood of precum that dribbled down his shaft, some soaking into the sheet. I lapped up the remaining precum and sucked his dick into my mouth while I proved his hole with a finger. I risked pulling out and forcing a second finger into his tight opening. He grunted, but this time it sounded more like pain than pleasure. I held two fingers in place, fearing to move them in or out and make it worse for him.

I focused on his dick, licking and sucking the smooth skin to distract him from his ass and help him relax. It seemed to work, his ass released its vice-like grip on my fingers and let them slip back inside him. I found his prostate again and pressed it as I sucked him. My mouth filled with his precum as he began to grunt and moan.

"I'm gonna cum" he said, though it was hardly a warning since he immediately started to unload inside my mouth. I continued to jam my fingers into his prostate as I felt his warm cum fill my mouth. I swallowed his seed, relishing the bittersweetness of it. When I had squeezed every last drop from him, I let his dick fall with a heavy thud into his abs and slipped my fingers from his hole.

I pulled the sheet away and sat back, admiring Evan's body in the warm morning sun.

His eyes were closed, his face a visage of pure bliss. The blond hairs of his beard caught the light and glowed like embers. His chest hair sparkled in the sun like diamonds. His heavy cock rested in a spit soaked bush of thick dirty blond hair. I crawled up beside him, running my fingers through his chest hair, my unrelieved cock pressing into his side. I knew I'd need to get up soon, but I never wanted to leave his side again.

His hand played through my mop of bed head hair and came to rest on my neck, gently stroking it. I drifted off to sleep once again.

I woke with a start, hearing my phone buzzing alerts. I sat up and grabbed my phone, realizing how late it was. My boss was going to kill me, for missing the morning meetings again. I was only a little late as a scrambled to find my earbuds and join the call.

Evan opened his eyes and watched me as I tapped through missed messages and emails.

"Sorry I'm late" I said without further explanation. I'd found excuses to be lame and unneeded. A simple apology and then moving on to the subject of the meeting sufficed. I didn't have my laptop handy, but I managed on my phone as I spoke with my team about the latest issues and status.

I was so focused on the small screen, I failed to notice Evan moving down the bed.

"Oh!" I suddenly gasped as his mouth enveloped my cock. "No, sorry, please continue" I said, then pressed the mute button as Evan gummed my shaft back into life.

I now found it nearly impossible to focus on what the junior developer was asking, and I found I had to ask her to repeat things twice. Evan gripped the base of my now fully hard cock and slipped his tongue down the steely shaft. He took as much as he could down his throat before he started to gag loudly. I mashed mute again, fearing my colleagues would hear him choking in the background.

"Check in what you have and let me review it later" I finally said after not comprehending the problem she was describing for the third time. Evan spit on my cock and began to stroke me using an almost too tight fist.

I moaned softly, then quickly checked that the mute was on. I was relieved to find it was. In a moment of panic, I double-checked the camera was disabled. I'd seen the videos that had circulated where people on work calls showed up naked, not realizing their cameras were on. I didn't want that kind of scandal.

The meeting droned on in my ear as Evan stroked the bottom half of my cock while sucking the top half. His mouth felt so good, he wasn't bad for a novice.

"I'm close," I warned him. Then heard in my ear, "close to what?"

Shit, I thought, I'd forgotten to mute again. "I'm close to solving that issue with ..." I launched into an explanation of a problem I'd been working on. I knew it was out of context for what we'd been discussing, but I had to cover for my outburst somehow.

I mashed the mute again and double-checked it. Evan hadn't stopped what he was doing, stroking and sucking me closer and closer to climax.

"Oh fuck, I'm gonna cum" I said softly, still nervous that the mute wasn't working. Evan heard me because he looked up into my eyes. I dropped the phone on my chest and stared into his eyes as I unloaded into his mouth. He took my load without flinching, continuing to stroke the bottom half of my cock while he kept my head in his mouth.

I heard someone saying my name. "Oh, sorry, can you repeat that?" I said, still coming out of my post orgasmic haze.

"No, I don't have anything else to bring up. We can end the call. Thanks everyone, great work!" I said as faces began to disappear from my screen. I hit the end call button and sighed in relief.

I looked down at Evan, who was still suckling on my softening cock. He let it fall from his mouth and beamed up at me, a mischievous grin.

"You bastard!" I said with a great deal of mirth. "I could have gotten in trouble" I said, lightly slapping his cheek. He didn't say anything, only leaned forward and kissed up my abdomen and chest until he found my lips. We kissed, sharing the taste of my cum on his tongue. He no doubt could also taste his cum still on my tongue. I was again shocked at Evan's behavior. I wasn't expecting him to reciprocate, much less swallow my load.

Much as I would have loved to stay in bed with him all day, my phone was buzzing as work demanded my attention.

"I'm sorry, I've got to get to work" I said when we finally broke our kiss.

"It's all good" he said smiling. It was a contagious smile and made me feel warm and tingly inside.

I got dressed, though I hardly needed to for work these days. I rarely had to be on camera for meetings and didn't need to leave the house if I didn't want to. But it had been engrained in me that I should dress appropriately for work. This typically was jeans or shorts and a teeshirt. I have some standards. It was only because I was late I even considered joining the call from bed, still naked.

Evan slipped on his shorts, which was his typical work attire. He headed to the kitchen while I cleaned up a bit in the bathroom. It had been a perfect night and an even better morning, but I knew a storm loomed on the horizon.

I'd not had a chance to tell Evan about my confrontation with Cassie yet. It was in the back of my mind, but I avoided it for as long as I could. I wasn't sure how he'd react to the news. If I let it go too long, he'd wonder why I didn't tell him sooner when he eventually found out.

I took a deep breath and steadied myself as I headed downstairs and into the kitchen. Evan had started a pot of coffee and was rummaging in the fridge for something to eat.

"Hey, I've got to talk to you about something" I said gravely. He turned and looked at me, sensing the mood shift in my tone of voice.

"What's wrong?" He asked.

"I saw Cassie yesterday" I started. His face dropped. His expression was one of longing and sadness mixed with a touch of anger and fear.

"Oh," he said, tensing up.

"Yeah, she asked if you were staying here" I said.

"Everybody knows that by now" Evan said.

"But she asked if we were sleeping together" I finally said, finding it hard to come out with the statement.

"What!!" He said, in shock. He looked around in panic like someone was hiding behind the refrigerator, spying on us.

"How did she know!" He asked.

"I don't know. Maybe she just guessed" I said.

"Fuck!" He said, slumping to the floor.

"There is something else" I said. I hated to continue to drop bad news on him, but like ripping off a bandaid, it had to be done.

"She was furious about something she found on the computer" I said. He grew silent and his face flushed red.

"Oh shit, she must have found my browser history, fuck" he said.

"It's ok." I said.

"No it's not, she'll use it against me" he said. "Fuck! Why didn't I erase it?"

"It's not that bad, is it?" I asked.

He looked up at me and shook his head.

"How bad?" I said, seeing his reaction.

"I was curious after Jake and I ... you know." He said.

"I don't blame you" I said.

"Fuck! Now she'll think we've been having an affair all this time," he said, despondent.

"She'll have no proof of that, just some browser history that proves only that you were curious. That's it. " I tried to reassure him.

"What am I gonna do?" he said. I knew this would be hard for him. His straight persona would be shattered, everyone would learn of his interest in dick. I could empathize. I'd hidden who I was for years before I finally came out. I don't know how I would have reacted if, instead of making that choice when I was ready, I'd had the closet door thrown open for me.

I got down on the floor with him, ignoring work for a moment, and held him. I gently rubbed his back, trying to find words to comfort him, but let actions speak for me.

"It's gonna be ok" I finally said. He sniffed as if holding back tears. Finally, he stood up and gathered his tools, forgetting the coffee he'd brewed.

"You can stay here as long as you want" I told him as he headed out the door. I wished it would be forever, but I still didn't know if that was in the cards. He was just finding himself, and he had a long road ahead of him.

I settled down to work but found my focus drifting ever back to him and the feelings I was developing for him. What had started out as a simple gesture of help to a neighbor in a time of need was developing into something so much more. I wasn't sure either of us were ready for what came next.

Chapter 16
Role Play

The air was filled with iridescent bubbles, swirling aloft on invisible currents. The source of the bubbles was a bubble gun welded by Jake's daughter.

"Hey," he said on seeing me as he pushed the stroller up the block through the stream of bubbles.

"Hey, how's it going?" I said.

"Heading to the playground" he said.

"Have fun" I said, fishing me key fob from my pocket.

"Oh hey, Nat asked if you guys wanted to come over for dinner Sunday, we could watch the game after" he said vaguely. I suspected there would be more too it than watching a football game.

"Yeah sure, I'll check with Evan when he gets back" I said.

"Cool, see you Sunday, if not sooner," he said with a wry smile and a wink. My dick jumped as I contemplated what he might have in store for us on Sunday.

The trio sauntered up the block, leaving a trail of bubbles in their wake that lingered until they landed softly on the sidewalk, winking out of existence one by one.

I wanted to tell him about Evan fucking me, but it wasn't an appropriate time. That news would have to wait until I saw him in his running shorts a couple of days later.

"Evan still isn't back?" He asked.

"No, and I'm starting to get worried" I said. He'd not come home, the evening after I told him about the confrontation with Cassie. I assumed he must be staying on the boat he was working on. I'd texted him but had gotten no reply.

"He was upset about her finding out about us, he took his tools and left. I've not been able to reach him since" I said.

"Huh, I guess give him some time, I'm sure he's fine," Jake said.

"I know I just worry" I said.

"Sounds like you're starting to have feelings for him" Jake said as we turned the corner and jogged into the park.

"I did feel something between us, it was more than just fucking" I said.

"He fucked you?" Jake asked, nearly tripping over his left foot with his right.

"Yeah, he came to bed after I'd fallen asleep and the next thing I knew his dick was pressing against my back door" I said.

Jake reached down and adjusted himself.

"He just started fucking you in your sleep?" He asked.

"I think he was asleep himself. I wondered if he thought he was fucking Cassie at first. He didn't really get very far before he woke up and kinda freaked out" I said.

"Fuck! I'd kill to be in your place. Maybe that's why he left? He's feeling weird about that?" He speculated.

"No because I followed him into the kitchen and that's when we really fucked" I said.

Jake stopped in his tracks and turned to me, eyes wide and mouth open in shock.

"Ok now you've got to tell me everything" he said, his dick was already hard and pushing against the jockstrap he was wearing under his tight shorts. The straps were clearly visible against the slick red fabric.

As we jogged toward our spot, I filled him in on what had happened.

"He fucked you twice in a row!" He said when we reached the spot hidden among the brambles and kudzu vines.

"Then in the morning he let me rim his hole and finger fuck him till he came in my mouth" I said.

"Holy shit, no way!" He said, yanking down his shorts to reveal his hairy ass framed by the straps of his jock. We were both covered in sweat and beyond horny. I let my shorts fall to the ground. My dick was already rock hard from reliving in what had happened with Evan. It had been a few days since I'd even jacked off. I'd waited, saving my load for him, but he'd not returned that night, and so I waited again and still no sign of Evan.

I bent down and spit on Jake's ass and licked it up, tasting the salty sweat gathered between those soft white globes. I snaked my tongue into his hole, feeling it open for me.

"Give me that big cock!" Jake insisted as he pushed out his ass, taking another finger. Nothing less than my thick cock would do now. Maybe he was imagining it was Evan's even bigger cock that was entering him.

He was in heat. He pushed his ass back, impaling himself to the root of my cock with a loud grunt. If he regretted moving too quickly, he didn't show it. He gripped the tree branch, white knuckled, as I gave him what he wanted. He was so tight and warm, and I was so amped up and ready to cum, that I barely took a dozen hard strokes before I was ready to cum. I couldn't hold back.

"Oh fuck!" I screamed as I loaded Jakes ass with the cum I'd been saving for Evan. I stayed fully hard after my cum filled his hole. It lubricated my continued thrusts. I kept pounding his hole, envisioning it was Evan, taking my cock like he took my fingers.

"Yeah, fuck me, Evan" Jake said as I pounded him. "Fuck me hard, bud, with the monster cock of yours!" He went on. I was a bit taken aback at first but realized he was playing out a longtime fantasy with me. I went along with it.

"You want your buddies cock, bro?" I said, pulling out so that just the tip, slick with cum, was at the entrance to his gaping hole.

"Yes! I've wanted it since the first time I saw it," Jake said.

"I never knew you wanted it so badly," I said, mimicking Evan's slight Canadian accent.

"Yes, I want it in me" Jake said, pushing out his ass to try to fill it again with Evan's cock.

"I don't know. I don't think it'd be right to fuck my best friend like this." I said.

"Please," Jake begged as I teased his hole and smacked his ass with my hard member.

"You really want this cock, don't you?"

"Please fuck me Evan" Jake pleaded.

"That's right, beg me for it" I said, getting more cocky.

"Please sir, take my hole! Use me!" He said, wiped up into a frenzy by the role play.

"You want me to bend you over the sofa while we watch the game?" I said, pushing his back down and pressing my dick along his sweaty crack.

"Yes! Fill me with that thick monster" he gasped.

"What was that?" I said.

"Fuck me sir!" He said apologetically.

"That's better" I said, pressing the tip to his hole. Some of my previous load leaked out around my head. "You'll be my little slut, won't you?" I said.

"Yes, I'm your slut, use me, breed my hole, sir" he said, his voice going higher. I jammed all 8 inches inside him in one quick mention that took his breath away. It felt like his legs were giving way.

His hand worked frantically on his cock as I started to pound him hard with long strokes nearly all the way out then back in as deep as I could go. My balls ached as they smacked his ass loudly.

"Take it slut!" I said, and Jake whimpered in delight. His ass quivered and tightened around my cock as his cum splatted the dried leaves and dirt at the base of the tree.

I hadn't cum again, but I was getting close to a second load as his balls drained, and his ass gripped me tightly. I pulled out. My dick was sticky with wet cum and sweat.

Jake turned to press his back against the tree and steady himself. I stepped up to him, my hard, sticky cock looming in his face.

"I'm not done here! Clean it up bitch" I said now acting as if I were Evan and Jake was Cassie.

"Yes sir" Jake said, leaning forward and taking my dirty cock in his mouth. He licked my cum and his juices from me, then gave me the sloppiest blowjob I've ever had. His drool ran down my balls and leg as he used one hand and his mouth to bring me ever closer.

"Yeah that's it! Suck my cock! Take your buddy's load" I said, slipping back into the roles of Jake and Evan. Jake grunted and took my load, stroking me furiously with the tip of my cock in his mouth as each glob landed on his tongue.

I looked down at him, his stubbled chin was covered in spit that dripped down into his hairy chest. When he'd finished licking every last drop of cum from my dick, he stood with my help. He looked a little wobbly, my legs felt like rubber as I held on to his shoulder, balancing against one another.

"Holy fuck!" Jake finally said.

"I know right" I said, wiping the sweat from my brow.

"That has got to be the hottest fuck I've ever had in my life!" Jake said, still trying to control his breathing.

"It was" I said. "It was a little weird at first, being Evan".

"Sorry about that, what you told me about him. I couldn't help myself" he said, flicking some cum that he'd gathered from his still dripping foreskin into the underbrush.

"I hope he comes back in time for Sunday" he said.

"I know you have something more than watching the game planned" I said.

"You can count on that" Jake said, flashing me that irresistible smile.

"And Nat is ok with it happening under your roof?" I asked.

"I hope this doesn't spoil things for you, but she is eager to join us" he said.

"Oh" I said, taken aback. I'd never truly been with a woman, apart from a few fumbling encounters in high school.

"She just wants to watch if that's ok" Jake said.

"Ah, ok sure" I said, relieved I wasn't expected to do anything with her. Not that she wasn't attractive. Like Jake, she took care of herself. She was still in the process of losing some of the extra weight she gained after their second child was born. Honestly, it looked good on her.

"Cool! I'm really looking forward to it. I hope Evan comes back in time" Jake said, pulling his shorts back up and tucking his shirt in the waistband.

"I hope so too" I said with an anxious smile.

Chapter 17

Houseboat

When Evan didn't come back, I went looking for him Saturday morning. I had no idea if I'd even be able to find him among all the boats at the pier. I didn't even know if the boat he was working on was at this one or one of the others dotted around the harbor and beyond.

I was about to give up when I spotted his truck parked in the lot near the entrance. My next obstacle was the locked gate at the end of the pier. I stood pondering what to do next. Maybe he'd come this way, but I could be waiting hours before he showed up.

"You lookin for someone?" said an older gentleman wearing a robe and pulling a cart from the marine terminal to the pier.

"Uh, you know a guy named Evan? He does work on boats around here" I asked.

"Of course I know him, he's fixing my boat" he said, then he eyed me cautiously. "What do you want with him?"

The question hit me on so many levels. What did I want from him? What was I expecting? I fumbled to reply.

"I ... I'm a friend of his. Just wanted to see him" I said, not sounding at all convincing. The man eyed me with suspicion again but seemed to accept my answer anyway. He pulled out a key and slipped it into the lock, and the heavy metal gate swung open.

"After you" he said, ushering me in. He followed closely behind me, the cart rumbling as it rolled over the uneven wooden slats. He led me along a maze of piers until we came to a 44-foot houseboat.

The man hopped aboard, more spryly than I expected. I helped him pull the cart over. He took a minute to look below, then retuned.

"We'll, he ain't here" he said. "Might've gone to get a part or something. You're welcome to wait for him here" he said, taking a seat on the "porch" and gesturing to the seat next to him.

I didn't have anywhere else to be, so I settled into one of the comfortable chairs arranged around a small bolted down table.

"I'm Steve, by the way" he said, holding out his hand. I shook it and introduced myself.

"So, how did you get mixed up with Evan?" He asked, spreading his legs open a bit and relaxing into the chair. He must have just come from the shower because he was just wearing a robe and, to my surprise, nothing underneath it. His hair was still damp, and he wore a weathered pair of flip-flops.

"He's my neighbor." I said.

"Really? Oh, Can I get you something? Coffee, tea ...?" He said. And I instantly heard the word "me" echo inside my head.

"Some coffee would be great," I said.

He got up, his robe slipping open, so I had a quick full view of his hairy body and thick pubes resting above an impressive semi-hard thick cock. He closed the front and adjusted the tie before he headed inside. A little while later, he returned with two steaming mugs.

"Cream?" He asked, standing over me, his cock once again visible through the barely cinched opening of his robe.

"Ah ..." I looked up to find him holding a small cup of cream. I nodded and he poured some in. I got the distinct impression he was also offering another kind of cream from a very different source. Despite myself, I found I was getting aroused.

"May I ask you something?" He asked, taking his seat next to me again.

"Sure, I guess" I said.

"Is everything ok with him?" He asked.

"I'm not sure what you mean?" I said knowing exactly what he meant.

"I live here and hired him to do some work on her. " He said, gesturing to the boat around us. "A couple of nights ago, I found him sleeping on the deck. I let him crash on the sofa. Did his wife kick him out or something?"

"Yes, they are getting a divorce" I said.

"Oh, that explains it. He was real upset about something. I didn't have the heart to make him leave, but he really can't stay here forever," he said in a low voice.

"He had been staying with me for a few nights. I came to find him because he didn't come home" I said. He looked me up and down again when I slipped up and used the term "home" by mistake.

"How'd he end up with you?" He asked, raising an eyebrow.

"He was sleeping in his car after his wife kicked him out. We've been neighbors for a while. I didn't really know him other than a friendly hello in passing," I said, trying not to look up the robe where his balls were clearly visible along with just the tip of his uncut cock. It looked incredibly thick, with just a half inch of his head pushing out from the hood.

"Ah, so his wife found out about you two?" He said, with a sly grin on his face.

"Oh no, it had nothing to do with that" I said, finding I'd slipped up again.

"So there is something going on between you two" he said, giving me a knowing wink.

"I mean ... it wasn't like that. She kicked him out before I even knew him," I said now completely flustered.

"It's ok, I wouldn't blame you. He's got one hell of a body and a cock that belongs on a horse" he said.

My jaw nearly hit the deck.

"Don't worry, I didn't make the moves on him or anything, if that's what you're worried about. I was a perfect gentleman. I just happened to find him sprawled out on the sofa this morning naked as a jaybird with wood to peck" he said.

"That sounds like him" I said, shaking my head.

"If I'd have known he swung that way I might have offered to help him out" he said grinning from behind his scruffy gray beard.

"I thought he was straight, too." I said. You dirty old man, I thought. But then again, I wasn't much better the way I spied on him in the shower.

"So how did you two end up ..." he said, filling in the missing last word with a nod.

I was a bit taken aback by his directness. He didn't try to cover up his growing cock as he sat back down in his chair. It slid down and rested on his balls, then crawled toward me like a slug inching its way along the seat cushion. I gulped, finding my throat dry. He wasn't my usual type, but then again, what was my type exactly. He was older and heavyset with a barrel chest covered it thick dark hair that crawled out from the loosely tied robe.

"I took him in and one thing led to another. First there was the shower ..." I said, then recapped the highlights of our escapades. His dick grew harder with each tale. I didn't know why I was telling this total stranger all about our sex life. I got a bit of the thrill from it, knowing the reason his cock was lifting itself off the seat and drooling was because of what I was telling him.

"Damn! That is about the hottest thing I've ever heard" he said, his hand openly pawing at his hard member. He looked down at it and back up at me. "You've made me leak!"

I grew flush in the face. What was happening here? I was also hard and leaking inside my jeans.

"Looks like he might be a while, maybe we can pass the time inside" he said grinning. I knew exactly what he was implying. Without waiting for an answer, he got up and went inside, dropping the robe the minute he was inside the door. Thought his ass sagged a bit, it was still ample and covered in a light sprinkling of salt and pepper hair. He bent down and picked up the robe, showing off his ass and heavy balls as he headed toward the bedroom.

I knew I shouldn't have, but I got up and followed him inside, slipping off my clothes as I went, leaving them in piles leading into the bedroom. The ceilings were a bit low for me, so I had to duck below the bulkhead or hit my head on the way in.

He was sitting on the edge of the bed watching me remove my underwear with mounting anticipation.

"Damn! You give Evan a run for the money" he said, reaching up to grab me.

"You're not so bad yourself" I said, stooping down to grasp his thick tube. The outer skin felt warm and soft, moving effortlessly over the steel core. I sat down next to him on the bed. We stroked each other's cocks until we were both leaking.

He laid back on the bed and nodded for me to come forward. I straddled his chest, hanging my heavy dick over his bearded face. He licked the underside of it from my balls to the tip before slipping it into his mouth. He was a pro at sucking dick. He had me ready to cum in seconds. I bit my lip to keep from cumming too soon. I looked down to see his bald crown ringed with closely shaven hair. My dick was completely in his mouth, my pubes pressing into his nose. He pulled back, flicking the underside of my dick with his tongue as we went. There is something to be said for age and experience.

I leaned forward and fucked his face, pounding the silky wetness of his tongue and throat. The boat rocked gently as I became lost in the sensation.

"What the fuck are you doing here?" Came the angry voice of Evan behind me.

"Oh shit" I said as my balls clenched, and I passed the point of no return. As I stepped back, cum shot from my dick and splattered Steve's face and chest.

Evan stood in the doorframe, his face reddening at the sight of us.

"I'm sorry, I came to find you and ..." I started to say.

"And you figured you'd fuck my employer while you waited" he said, his voice dripping with anger.

"I ... I ..." I looked for something to say, some way to excuse my behavior, but there was no excuse. I knew I shouldn't have done it. I knew Evan would be along any minute. Why did I do it?

"Because of you, my wife thinks I'm a ..." he stopped himself saying the word that I'm sure was on his mind. His fists were clenched and his knuckles white. I was afraid he might give me a black eye. "Not to mention the whole fucking neighborhood probably knows by now!"

"It's my fault," Steve said.

"Huh?" Evan said, looking down at Steve below me. His cock was still hard and dripping precum. Evan looked down then looked away, like he was struggling to look and not look at the same time.

"I was horny. With you being here the past few days, I've not been able to get off. So when your friend here came along, I pounced at the opportunity. I'm sorry" he said.

"I wasn't talking about today," Evan said, set off balance by his employer's admission.

"I'm sorry for how it went down, but it sounds like it had nothing to do with me, she found your porn stash" I said, bitting back my anger. I was only trying to help, and this was the thanks I got. Even looked like I'd punched him in the gut. He sank against the wall.

"He told me what happened," Steve when on. "It's alright, I'm not gonna judge. There is a reason I've remained a bachelor all my life" he said, giving Evan a wink. He wiped the cum from his chin and licked it off his hand.

"So he told you about ..." Evan said, looking down at his feet.

"I asked him what was going on, I'm worried about you and so is he" Steve said.

Evan slumped down onto a built-in seat in the bulkhead. I took the opportunity to slip my underwear back on quickly. The rest of my clothes were out in the other room.

"I'm sorry," I said.

"You don't need to apologize, it's not like ..." Evan said, then stopped mid-sentence. It occurred to me then that maybe he'd felt the same things I'd felt the last time we were together, and his anger might contain a touch of jealousy.

"I've missed you" I said, taking a seat next to him. Steve took the hint and left us alone to fetch his robe.

"I've missed you too" he said, looking up at me glassy-eyed.

"Why didn't you come back?" I asked.

"I don't know. Guess I was too embarrassed to show my face knowing how everybody talks" he said.

"Nothing to be embarrassed about" I said. He responded with an incredulous look. I could see where he was coming from. In little over a week, he went from being a straight married dad to being a soon-to-be divorced gay man, well gay might be a stretch, at the least bisexual.

"I know it's been a crazy rollercoaster, but you don't have to go it alone. You have me, and you have some very supportive neighbors." I said.

"Like who?" he said.

"Jake and Natalie, to start" I said. He still looked deeply depressed.

"Speaking of which, Jake and Nat invited us over to dinner tomorrow to watch the game," I said.

"And Steve seems like a cool guy" I said, jabbing him in the ribs a little. He gave me a weak look.

"The guy really knows how to give a good blowjob" I added. Jake pushed me over, so I nearly fell off the bench. I laughed, and Evan couldn't help but join in. It was nice to see his smile break through.

"Oh and Jake has something special planned for Sunday" I said.

"Oh yeah?" Evan said.

"If you are up for it" I said.

"What is it?" He asked.

"It's a surprise. I can't tell you" I said.

"Tell me!" He said, grabbing me and pushed me into the bed, straddling my waist and getting ready to tickle me.

"No, I can't tell" I said between giggles.

"You'd better talk" he said, tickling me. I tried my best to resist, but in the end I was doubling over trying to get away.

He grabbed me and pulled me back when I tried to roll away. I pushed off a little too violently, twisting to my side while he grabbed me and pressed his fully weight against my back.

"If you break my bed, I'll take it out of your ass" Steve said from the door.

We stopped and looked up. He'd put on his robe, but it did little to hide his still hard dick poking against the terrycloth.

With Evan on top of me, I could feel a stirring from his crotch pressed against my left ass cheek.

"Oh sorry, about that" I said, trying to move off the bed and get up. Evan wouldn't let go.

"Now if you were to break it fucking each other, I'd be much more understanding" he said with a sly grin. His hand dropped to his robe and the mound of flesh not well hidden below.

I felt Evan tense like he was unsure where this was leading. I pushed back, my ass pressing hard into his thickening cock. He looked down at me, then back at Steve. Something seemed to shift in him. He pulled back from laying on top of me. For a moment, I felt disappointed and regretted starting this.

Then with a loud rip, he yanked open my underwear, exposing my hole where the tattered cloth once was. He smacked my bare ass. The sound was loud but muffled by the low ceilings.

"This what you want?" Evan asked, pressing forward. His hard cock poked at my opening, white-hot like his welding torch.

"Oh fuck," I heard Steve say breathlessly as he watched Evan hump my ass without penetrating me. I pushed my hips back, so I was doing the downward dog. He grabbed the waistband of my underwear and grasped it tightly while ripping the opening he's made wider. My balls hung out the opening, while my hard dick remained pressed into the front of the underwear.

"You want this cock you little slut" he said batting my hole a few time with his thick head. I nodded.

Evan pulled back and spit on my ass, it oozed down my crack. He slipped it into my hole roughly with two fingers. I tried to breathe deep and prepare myself for what came next. He slammed it into my hole. I cried out in pain as my ring ached to accommodate the sudden onslaught. I tensed with only made matters worse for me. I deserved the rough treatment, even welcomed it.

I turned my head to the side and let out a grunt. Then I felt something heavy rest on my cheek. I opened my eyes to find Steve's thick tube resting there, leaking precum in a slimy trail toward my lips.

His robe was untied and open at the front, showing off a thick strip of hairy belly and chest. My ass quivered and tried to expel Evan's dick, but he held firm, not moving an inch out of me. I clamped down hard, feeling the strength of my ring wavering.

"Go on, take us both, you dirty white!" Evan said. I was shocked at his language but complied.

I pushed myself up off the bed, so I was now on all fours. I lapped at the half inch of exposed head beyond Steve's foreskin and tasted the salty sweetness that was dripping from the wide piss slit.

Evan pulled back and spit on my ass again, the sticky wetness dripping down onto my balls. He took a few tentative thrusts, and I gritted my teeth, willing the discomfort to go away. I wanted him to fuck me. I wanted him to completely own my hole like I had role-played with Jake, just in reverse.

"That's right bitch! Your ass is mine" Evan growled.

Evan tightened his grip on my waistband, knotting it in a ball as it cut into my skin. His dick began to slip in and out of me. I was finally able to let go and let his thick nine inches invade me fully. I felt that indescribable full feeling. I grunted as he began to pound me. I whimpered and took the pounding I deserved. He took his frustrations out on my poor abused hole.

I felt something wet smack my lips. I'd neglected what I'd begun with Steve. I opened my mouth, and he fed his dick into it. I slipped my tongue over the foreskin, looking for an opening. It slipped in alongside his head and I heard him gasp. I flicked my tongue over the sensitive skin inside, lapping up more precum. He pushed past my tongue and slipped to the back of my mouth as I gripped his foreskin, letting it pull open inside my mouth. He pulled back, and I cinched the skin closed around the head once more. I bit down on the tapered foreskin, nibbling the soft flesh. He seemed to enjoy that as he grabbed hold of my head and held me there. Evan's fucking made it difficult to hold still and focus as each new thrust into me pushed me forward. I let Steven slip back inside me and used Evan's thrusts to press Steven into my throat.

They worked up into a rhythm using me from both ends. My trapped dick began to tingle as it pressed into the overstretched material of my underwear. Evan pounded me hard and relentlessly until I lost all feeling in my ass. His dick hit my prostate over and over again, milking precum into my soaked underwear.

"Oh fuck!" Steven cried, seed spilling into my mouth. I lapped it up and swallowed the warm, ripe spray. Steven cumming set Evan off. He pounded me hard and with frenzied motions, stabbing at my prostate. I felt my ass camp down hard and my underwear soak with warm cum.

"Oh shit!" Evan cried, feeling me tighten around him. He made a few last jabs into my rock-hard prostate before he held it there. I felt his dick pulse and paint my insides with his seed. He took a few more thrusts, depositing what must have been several days worth of cum into my aching ass. My legs and arms gave out as I crumbled onto the bed.

I felt the wetness of my load seeping from my spent dick onto the white linen. I feel the bed shift as Evan fell to my side, having pulled his cock from my ass with a grotesque slurp.

Our host sat down on my other side and lightly caressed my hair as I purred in delight. I must have slipped into unconsciousness because when I came back to my senses, Steven and Evan were gone, and I was alone in the bedroom. I could hear muffled talking from the next room.

"If you need more work, I know this guy with a yacht who is looking for mechanic" Steven was saying.

"Yeah, I can always use more work" Evan said.

I slowly sat up and looked into the living room. Evan and Steven were both still naked, sitting across from each other having coffee.

"Hey" I said as I wandered over to them looking for my discarded mug.

"Here let me warm that up for you" Steven said grabbing the pot and pouring steaming hot coffee into the cold coffee. I sipped the warm beverage, trying to shake the fog from my head.

Evan was rattling off a list of things that needed fixing on the boat, while Steven nodded gravely.

"I love living on the water, but the upkeep is so expensive." Steven said.

"I bet" I said. Evan seemed totally at ease now. His still impressive soft cock resting against his thigh.

"I'd better get to work on that pump" Evan said, standing.

"Are you coming back tonight?" I asked, discarding my ripped underwear and pulling on my shorts.

"I'll be there," Evan said, getting up and slipping on his shorts.

"Cool, Jake will be happy to see you" I said.

"You never told me what the surprise is" Evan said.

"You'll have to wait and see." I said.

Chapter 19
Domesticity

"You made it" I called out from the kitchen when I saw Evan come through the door.

"I'm sorry it took me longer to fix than I thought" he said putting his tools.

"That's ok, I'm still working on dinner" I said, stirring some sauce in the pan.

"I'm gonna grab a shower then" he said, dropping his shorts where he stood. Though he was covered in grease and grim, I was tempted to let dinner burn and drop to me knees in front of him. He smiled at me, scanning down his body, and then walked into the kitchen.

He kissed me softly on the cheek before turning to head up the stairs. I stopped to watch him go, feeling the ghostly impression of his lips on me skin for minutes after he'd gone.

I slipped off my shorts and shirt once I was done cooking and waited for him to return as I played the food.

"Smells delicious," he said, walking into the room, rubbing his fingers through his still damp hairy chest. As I had hoped, he hadn't bothered to dress for dinner. I poured some wine, and we sat down at the table.

"That Steven is a character huh" I said.

"He sure is. I had no clue he was gay." Evan said.

"I got vibes from him the minute I stepped onboard" I said.

"You'll have to teach me all about these Jedi powers you gay boys have" he said.

"Didn't take any Jedi powers, his dick was practically falling out of the robe the whole time" I said. He laughed.

After dinner, he cleaned up the dishes then joined me in the living room. I'd picked out a movie to watch.

"I love this movie!" He said, flopping down next to me. I never would have pegged him as a Star Wars fanboy, but he suddenly launched into a giddy conversation about some lesser known plot points and characters.

"Oh that's right, I forgot you dressed as a stormtrooper for Halloween last year" I said. I recalled how good he looked in the outfit and how much I wanted to get a look at what was under that molded plastic codpiece.

"Yeah, I know I'm a geek" he said. Huge dick and he was a geek like me too. This guy was too good to be true.

I started the movie and sank in next to him, resting my head on his chest. He put his arm around me and rested his palm in the middle of my chest. It was nice to just relax and cuddle up with a good movie for a change. His typical nervous energy had faded, and he seemed content to just sit with me as well.

"This thing tomorrow, I take it that it will involve sex?" He said after the movie was over.

"I can't say" I said with a grin.

"Ugh, if I know Jake it does, but why is that such a surprise." He said.

"Did you tell him about the other day?" He asked.

"About what in particular?" I asked, knowing full well what he was asking.

"You know, what happened in the kitchen" he said.

"I might have mentioned something" I said.

"You bastard, you really are terrible at keeping secrets" he said.

"I'm sorry, I figured there wasn't any harm." I said.

"How'd he react?" He asked.

"He was ..." I wanted to say "champing at the bit to have you fuck his ass" but I said "curious".

"Curious about?" He persisted. I got flustered and red in the face.

"How it felt to take this monster," I said, reaching over and grabbing his perpetually semi-hard cock.

"You think he wants to get fucked by me?" He asked.

"Yes! I think he's wanted to ever since you two started fooling around" I said.

"Really? He's such a freak" he said.

"He sure is" I laughed.

"Bed?" He asked.

"Sure" I said, yawning and stretching.

He headed upstairs while I got the lights and made sure the doors were locked. He was brushing his teeth when I reached the top of the stairs. The door was wide open, and I could see his face in the mirror and his back and ass in the bright glow from the overhead light. I stood admiring him for a moment before I stepped up behind him.

I leaned in and pulled him close to me, my semi pressing into his ass crack. He leaned forward, pushing out his ass against me as he spit into the sink. My head touched his opened for a moment and I started to harden.

"Didn't get enough earlier?" He asked.

"With you around, I'll always be back for more" I said, grinning.

He tilted his head toward me and we kissed. My mouth was full of minty freshness as our tongue met. My dick hardened, pressed against his hole. I fucked his opening a few times before he turned around, his dick already hard.

He pivoted me around and got down behind me. I felt a cool feeling touch my hole. It built into an icy heat. His tongue flicked at my hole.

"The toothpaste is kinda burning" I said, pulling away and touching my hole. It tingled unpleasantly. I got in the shower and washed off the residue.

"Sorry about that, I wasn't thinking" he said.

"It's ok, just felt weird" I said, grabbing the toothpaste.

"Maybe wait until after" he said, stopping my hand.

"After?" I asked. He responded by turning around and showing off his ass. He leaned forward over the sink invitingly. I took the hint and got down on the plush bathroom rug and pulled open his cheeks. There was his bright pink pucker, the soft blonde hairs sparkling in the harsh bathroom light.

I leaned forward and licked his hole tentatively. He let out a moan. I dove in and licked and sucked his hole, biting down on it at times. He began to whimper as I pressed my tongue into his opening.

He reached back and pressed my head into his ass, working my tongue into him. I couldn't breathe, his ass was covering my mouth and nose. He finally let go, and I came up gasping for air.

I pressed a finger to the sticky, wet flesh. It slipped in an inch or so. I moved it around looking for his prostate.

"Oh fuck" he said when my finger punched at it. His dick jumped and a line of precum oozed from his dick into the bowl of the sink. I pulled out and spat on my fingers, getting them wet before plunging two into him. He whimpered in pain, then sighed as I hit the spot again.

I was eager to be inside him, maybe too eager. I licked his hole again, getting it wet, before I stood and pressed my dick where my fingers had just been. He was sealed shut, tight. My head pressed against his hole but wouldn't budge. I took short strokes just on the outside, pressing in a little more each time I came forward. He inched opened until, suddenly, I slipped in.

"Oh fuck" he cried and pulled away, my dick slipping out of him. There was a pained look on his face.

"I'm sorry, went in a little too quickly." I said, kicking myself for being too eager. His virgin ass needed a slow, patient touch.

"It's ok, I'm not sure I'm ready for that" he said, turning around. His dick had softened a bit but was still impressive.

"Sure, no problem" I said.

"You won't be disappointed?" he asked.

"No, why would I?" I said, leaning in and kissing him, our dicks pressing into each other. As we kissed, our bodies writhed against each others. His hands ran down my back and rested on my ass. When he tugged them apart, the cool air kissed my puckered hole. I could still feel a bit of the minty freshness from the toothpaste.

"Take this to the bedroom?" I asked. He smiled and slapped my ass in the direction of the hallway. I turned and headed out into the darkness, knowing he was right behind me, looking at my ass as I headed into the bedroom.

He slipped into the bed next to me. In the dark, I groped around for him, feeling the soft hair on his arms and chest. I leaned in and licked up his armpit, tasting the strong funk that had built up there even though he'd showered a few hours ago. I buried my nose in it, licking and sucking the hairy skin. I made my way over to his nipple, sticking up prominently. I sucked it to a point, then bit down on it lightly. I felt his dick jump and press into the back of my arm. I made my way down his body, tracing the outline of his tight abs as I went.

He giggled when I stuck my tongue into his belly button. I moved further down until I found his cock rising in an arc over his abs. I stroked it gently as I moved down to his balls.

I caressed them with my tongue, trying to stuff them in my mouth. They were too large and full to fit inside. I licked around them and down to his perineum, feeling the soft hairs catch between my teeth.

I licked up his balls to the base of his shaft lovingly. I explored every inch of his cock with my tongue, tracing each vein and ridge. I felt it pulse when I hit his frenulum. I teased it with the tip of my tongue, feeling him push back against me each time. He was leaking precum from his wide piss slit. I lapped it up and then finally plunged his dick into my mouth.

He gasped as I sunk down his poll. I started out slow, but he got impatient and started to push up into my mouth. I held him tight at the base and slurped his head and sensitive shaft. I could taste a steady stream of precum seeping from his piss slit.

"Oh fuck" I gasped as I felt his load fill my mouth. His hips bucked wildly as his balls drained. I swallowed most of it but kept some in my mouth. I spit it down onto my cock and stroked myself. I grunted loudly as I shot my load across his dick and hairy abs. I bent down and licked up my load, cleaning up a little more of his cum that had seeped out as his dick deflated.

We kissed, and he got a taste of both our loads as I snuggled in next to him. My dick pressed into his leg, leaving a slime trail behind. I wished I could have fucked him, but I loved being able to take his load in my mouth. I drifted off to sleep, more contented than I'd been the past few nights in my too large, empty bed.

Chapter 20
A Hot Grilling

"**H**ey! Wanna beer?" Jake said, grabbing Evan's arm and patting his shoulder.

"Sure" Evan said. Jake handed us both beers and then went to check to the grill.

"Hi boys" she said looking at us like we were the meat she was carrying out to the grill. I had a hard time meeting her gaze, knowing what she'd planned for us later. I needed a few more beers before I could relax.

"It's good to see you" she said, smiling at Evan. "Jake said you've been working on some boats down at the harbor".

"Yes, I'm working on a houseboat now, but hopefully, I'll have some others lined up soon" he said. Steve said he'd definitely recommend Evan to his friends, some of whom had a great deal more disposable income than him.

"That's great to hear" she said. "Could one of you help me bring out the rest of the food?"

"Sure," Evan volunteered, following her inside.

"You're still cool with this?" Jake asked, dropping sausages onto the grill with a hiss. Sausages, how fitting, I thought.

"I guess so" I said, still a bit hesitant.

"It's no big deal, you'll hardly know she is there" he said confidently. I was anything but confident that would really be the case. I'd not been with a woman since experimenting a little in college. It was enough to convince me it wasn't for me. When I pulled up porn, I cringed when an ad for straight porn popped up. I hated when I saw breasts bouncing up and down as a woman screamed what seemed an obviously fake orgasm. I gave him and nervous look and downed half my beer.

"How about Evan, is he cool?" He asked.

"I actually didn't tell him, I just said it was a surprise." I said.

"Oh really? That could be interesting" Jake said, appearing lost in thought.

"Yeah, I wasn't sure how he'd react. He guessed that it involves sex" I said.

"God, I'm so fucking horny right now! I could just skip dinner" he said, lifting his apron to show me the bulge in his shorts. I reached over and rubbed my hand along the stiff rod.

"I know what you mean, I can't wait to see if Evan fucks you" I said.

"You think he will?" Jake asked. I could feel his dick jump and pump out precum into the fabric at the mention of Evan fucking him.

"I told him about our conversation and hinted that you were curious about what it would be like" I said. It was as if I'd squeezed a whole bottle of lighter fluid on the grill. He's dick felt like it would burst out of the jock and shorts he was wearing.

"Fuck!" Jake said, closing his eyes. I could probably make him cum just by rubbing his sensitive cock.

"You can't wait to feel that thick cock inside you. You want him to breed your hole don't you" I whispered, though I didn't need to.

"Fuck yes!" He said under his breath. His body trembled with excitement.

"I talked with her, she's staying with her mom for a while." We heard Nat say coming back out with rolls and condiments, with Evan following behind carrying bags of chips and some other sides. I pulled my hand away, but not before Nat saw and gave me a wicked grin. I felt my face flush red.

I helped set the table, feeling the tension building between her and Jake. Evan seemed clueless, though he had some warning about what was in store.

"I hope I can see my girl soon" he said. I knew he missed his daughter more and more each day. I remember how good he was playing with her in the yard or tossing the ball to her on the sidewalk. She would grin from ear to ear when she saw him.

"Can you pass the potato salad?" Jake asked when we sat down to eat at the outdoor table. He sat to my right, while Evan sat across from me and Nat across from Jake.

Jake picked up a sausage and ate it seductively. It was as thick and long as Evan's dick. Evan's eyes grew wide, and he nearly choked on the beer he was drinking. He coughed as he watched Jake lick the mustard from the tip like it was precum oozing from the slit. Jake giggled while Evan shifted uncontrollably. I was getting hard again, the anticipation was killing me.

Conversion died down as we finished eating, and I downed the dregs of my beer. Being nervous, I had not gone easy on the beer. I could definitely feel the effects, and I was not alone. Jake got up and staggered as he went to turn off the forgotten grill.

"The game will be starting soon" Nat said, getting up and gathering the plates and utensils.

"Let me help clean up" I said, trying to be a good guest.

"Don't worry about it, why don't you all go downstairs and put on the game." She suggested.

"Thanks hun" Jake slurred as he kissed her. She whispered something to him before slapping his ass and sending him up into the house with a plate of leftovers.

"Come on boys" he called out after us. I looked at Evan, who was looking over at me apprehensively. We got up and grabbed a few things to take in with us. The minute we set things down Jake was there with more beers in hand. I accepted another, though I was less inclined to drink it now. After opening his, He headed toward the basement door and nodded for us to follow. We followed him down the stairs to his "man cave".

In the corner was a small bar with a couple of stools and rows of bottles lined up on the shelf with glassware and shakers. On the far wall was a framed signed jersey along with some other sports memorabilia carefully framed with great reverence.

Dominating the room was an 85-inch flat screen mounted in the center of the wall. It took up nearly the entire wall. In the middle of the room was a sofa and recliner.

The floor was carpeted with soft beige carpet. The room was bright with recessed lights, which Jake dimmed to a soft glow before flipping on the tv. The picture was so crisp and clear you could make out the nose hairs on the coach standing on the sidelines.

I debated for a moment where to sit. Should I sit at the end next to Evan or between him and Jake? I reserved the recliner, assuming that would be where Nat would be sitting. Evan made up my mind for me by taking the end, so I was left with the middle between them.

We drank our beers and only half watched the pregame commentators drone on in the background. I could make out the outline of Jake's already, or possibility still, hard dick inside his shorts. I could see the straps of his jock wrapping around his leg toward his ass. When I looked up, I could see he was looking behind my head toward Evan. Evan's face was aglow with flickering light. His beard set in sharp relief as the soft curls caught the flickering light. He was facing the screen, but I could see his eyes were darting down back and forth between our crotches.

Someone had to break the ice and start something or the tension was going to kill me. I reached over and placed my hand on the lump in Jake's shorts, gently massaging the slippery fabric over the knitted jock beneath. Evan's eyes grew wide as he turned to watch my hand play over the fabric.

He looked around nervously, knowing Nat was just upstairs. I could see the growing mound in Evan's shorts as well, and reached with my left hand into his lap. I fondled them both as my dick pressed against my shorts, longing to be let free.

I slipped my hand into the warm pouch of Jake's jockstrap and felt the hot steel come in contact with the back of my hand. I reached past it and fondled his balls, hanging loose in their sack.

I slipped my other hand into Evan's shorts, finding his dick tenting out the front of his shorts and straining at the fabric for release. I went to pull it out into the open air, but he shook his head, looking over his shoulder at the stairs. If only he knew.

I contented myself with stroking him inside the shorts for the moment. I felt Jake move and shifted my attention toward him. He's lifted his ass off the sofa and pulled his shorts down to his knees.

Evan mouthed the words, "What the fuck are you doing?"

Jake's answer was to let his shorts slide down his legs. He flicked them off and flung them at the tv, landing in a pile on the floor. I pulled his dick out of the side of the jock into the cool basement air.

Evan looked around again nervously. I leaned in and took Jake in my mouth, loudly slurping on his dick while Evan watched, his dick jumping in my hand. Jake ran his fingers through my hair, lightly pushing me down on his cock. I could taste his sweet precum as I lapped at the soft skin. Jake moaned softly, pushing up his hips so that his cock jabbed at the back of my throat.

I sat back and yanked at Evan's shorts to pull them down, but he held them up, shaking his head. I leaned in and licked the blond treasure trail to his waistband. I pulled up the waistband and licked down to the base of his cock.

I felt Jake pull my dick out of my shorts as I nuzzled my nose in Evan's thick pubes. I felt Jake's lips close around the head of my dick. I moved my hand into Evan's shorts once again, this time weighing his balls in my hand.

"You started without me?" Came Nat's voice from the bottom of the stairs. She walked like a cat on the stairs, so none of us had heard her until she was already in the room.

Evan jumped up, yanking my hand from his shorts. He stood facing her. Jake continued to suck my dick without missing a beat, as if she wasn't there.

Chapter 21
In the Man Cave

I saw Evan look up at Natalie and then back down at me as Jake stroked my spit covered dick openly, beaming up at her.

"It's ok, carry on" she said, rounding the sofa to watch her husband sucking my dick. Evan seemed a little dazed.

"Surprise" I said weakly to Evan

"This cool with you?" Jake asked, looking up at him from behind my dick.

"Uh," Evan said, looking back and forth between Jake and his wife, now taking up a place in the recliner.

"I shouldn't have kept it a secret" I said.

"It's ok, it was my idea, I wanted to see what you boys have been up too" Nat said, giving us a wicked grin.

"You're cool with this" Evan asked, looking down at my wet dick as Jake lapped along the shaft.

"Absolutely! Jake tells me everything" she said.

"Oh" he said, relaxing just a little. His dick had not lost any of its stiffness, from what I could tell.

"He said you both had the biggest dicks he's ever seen" she said.

I grew red in embarrassment.

"Clearly he wasn't exaggerating" she said, looking down at her husband gaging on my thick cock.

I sat back and looked at Jake, then over to Evan, who hadn't moved. Jake held up my dick like it was a prize trophy.

"Damn, that's nice." She commented as some of Jake's drool rolled over his fingers.

Evan still stood immobile. I nodded for him to go ahead and pull out his dick. He reluctantly reached down and pulled at the waistband of his shorts. Out popped his bone hovering in front of him, defying gravity.

"Oh shit! It's even bigger than you described." She said. Her hand was already in her lap, rubbing at the fabric. "You've got your work cut out there" she said to her husband. He grinned at her and then got down from the sofa and knelt in front of us. First, he took my dick in his mouth, slipping his tongue along the sensitive skin. It was strange to have her watching and rubbing herself as her husband pleasured me.

Next, he moved over to Evan, taking hold of his buddy's cock and stroking it a few times, looking up into his face. Evan looked down at his buddy staring submissively up at him. He got a shy expression on his face and tore his eyes away from Jake's gaze. He didn't protest, though. Jake slipped it into his mouth. Evan looked back down as his dick slipped into his mouth. Jake's cheeks puffed out, and his lips stretched over the thick rod as he attempted to take as much as he could inside him. I stroked myself, feeling self-conscious, knowing Nat was watching.

"He tells me you really know how to rim" she said to me. I blushed, imagining the conversation Jake must have had with her. I took that as an invitation to demonstrate. Jake directed Evan to sit back down as he got up and bent forward over the ottoman, face in Evan's crotch. Evan looked over at Nat, watching as she slipped a hand inside her slacks.

I knelt down behind Jake and looked up at his hairy ass spread open in front of me. I blushed, knowing I had an audience, but I couldn't resist that hairy pucker. I plunged my tongue in.

"Oh fuck," Nat whispered, watching me tongue her husband's tight hole. I started to get into the performance, exaggerating what I was doing like I was auditioning for a porn. I looked around for a moment, wondering if Jake might have set up a camera to record the action, but I didn't see any.

Jake moaned around Evan's dick as I pressed my tongue into his hole. He'd clearly worked open his hole and cleaned it out prior to us coming over. My tongue could slip inside him an inch or more. I could taste some flavored lube already applied. It tasted sweet and sticky like sour apple candy. I worked a finger then another into his hole, feeling around for his prostate.

"Oh fuck" Jake whimpered as I massaged the hard lump.

"Go on, fuck him! I want to see him take your big dicks" Nat said. She had her pants pulled down and her hand inside black lacy panties. Evan was watching her finger herself while Jake sucked his dick. She unbuttoned her blouse, exposing her barely covered breasts. Evan continued to stare at her as she unhooked her bra and let her bare breasts rest against her chest. I looked away, feeling more and more uncomfortable. It only served to remind me that though we were fucking, he was still genuinely interested in women.

I noticed a bottle of lube on the built-in shelf and grabbed it, squirting some on my dick and slicking it up. Jake was on all fours on the ottoman, head in Evan's lap and ass sticking up. Nat swiveled the recliner so she was facing me. From that angle, she could easily see Jakes ass splayed open and ready to take me.

I eased up behind him, grabbing his hips and getting ready to slip inside him. But before I could, I felt something shift my arm up. Nat was standing next to me, holding up my arm so she could see the moment of penetration.

She held open his ass cheek as I pressed my head into his crack. It slipped in without much resistance. Jake grunted with his mouth full, so it came out muffled. Nat sat back down but, not before stripping off her top and dropping her wet panties to the floor. I looked at Evan and his eyes grew wide looking down at her pussy. I wasn't jealous, exactly. Here I pictured Evan was some closet case and was really gay, but seeing the way he looked at her, I realized he was much more straight than I thought. I guess it shouldn't have come as a shock to me after all, but it left me feeling a little lost as to how I fit in all this.

I'd developed feelings for him, and I thought he might be developing feelings for me too. Maybe I was projecting too much. I realized after a few minutes that they were both now staring at me. Even Jake was looking over his shoulder in anticipation.

"Oh sorry" I mumbled as I stroked my cock back up to full hardness. My nerves had gotten the best of me and my dick had started to go soft. It was a vicious cycle. The more I thought about getting hard, the less hard I got. I was panicking.

"It's ok, take your time" Jake said, rolling onto his back. Evan's cock dangled over his forehead. I took a deep breath and tried to relax. Nat took her place back in the chair behind me to the left. I focused on the men in front of me. Jake's dick was hard and leaking as it bounced slightly with every beat of his heart. Evan stroked his cock coated in Jake's spit as he looked down at my dick and smiled. I looked down and found I was hard again, my dick bobbing and weaving in front of me. Jake pulled back his legs and held them behind his head. His ass was hanging over the edge of the ottoman. I bent down and pressed my hard dick into his hole once again. This time I remembered to keep my arm up, so Nat could see in.

"Oh fuck!" Nat whimpered in the background, and both Jake and Evan looked over at her. I resisted looking back and continued to plow on until my dick was buried to the pubes inside her husband.

Jakes eyes rolled back as I began to fuck his hole. He was hard, and his cock leaked a stream of precum down into his neatly trimmed bush. I wanted to lean in and lick up his juice, but to my surprise, Evan beat me to it.

He sat down next to Jake on the sofa and stroked Jake's wet cock, watching Nat for her reaction. She gave him a nod of approval. He leaned forward and licked the precum off his shaft while she watched intently.

Seeing Evan sucking Jake's dick made my dick jump, stretching Jake open wide. I loved how warm and wet he felt inside. I got lost in fucking him, forgetting that Nat was behind me until I heard her whimper slightly. I looked back to find her flicking her fingers around her pussy. The image became burned in my brain. It excited me to know the fact that I was fucking her husband was turning her on so much.

The beers helped me relax, but also helped to prevent me from cumming too quickly as well. The room spun as I continued to fuck Jake with long, slow strokes. I felt my balls tighten, and my shaft tingle as Jake's ass clamped down on my hard dick.

"Oh fuck!" Jake yelled as I felt something hot and wet hit my abs and run down to the base of my cock. His dick was erupting all over the place. Cum landed on his chest and belly and even ran down onto my dick. I pressed his cum into his hole as his abs tightened, and he jerked his head up. His eyes were wide open in surprise and wonder. I couldn't take it anymore. I slammed into his quivering man cunt as fast as my hips would allow.

"Yeah! Breed my husband's hole!" Nat cried out, pounding her fingers into herself. I grunted as wave after wave of pleasure coursed through me. Shot after shot filled Jake's ass and seeped around my cock. The room was spinning even more now as I pulled out and fell back onto the sofa.

I looked over at Evan, who was focused on my wet dick. He stroked his cock like he was getting ready to cum all over Jake's stubbled chin.

"Wait" Jake said, reaching up to stop Evan from finishing. Evan looked down as Jake holding him steady. Jake spun around and flipped over on the ottoman, so his ass was facing Jake. "I want you to unload in me!" Jake said.

Evan looked down at my cum seeping slowly down Jake's thigh, contemplating what to do.

"Please fuck my husband!" Nat said, standing up in front of him. She mashed her pussy into Jake's face. He licked her out, grunting uncontrollably. I sat back, watching, feeling my dick harden again as Evan stepped closer. Nat leaned in and took Evan in her mouth, moistening his dick before giving it a few wet strokes.

She guided him toward Jake's waiting hole. Jake took a break from eating out his wife to look down and watch as Natalie lined Evan's dick with his hole. She felt around his used hole as Evan's head pressed into the opening. Jake grunted loudly as Evan slipped inside him. Evan reached out and cupped her breast as he began to pound Jake's hole. Jake went back to eating out, Natalie, while Evan used his hole mercilessly. The basement filled with the sounds of skin slapping skin and the wet slurping of Jake's tongue. I stroked my hard cock, focused on Evan's dick disappearing inside Jake's hole.

Evan pressed his facing into Nat's bosom and licked her extended nipple. Another image burned onto my mind that I didn't want. I began to feel more distant from what was going.

Natalie moved forward and began to kiss Evan as she sat down on her husband's cock. She began to ride him in time with Evan's thrusts inside him. When I saw Evan kiss her, something snapped inside my head. I was never the jealous type, in fact, I loved seeing Evan fuck Jake, but seeing him kiss Natalie was somehow too much for me.

"Oh fuck!" Evan grunted with his head pressed between her breasts as his flooded Jake with his load. She whimpered loudly as Jake's cock brought her over the edge. Her body shook trying to hold herself up while her thighs clamped down around Jake's legs.

Evan pulled his cock from Jake's ass with a loud, wet slurp. It was still hard and covered in the combination of his and my cum. Suddenly, he slid his cock alongside Jake's into Natalie's cunt. Her eyes grew wide as his big cock joined her husband's inside her. She remained still while Evan drilled his dick along Jake's. I didn't want to watch this but found I couldn't look away.

Nat writhed in pleasure as the two studs mounted her. I felt like I was superfluous, and they didn't even know I was still in the room.

I saw Jake look over at me, then down at my cock. I was hard again, despite my mixed feelings about what was going on. He nodded to me to join them. I stayed put, not sure whether I wanted to. I watched Evan fuck Natalie, as he held on to Jake's hairy legs. The scene was incongruous and strange but undeniably hot. I stroked myself watching those dicks pound her hole simultaneously. She began to buck and scream as she began to cum again.

I found I was stroking my cock and nestling another orgasm. I stood up and stepped up to Jake. His face was covered in spit and Nat's juices from when he was eating her out.

I spotted Evan's face over Nat's shoulder as he licked her earlobe. He looked up at me, then down at me stroking my cock over Jake's face.

"Oh fuck!" He cried as he came a second time, this time inside her alongside Jake's cock. His eyes opened wide as he stared into my eyes. I couldn't believe it, but I felt I was ready to cum again.

Evan reached around Nat and braced me against them with a strong hand across my shoulder. He leaned forward and kissed my cheek and licked my ear. The intimacy of the action sent me over the edge once more. I painted Jake's face and chest with my load.

Jake reached back and felt around his used hole, feeling around his expressed opening.

"Oh fuck!" Jake said through cum covered lips as he licked my cum from them. Jake's dick began to erupt again, spraying another full load inside Natalie with joining Evan's cock and cum inside her. Evan stepped back, pulling his dick from Natalie's cunt, letting Jake drop his legs to the floor as his head lolled back. I fell back into the sofa and Evan sat down beside me.

I looked over at Evan's dick, knowing it was covered in his cum, my cum, Jake's cum and Natalie's juices. He gave me a weak smile as I leaned into his chest, relaxing against his warm flesh. We sat in silence long after, still basking in the glow of what had happened.

Natalie was the first to get up. She leaned into her exhausted husband and kissed him, licking up some of my cum from his chin.

"Thank you" she said to us both as she walked around the sofa and headed upstairs nude.

"Fuck that was the hottest thing I've ever done" Jake said, finding the strength to sit up. He stood and waddled toward the stairs, bowlegged nursing his tender ass. "I'm not going to be able to sit down for a week." He said as he made his way up the stairs.

I stayed with Evan, nuzzling into his chest as the coolness of the basement made gooseflesh rise on my skin.

"You ok?" He asked.

"Yeah, why?" I asked.

"You looked a little concerned at one point" he said.

"I ... I," I held back, saying what was on my mind. I knew he liked women and I wouldn't get in his way if that was what he wanted.

"Something is bothering you about what happened?" He said, pulling me away from his chest to look me in the eye.

I looked away, avoiding his gaze. "I ... I know you liked her, I guess I just ... never mind" I said, getting up and fleeing toward the stairs. I didn't even think about the fact that I was completely naked. I ran outside, tears streaming down my face as I ran into my yard, stones cutting into my bare feet.

Chapter 22

Aftermath

"**H**ey, could you let me in!" I heard Evan call from the other side of the door. The cold wood pressed against my back as I leaned against it, crying. Why the fuck was I crying. I should have known better than to let this happen. I'd enjoyed it, but Evan was right that something about the experience that's bothered me.

"You want me to get arrested?" Evan called through the door. I turned and looked out the small rectangular window in the center of the door. Looking down, I saw Evan was standing on the step, completely naked. Looking in at me. He must have only been a few steps behind me as I ran from Jake and Natalie's house.

I opened the door quickly, fumbling with the handle. He stepped inside, letting the screen door close behind him. He grabbed hold of me and I felt my chest heave as I let loose a sob.

"What happened?" he asked, rubbing my back gently.

"It's just, I saw the way you looked at her and ... I realized the world I'd imagined with you was impossible" I finally said when I got control of myself.

Evan looked at me as if trying to find the right words and, failing that, gave me a sad smile. I turned away from him, expecting the worst.

"Listen, I really like you, things are just really complicated." He said.

"I know, I just ... I didn't know what I was expecting" I said.

He folded his arms across my chest, pulling me close. I could feel his soft dick press against my ass.

"I never expected this to happen. I never thought I'd fall for a guy" he said softly.

"Huh?" I said, not sure I'd heard him right.

"You heard me, it's got me all messed up inside. I think I'm falling for you" he said. I turned, and we kissed gently at first, then deeply and full of passion. Though I'd just cum twice in a row, I was ready to go again. I felt giddy with excitement. I felt his hard dick poke into my abs as we kissed in the doorway.

I heard a soft tapping on the screen door and looked back to find Jake standing there on the other side of the screen door. He was dressed in sweatpants and a teeshirt and looking a bit embarrassed. Which for Jake seemed impossible.

"Is everything ok?" He asked.

"Yeah, sorry, I had a mini panic attack back there." I said.

"You left this" he said, holding up a bag with our clothes stuffed in it.

"I hope none of the neighbors saw us" I said, getting red in the face.

"I'm sure Mrs. Sanchez got an eyeful" Evan said. She was my neighbor across the alley. "She was taking in her trash can when I came around the corner".

"Oh shit" I said. I opened the door and let Jake come in to hand me the bag. He reached down and grabbed hold of my hard dick.

"Am I interrupting something?" He asked.

"No, it's fine" Evan said, stepping further into the kitchen.

"I hope it's nothing we did" Jake said apologetically.

"No, I just, never mind, it's complicated." I said.

"I know Nat got a little excited and joined in when she said she was just going to watch. I'm sorry" he said.

"No it's fine." I said. It was ok that she did it. The guys seemed to really enjoy her being there. I guess that was the heart of the problem for me. I wanted them to look at me like they did at her. I knew it was a stupid thought. I knew they were bisexual and would always be that way. I'd have to accept that.

"It was really hot, I think we all had a good time. Maybe we just overdid it on the beer" Evan offered.

"Oh ok. I hope we can do it again sometime" Jake said, looking sheepish.

"I hope so" Evan said. I just nodded. I wasn't sure I'd join them next time, if there was a next time.

"I'll let you get back to whatever I interrupted" Jake said. I could see he was still hard, and his dick poked up against his sweatpants. He followed my gaze down. "I took a little something, and now it won't go down".

Evan laughed as I swatted at the hard lump.

"I've never tried taking anything, don't guess I need to" Evan said, pulling down his hard cock and letting it fly up and hover in front of him. Jake reached over and grabbed it, measuring the girth with his thumb and forefinger.

"Damn, I can't believe I took this monster" Jake said, beaming from ear to ear.

"Shame it took you so long to try," Evan said, punching him on the shoulder.

"I'm willing to make up for lost time" he said. "Though maybe not tonight, I'm pretty sore back there".

"We sure did a number on you" I said.

"It was worth it. I'd take you both again." Jake said.

"I bet you could one day take us both at the same time, like you did with Nat" I said, reaching down to pull Evan's dick closer so that it lined up next to mine.

"The two of you at once would rip me in half" Jake said, though he got a look of curiosity on his face.

"You wanna give it a try don't you" Evan said.

"Don't tempt me" Jake said. I reached my hand inside his sweatpants and felt for his leaking hole. My finger easily slipped inside him. When I pulled my finger out, it was covered in cum.

Cum had also soaked into the back of his sweats, leaving a dark stain. I wanted to be back inside him, feeling Evan's cum around my cock. Jake relaxed and let me finger him while he stroked Evan's dick.

His phone buzzed, bringing him out of his trance.

"Shit, I've got to go pick up our kids from their grandparent's" he said looking down at the screen. He looked down at both of our cocks next to each other and put his hand around them. He pulled it away, keeping the wide arc of his fingers.

"I'm gonna need a bigger dildo to practice on" he said.

"You'd better take care of that before you pick up your kids" I said, nodding at the wet spot on the back of his sweats.

"Fuck, I'll have to go home and change first. See you boys later" he said. And with that, he turned and went back out the screen door.

Evan stood there in the soft light from the living room and smiled, shaking his head. I smiled and laughed as well.

"We never did finish watching the game" he said, heading to the living room. I followed as he turned on the tv and flipped through the channels. We stayed naked, leaning into each other, and watched the second half. It was nice to just relax for a while with Evan close to me. I didn't know what the future would hold, so I tried my best to just cling to these rare moments together.

We headed upstairs a little early. I drifted off to sleep nearly as soon as my head hit the pillow.

I was back in Jake's man cave. He was bent over the ottoman, and I was fucking him. Evan was standing in front of him with his dick in Jake's face. I was getting into it when Jake rolled over onto his back. I looked down to find he had breasts, and I was fucking his pussy, not his ass. I jolted myself awake.

My cock was hard and tenting the sheet. I looked over to see Evan was also hard. The sky was beginning to take on a lighter tint, but it was still dark. Evan stirred in his sleep like he was waking up. I couldn't get the odd dream out of my head. I needed something to replace it in my thoughts. I reached over and grabbed the lube from the nightstand. I slicked up my dick and then fingered my hole. Evan's cock swayed under the sheet. Recalling how hot it was to see Evan's dick slip into Jake's ass, I sat up then straddled Evan. His dick pressed into my crack. As I sat back, pressing his head against my hole, his eyes opened to slits. He looked up at me, then down at my dick touching his abs.

"Mornin" he said, yawning and stretching like a cat.

"Morning" I said, leaning down to kiss him. I reached back, pressing his dick into my crack.

"What time is it?" He asked.

"Time for you to fuck me" I said, grinning.

"Really? I should get up and get to work" He said, pushing up his hips so that his dick slid along my crack a few times.

"We've got time" I said grinding back against him teasing my hole.

"If we must" he said grinning. I gave him a mock slap across the cheek. He grabbed me and pushed me over so I rolled onto my side. Instantly, he was on top of me, his dick pressed into my crack again. I squirmed, but he grabbed my wrists and held them tight.

He locked his legs around mine. I was pinned down on my stomach, my dick pressing into the mattress while his dick pressed against my hole. I pushed up my ass, letting him sink into me an inch. He humped me without penetrating me any deeper. I felt his precum begin to drip into my crack. He pulled out and humped my crack, teasing my hole with his shaft as I felt more drops lubricate my crack.

He began to fuck my crack, sliding up and down it, each time resting for a moment on my hole before moving past it and up my hairy crack. I pushed my hips back, wanting desperately for him to enter me.

He continued to hump me without penetration, and I found I was actually enjoying it. I loved the way his body moved over me and how hot his dick felt pressing into my ass. I began to hump the bed in time with his strokes. He leaned in and kissed my neck and licked the back of my ear. I shivered at the sensation of his scruffy beard tickling the hair on the back of my neck. He continued to hump me, kissing down my back between my shoulder blades.

The pace quickened, and he began to grunt loudly as he pounded my crack. He balls slapped against my taint and I found myself getting closer.

"Fuck!" He roared as I felt hot cum land in the middle of my back and roll down my crack. More grunts and more cum seeped into my crack. There was something incredibly hot in feeling his warm cum on my skin like this. Finally, he collapsed on top of me, his cum glueing our bodies together.

I pulled my arms in, and he reached under me, embracing me close. It was an incredibly intimate moment. He nuzzled my neck and kissed my scruff tenderly.

"Your turn" he said a few minutes later, getting up and laying beside me on his stomach.

"Like you did?" I asked. He nodded, looking back at me over his shoulder. I got up on all fours, feeling some of his cum roll down the side of my back and still more roll down my crack onto my balls.

I scooped up some of his cum and pressed it into his crack, matting down the thick blond hair. I mounted him, legs on either side of his pelvis. He brought his hands up over his head, and I placed mine on top of his wrists. My dick slid into place along his crack. I felt his warm skin against my dick as I raked into over his hole, then pushed up his pillowy ass. I began to fuck his crack, teasing his hole on each pass. My balls began to slap his taint as I got more into humping him. I leaned in and kissed the small of his back, then licked up between his shoulder blades to his neck. He purred softly as I tickled his hairs.

I couldn't believe I was getting close already just from mock fucking him. It felt so good to be so close to his hole, and yet so frustrating to not enter it. I pressed into his wet hole a few times, still not penetrating him but feeling his creeks press in against the head of my cock.

Suddenly, I was painting his hole with my cum. My dick spasmed as I shot warm cum into his crack. It leaked down his taint and coated his balls. I fucked upward and launched a stray across his back. I formed a small pool in the dip next to his spine. I continued to hump his crack, dribbling cum into his fine dirty blond hair.

Spent, I collapsed on top of him, feeling my softening cock press into his hole, aided by my cum. I held it there, feeling his sphincter tighten and relax around the head of my dick. I lay there with my dick just on the edge of penetration as my breathing slowed, and I felt him rise and fall under me. He squirmed a bit under me as my dick snaked another inch inside him. It felt so soft and warm and tight against me. I didn't try to fuck him, I just held my dick there at his entrance, enjoying the bond between us. I worried my weight might be crushing him, but he didn't complain.

My alarm droned on for a minute before I reluctantly rolled off him, my soft dick pulling from his ass like popping the cork of a wine bottle.

I helped wash my cum from his ass, feeling his wet ring with my fingers, teasing his hole. We switched, and he did the same to me, slipping a wet finger inside me. I started to get hard again, but I knew it would have to wait, a mountain of neglected work was calling to me.

He grabbed his tools and I joined him at the door. He turned and kissed me, then smiled and was gone, leaving me alone, feeling the empty house around me.

Chapter 23
Business Trip

"**H**ow long is it?" Evan asked.

"Just five days," I said. It had been planned for months, I was going to a conference in Los Vegas. I'd been looking forward to it but had forgotten all about it when Evan arrived in my life. Now I was dreading being away from him for a week when things were just getting interesting.

"That's not that long. Lucky you, getting to go to Vegas!" Evan said.

"Yeah, real lucky," I said, rolling my eyes. I'd been to these conventions before, and they always proved more exhausting than anything. Sessions all day, client dinners at night, little free time to enjoy the city. Not that I really was all that into Vegas anyway. Gambling wasn't my speed, and there wasn't time to venture out into the surrounding area to enjoy the natural wonders beyond the fake glitz of the city.

"I'd invite you to come with, but I've got to share a room with one of my coworkers" I told him.

"That's ok, I've got to finish work on Steven's boat, and then he said he'd introduce me to a friend of his that needs a good mechanic." He said.

"That's great! Things are really taking off for you," I said.

"Yeah, thanks to you" he said, giving me a heartwarming smile.

"You'll have the place to yourself till I get back" I said.

"Maybe I'll invite Jake over" he said. I felt a twinge of jealousy, or was it envy? He caught the look and added, "what about you? You might get lucky in Vegas".

"I very much doubt that, the guy I'm rooming with is straight" I said.

"And your point?" Evan said, looking down at his naked body.

"He's also a coworker, I'm not about to try anything and risk my job" I said.

"What happens in Vegas ..." he started to say.

"Comes home with you in the form of a sdi" I said, rolling my eyes.

"Let's hope not" he said.

"Do you mind giving me a ride to the airport?" I asked.

"Sure" he said.

My flight was at 7:20am, which sucked since we had to get up so early. I wished there had been time for the usual leisurely blow job to wake him up before work, but I wasn't about to get up any earlier or risk missing my flight.

When he dropped me off, I leaned over and gave him a kiss. He looked around like someone might be watching. I doubted anyone he knew would be there at that moment to witness him kissing a guy. I knew this was all new to him, and I'm sure he was still feeling weird about it.

"Have a safe trip! See you in 5 days" he said before driving off.

The flight was uneventful apart from a little turbulence. The cute flight attendant gave me a few free drinks to help calm my nerves. I didn't mind flying, it was the crashing I could do without. I was also horny the whole flight, feeling the hum of the engines through my cramped legs. I wondered if the flight attended would help me join the mile high club, but I knew what those bathrooms were like, they were anything but sexy.

I dreaded the next five days, if I was already throwing boners just sitting on a plane, I hated to imagine what it was going to be like with no outlet to even masturbate while I was here. I was tempted to download a hookup app and see about a random hookup but thought better of it.

I hailed a lift to my hotel, a pretty nice place just back from the strip. I went to check in and found the guy I'd be rooming with had already checked in.

"Hey roomie" said Daniel when I entered the room. I'd never met him in person, but I'd been on calls with him from time to time. He was married with 3 kids. He wasn't bad to look at, 6' 2" and only slightly overweight, in his early forties I guessed. He had a neatly trimmed beard and a fade style short haircut.

"Hey," I said, hoisting my suitcase onto the stand and dropping my laptop bag on the desk.

"Not a bad room, look at the view!" He said, pointing toward the picture window. The strip stretched out 20 stories below with its flashing lights and spraying fountains. Beyond the city, mountains of ocher loomed in the distance.

"I'm going down to get my badge then we have the keynotes speaker and dinner" Daniel said, scanning the event app.

"I'll unpack and meet you down there" I said.

"This place is a maze, I might never see you again" Daniel joked. He made no attempt at leaving. I was hoping I could change and rub one out before dinner, but that looked unlikely now.

I messaged Evan I'd made it to the hotel and sent him a picture of the room and the view. He sent me a picture of Jake's wet cock in his hand. He didn't waste any time, I thought, quickly flipping off the screen before Daniel could see the picture.

Dinner was dull and lasted longer than it needed to. There was a reception afterward that at least offered free drinks. I paced myself, knowing I wouldn't want to be nursing a hangover while trying to grasp the latest tech offerings at the sessions in the morning.

Daniel was not so foresighted, I had to help him back to our room, or he might have ended up wandering the strip all night or worse. He flopped down on his bed, fully dressed. I went into the bathroom to get ready for bed. When I came back, he was out cold and quietly snoring. He still had on his dress shirt and khaki pants, and even his leather shoes.

I debated helping him get undressed or at least getting his shoes off, but I felt that might cross a line. I felt my dick stir at the thought of it anyway. He was exactly my type, which these days seemed to be exclusively straight guys.

I risked pulling off my boxers and slipping under the light sheet. I stroked myself as quietly as possible. I kept an eye on Daniel, both to make sure he didn't wake up and also to contemplate what might be hiding under that bulge in his pants. There was a definite bulge in them, I'd been sneaking peaks at it all evening. I thought I'd been able to detect the rim of his cut head pressing into the material, but I could have just as easily been something in his pocket.

Exhaustion from traveling and the long evening, overtook me, and before I could finish I drifted off to sleep, dick still in hand.

I woke to the sound of water running, which only compounded the feeling that my bladder was going to explode. I got up and headed toward the bathroom. The door was closed, and I could hear the shower going.

"Is it ok if I come in and pee? I'm about ready to explode." I called through the door.

"Uh ... ok" Daniel said.

I swept into the bathroom in only my boxer briefs, pulling out my half hard cock as I approached the toilet. Relief came as the sound of my piss hitting the water mixed with the sound of the rain shower beside me. I glanced over to see Daniel's silhouette inside the fogged glass cube. I couldn't make out much more than his figure through the mist. It looked as if he were facing me.

"Sorry to intrude, but I couldn't hold it any longer" I said apologetically.

"No worries, I can relate. I woke up having to piss really bad too. Always do when I've been drinking." He said.

"You were really out of it" I said.

"I know, I hope I didn't do anything inappropriate at the reception, it's a bit of a blur." He said.

"No, you were fine, hilarious in fact. I loved your jokes" I said.

"Oh good, I've been known to go a little overboard" he said.

"It's cool, what happens in Vegas ..." I said.

"Stays in Vegas" he said as he shut off the water. I finished milking the last of the piss from my shaft and tucked my dick back in my briefs. I turned and was shocked to find Daniel emerging from the shower to grab a towel from the rack.

My eyes scanned down his wet body to come to rest on an impressive, soft cock held aloft by equally impressive balls. It wasn't the biggest dick I'd seen, but it was one of the most beautiful ones. You know how it is, some dicks are more beautiful than others. It's difficult to describe what makes a dick beautiful, maybe it's the tightness of the skin that makes it shine. Or perhaps it's the wide flared head or the soft red circumcision scar. Whatever it was about Daniel's dick, made my mouth water.

"Oh sorry, I'll get out of your way" I said, tearing my eyes away from that luscious cock.

"No worries. We're both guys," he said, lazily drying himself and not bothering to cover up.

"Nothing I don't see at the gym all the time" I said nervously. I wasn't exactly out at work, not that I was hiding anything either, it wasn't a topic that came up on work calls. Being totally remote had the disadvantage of very little social interaction with coworkers, which I missed. I knew he was straight from the fact that he'd mention his kids and wife occasionally, but since I wasn't dating anyone significant, the topic never came up.

I washed my hands but kept an eye on Daniel in the mirror. His chest hair was neatly trimmed down to his pubes. They were also neatly trimmed and only accentuated the meat hanging below them.

His balls were hairless, most likely shaven. I watched as he ran the towel over them, wicking away the moisture. I knew my dick was beginning to harden inside my briefs and if I lingered any longer, I could get myself into trouble.

"All yours" he said, nodding at the shower cube. I hadn't thought about taking a shower yet. I was going to take one before we headed down for breakfast.

"Oh, thanks" I said, looking awkwardly at him and the shower. He made no attempt to leave the bathroom, in fact, he headed toward me, or more specifically his toiletry bag sitting behind me on the counter. I changed places with him and stood outside the shower. I spotted him looking back at me in the mirror. Was he watching to see me get naked? I thought. It looked like he was pretending to busy himself at the sink while I got in the shower. I could now see his hairy ass protruding out. It was big and round and filled in with a stripe of hair down the middle that I would kill to bend down and lick.

I shook in anticipation as I pulled down my briefs and left out my growing cock. I heard a slight gasp and looked up to find Daniel's eyes trained on it. His eyes met mine and he quickly looked away. He was checking me out. I slipped into the shower, my dick hardening at the possibilities.

I heard the buzz of Daniel's razor come on as I adjusted the shower controls. I could still see out through lines left by water droplets. I studied Daniel's back muscles and the bit of stray hair that built into a mound at the top of his crack. As he leaned in toward the mirror, his ass pushed out. It was my turn to gasp as I saw his puckered hole appear. It looked so inviting, surrounded as it was with that soft brown ring of matted hair.

My dick was rock hard now, and I couldn't help was begin to stroke it, lusting after Daniel's dad bod. I wondered if he could see the way my arm was moving through the fogged glass. On some level,

I wanted him to see, wanted him to know how much his nude body was turning me on.

Something on the interior of the glass caught my eye. At the same level as my hard cock was a whitish glob oozing slowly down the glass in a lengthening string. Is that what I think it is? I thought. I put a finger to the gift he'd left me and felt the viscus fluid between my fingers, there was no question, it was his cum. I brought my finger to my lips and tasted the still warm sweet salty mixture. I was ready to stoop down and lick it off the glass when I caught movement outside.

"Don't take too long, we don't have much time to grab breakfast before the first session." He said, hanging up his towel and sauntering past, his dick swinging with each step.

"I'll be out in a minute" I said. A minute was all it took for me to plaster the glass with my load. I leaned in and licked up both of our loads from the glass, savoring his taste mixed with mine, wishing I'd been up a little sooner to get it from the source.

I waited until my dick had softened sufficiently before heading out into the room. I took a cue from him and left the towel behind. He was standing in front of the full-length mirror in just his underwear, white cotton briefs, while he buttoned up his pale blue shirt.

He glanced over at me with a grin on his face as I headed to my suitcase to find some clothes.

"Glad you aren't a prude" he said out of the blue.

"No, I'm anything but, at home I'm pretty comfortable walking around naked." I confessed.

"Must be nice, I don't have that luxury with kids around" he said.

"Bet it's nice to get away for a week, huh" I said.

"Don't get me wrong, I love my family, but yeah, it's nice to have a break from it for a bit" he said. I noticed him eyeing my still impressive looking cock as I picked out underwear, a shirt, and pants, doing my best to smooth out the wrinkles.

"If I had your equipment, I sure as hell would flaunt it" he said with an envious laugh.

"I've been known to" I said, grinning. He shook his head and turned to get his pants. His underwear looked very full and pushing out, like it was struggling to contain his cock and balls.

I could sense the tension but knew it was trouble, and besides, it was getting late. I reluctantly slipped on a fresh pair of boxer briefs and tucked my semi into the pouch. I could feel Daniel's eyes on me as I finished dressing.

After breakfast, I didn't see Daniel until our group dinner. He sat next to me as we chatted about the different sessions we'd attended and compared notes. Again, there was an open bar reception after dinner hosted by one of the sponsors.

I took a moment to write to Evan.

"How goes it?" I asked.

"Over at Jake and Nat's, they invited me to dinner" he said. I imagined what might be for dessert. I guess it was good I wasn't home. I wasn't sure I could stomach the thought of them fucking again.

"Hope you have a good time" I said, trying to be diplomatic.

"We will" he wrote. Then the three dots appeared and seemed to stay on the screen for a long time.

"Wish you were here" he finally wrote.

"Me too" I lied.

"Your girlfriend?" Daniel asked, holding up his phone with a message stream from his wife on it.

"Ah, no" I said, quickly hiding the screen as an image of Evan's cock in Jake's mouth filled the screen.

"Oh" Daniel said, flushing red. He'd seen the picture before I had a chance to hide it.

"I ... ah ..." I started to say.

"It's cool, I didn't know you were gay." He said.

"I don't talk about it much, never sure how colleagues will react" I said.

"I get that" he said.

There was an awkward silence as we both struggled to find something to say.

"You heading back to the reception?" I asked.

"I don't know, I don't want to over do it again, I was thinking I might turn in" he said.

"Yeah, I'm kinda beat myself" I said. Now that he knew I was gay, I wondered if he'd have problems with the sleeping arrangements. "You still ok sharing the room? I can see if I can find another room" I asked.

"Are you serious? No, it's totally fine with me. Besides, I doubt you'll find another room now. I bet the conference has most of the rooms booked already" he said.

I very much doubted that Vegas could ever truly run out of rooms, but I didn't argue. We made our way back to the room through a sea of blinking lights and tinkling sounds.

"That pic, was that your boyfriend?" He asked in the elevator. What was he exactly? Was he my boyfriend, he was living with me, and we were fucking, but had it reached that level?

"No, not exactly, it's complicated" I said.

"Oh ok, cuz I'm wouldn't be so cool if my wife sent me a picture of her sucking someone else's dick" he said.

"Oh, actually they are my straight neighbors, well, straight might be a stretch, bisexual I guess" I said.

"Wow? Really?" He said with a nervous giggle.

"That one has a wife and two kids, and this one has one kid and a soon-to-be ex-wife." I said, taking out my phone and showing the picture again.

"Damn, he puts you to shame," he said, pointing at Evan's massive cock stretching Jake's lips.

"We're about the same size hard, he might be a little bigger" I said. I knew he was bigger, but my ego couldn't let that be the case. Daniel tugged at the front of his pants to adjust the growing budge in his khakis.

"You both put me to shame" he said.

"I don't know, from what I saw you have a nice one" I said. I think the few drinks I had at the reception were stronger than I thought. I wouldn't have said that if I was sober. Daniel seemed to blush and look away shyly and shake his head.

"You've got three kids, you must be doing something right" I said joking as I jabbed him in the ribs.

"Not lately" he said softly.

"Oh" I said, feeling like I'd crossed a line and made it weird.

Suddenly, we both realized the elevator was taking far too long to reach our floor. In fact, wasn't moving at all.

"It helps if you push the button" I said with a laugh, trying to defuse the tension. The elevator began to move quickly up the 20 floors with smooth, rapid acceleration.

We reached the room and both went to our respective beds, lying down on them fully clothed. The tension was thick, I could tell he wanted to say something but seemed afraid to.

My dick was hardening, anticipating where all this might be heading. Suddenly, the lights went out. I heard him shift around in the darkness. As my eyes adjusted, I found he'd already gotten under the covers.

"Good night" he said softly.

"Good night" I said as I got up and went through my nighttime routine in the bathroom. When I came back, Daniel hadn't moved. I slipped off my pants, hung them up and got into bed, then pulled off my briefs.

I lay there debating what to do. Things had so quickly come to an end that I was left not knowing if he was flirting earlier or just curious. I kicked myself for saying what I did and doing what I told myself I wasn't going to do. I began to panic, thinking about the conversation I be having with HR if he reported it.

I heard his bed move and the sounds of him crossing the room. I held my breath, my dick involuntarily jumped in response. I saw the light go on in the bathroom and the door shut behind him.

I little while later, he came back out and went straight to his bed. I had my answer. I wasn't about to press the subject. I rolled over, but had a hard time falling asleep with my dick poking uncomfortably into the mattress.

Normally, I'd jerk off and that would help me drift off to sleep, but with him right next to me in the other bed and not black out drunk like the night before, I hesitated. I listened for sounds from his side of the room, but only heard his soft breathing. I wished I was home, cuddled up next to Evan. I imagined his night went better than mine had. I shook my head, not wanting the image of Nat getting drilled by Evan to be the last I saw before I slept.

I almost got up and went for a walk, but the warm bed against the strong air conditioning kept me in place, and eventually, I drifted off into a fitful sleep.

Chapter 24
The Vegas Strip

When I woke the next morning, Daniel's bed was empty and, to my disappointment, the bathroom was empty as well. I spotted Daniel on a break between sessions.

"Hey, missed you at breakfast" I said.

"Oh hey, I got up early and went for a walk, I've never been to Vegas, just wanted to see a few things before I go home" he said.

"Oh ok, hope I didn't say anything wrong last night" I said. He got a little red in the face, so I changed the subject, "what session are you going to next?"

He told me which one.

"Mine is in the same hotel, want to get lunch together after?" I asked.

"Sure" he said with a hint of hesitation. I knew it was a bad idea to let my hormones get the better of me. Now things were weird and awkward. I vowed to remain professional with him the rest of the conference. Lunch started out a little icy, but soon he warmed up, and we were talking about the sessions and what we wanted to do that evening. It was the one night we had to do whatever we wanted.

"I've been here before, I can show you around if you want" I offered.

"That would be great" he said.

"I know a nice place we can get dinner and maybe see a show" I said. He looked around to make sure no one we knew was nearby.

"I kinda want something wild, this is Vegas after all" he said.

"Oh, like how wild?" I asked, remembering the premise of numerous movies on the subject, many of which ended badly.

"You know like a strip club or something" he asked shyly.

"Oh?" I asked.

"It's Vegas! I can't go home and tell my buddies I didn't hit up a strip club while I was there" he said.

"I know of one, but I doubt it would be your speed" I said.

"Oh right" he said, looking anywhere but at me.

"I bet we could ask the hotel concierge, he would know of one" I suggested.

"You'd go with me?" He asked.

"Sure, on one condition" I said.

"What's that?" He asked.

"We stop at my place after" I said. He gave me an incredulous look and his face reddened.

"Sure, I guess if I'm going to subject you to titties all night the least I can do is let you see some dick" replied.

"Cool, I'll check with the concierge on my way back to the room since my session ends before yours" I said.

"Cool, looking forward to it" he said. The bulge in his khakis made that obvious.

I gave the concierge a nice tip, and he gave me a suggestion, even arranged for a car to pick us up for free. I headed up to the room to grab a shower and change.

"It's all set" I called out from the shower when I heard the door open and close. Daniel popped his head in the door.

"Really?" He said.

"Yup, set us up with the vip package." I said.

"Sweet!" He said.

"I shut off the shower and grabbed a towel to dry off.

"All yours" I said as I toweled off in the center of the room. He disappeared for a minute that came back in completely naked. I tried not to make a big deal about it. I noticed his dick looked like it was at half-mast. Mine began to chub up, so I quickly left him to get ready before things got weird again.

I got ready and messaged Evan to see how things were going.

"I'm going to meet Steven's friend tomorrow, wish me luck" he wrote.

"You'll do great, I know you'll land the job" I replied.

"I hope so, sounds like he's really rich" he said.

"Even better!" I wrote back.

Daniel came out of the shower and strolled into the room with a towel around his waist. I was disappointed he wasn't nude. Then I discovered why. I could clearly see his hard cock pressing into the fabric. There was no denying he was excited about this evening. He grabbed his clothes and changed in the bathroom.

We walked around, seeing some sights and found a nice place for dinner. We talked about our lives and the difference cities we lived in. His face lit up when he talked about his kids.

The town car arrived at 8:30 to pick us up. We'd been having a drink at the hotel bar. When we got to the place, I was impressed by the scale of it. The only strip clubs I'd ever been to had been little seedy looking holes in the wall. This place was decked out Vegas style with neon lights and topless waitresses carrying neon serving trays. I tried to look away, but with mirrors on the walls, there was no place to look and not see bare breasts everywhere I looked.

"Fuck!" Daniel said as we were led to a seat in an alcove off to the side with an unobstructed view of the stage. A busty red head came and took our drink order. The music thumped, and the drinks flowed as a stream of naked flesh danced across the stage. Daniel's eyes were glued to it, while my eyes were glued squarely on the movements in his crotch. It was like his dick was about to rip open his jeans and climb out the top.

I got up to pee and on my way back asked if I could get a champagne lap dance for my friend. I'd seen the one brunette he'd been especially following on the stage and requested her. I gladly paid the ridiculous fee and added a nice tip on top.

"I've got a surprise for you" I said when I returned.

"What?" He asked, adjusting his crotch for the third time in a minute.

"You'll have to wait and see" I said with a wink.

"This place of out of this world!" He said.

Just then, the brunette walked up with a champagne bucket, wearing a see-through negligée. She set the bucket down, set down two glasses, and then pulled out the bottle. She then proceeded to place the bottle in a towel between her legs like she was about to fuck herself with it. Instead, she tightened her legs around it and pulled the cork out. Champagne poured out from the bottle held between her legs as she grabbed a glass and filled it. She passed the glass to Daniel, then filled one for me. She started to inch up my legs, but I nodded over to Daniel. She gave me a wink and headed to him instead. I watched as she danced over his lap, getting her breast within inches of his drooling mouth. She turned around and pulled off her negligée, standing completely naked in front of him. Her ass was soft and smooth and her pussy hairless. Daniel's dick was trying to climb out of the top of his jeans. There was a dark patch in the denim where his precum was soaking through.

The dancer backed into him, hovering close so her neatly shaved pussy was inches from his face. She sat down in his lap and gyrated over his crotch. She rubbed her ass over his hard dick to the music. I thought he might have cum, the way his eyes rolled back in his head at the sensation of her actually making brief contact with his distended jeans.

She turned around and straddled him, pressing her breast into his face. I was surprised that she let him lick her nipples before she backed away. She ran her hands down his chest and across his bulge. She looked over at me and gave me a wicked grin. Maybe she'd seen the way I was looking at his crotch the whole time, she seemed to know what I wanted too.

She reached down and pulled the button on his jeans and slid the zipper down. His dick was straining the fabric so much the waistband was pulled back, leaving a gap between his dick and his neatly trimmed pubes. Now it was my turn to adjust my crotch.

She reached down and pulled his underwear open, exposing his dick to the cool air of the club. She put a finger to her lips seductively to wet it, and then ran the wet finger down his shaft. She cupped his balls playfully as his dick jumped and dropped buckets of precum all over his abs.

She teased him some more, then came in close once again, pressing her breast to his face and letting her long hair hang down in his face. Then she lowered herself and pressed her pussy onto his dick, not letting him penetrate her, but just enough to tease him. He involuntarily thrust himself up a few times before she stepped back and gave him then me a smile and a wink.

"Hope you boys enjoy Las Vegas," she said, throwing her negligée back on before walking away. Daniel watched her go leaving his dick out and drooling, his balls danced as if they were on the edge of exploding right there in the club.

"Wow! That was fucking awesome!" He finally said, looking down and realizing his dick was still out. He did his best to clean up the precum with a cocktail napkin before quickly tucking his dick back in his underwear. He had some trouble getting the zipper back up over his impossibly hard cock. I was doing my best to keep my cock in check, but I had to admit I was leaking too.

I knew if I didn't get some relief soon, I was going to have a massive case of blue balls. I'm sure that Daniel was in the same boat.

"Head back?" I asked.

"Aren't we going to your place next?" He asked.

"We don't have to, I was just kidding" I said.

"A deal is a deal" he said. I rolled my eyes.

"Are you sure?" I said. In response, he flagged down a blond topless waitress and asked for the check. He paid the rest of the bill, and we staggered out of the club. I fumbled for my phone to order a lift.

I'd picked out a place that had an all male review. I doubted it would have anything like a lap dance, at least not for a guy anyway. It would probably be filled with horny bachelorettes. I punched in the address and called a car.

Daniel swayed, holding on to me to steady him, which was like using a pool noodle as a cane. His hand idly tugged at the front of his jeans.

"Thanks again for that lap dance, that's one to tell the guys" he slurred, hanging around my neck and patting me on the chest.

"Of course, glad you had a good time" I said.

"I'm so fucking horny, she got me so close I nearly came all over her pussy" he said.

"I could see, that was fucking hot!" I said.

"It's been too fucking long" he said. Gone was the formality of our work personas, we were just two buddies having the night of our lives.

"You need to get laid!" I said, "when was the last time?"

"Not since our anniversary, back in September, last year!" He said. "Hasn't been the same since we had kids".

"I've heard that before" I said, thinking of Evan. "What do you miss the most?"

"Blow jobs" he said without hesitation. "She hasn't given me one since our wedding night." He continued bitterly.

"If it wasn't for the kids, I'd have probably left her years ago. I've been tempted to download a hookup app but if I got caught or got someone pregnant it would be over, and I wouldn't get to see my kids" he said.

"What if you could get a blowjob without getting caught." I said.

"Fuck I'd be there in an instant" he said.

"Would it matter who was giving it?" I asked. He thought for a minute.

"At this point it wouldn't matter, she could be ugly as fuck" he said.

"What about a guy?" I asked. He gave me an incredulous look.

"You offering to give me a blowjob?" He came out and asked.

"Not me necessarily," I said.

"That might be a little weird, being coworkers and all" he said.

"It would only have to be weird if we let it, but what if it was someone else, what if you could stick your dick in a hole and not even know who was giving you a blow job." I said.

"Are you talking about a glory hole?" He asked.

"Yeah" I said.

"Fuck, I didn't think they were real" he said.

"They are if you know where to look" I said.

"You just stick your dick in a hole and someone sucks it, no questions asked?" he asked.

"Yeah, some people get off on giving guys head" I said.

"Fuck, I'd like to see that!" He said as if this were purely a hypothetical.

I took out my phone, looked down the list of places I'd been looking at going. The other places were mostly gay bars and less strip clubs per se. I laughed out loud when a saw the last one. I wondered what he'd make of that one. There was only one way to find out.

I really wasn't in the mood to deal with screaming bachelorettes anyway, I updated the ride to the new address.

"Whatcha doing?" Daniel asked, looking over my shoulder.

"Making your wish come true" I said.

Chapter 25

Hot Sauna

"This doesn't look like a strip club" Daniel said when I arrived at an indistinct building.

"It is a club and does involve stripping, but it's not exactly a strip club" I said.

"What kind of strippers, men?" He asked.

"I'm assuming it will mostly be men inside." I said, "A bit of warning, this is a bit more wild than the last place, and more interactive" I said.

"Really? More than that!" He said.

"I don't know about you, but I need some relief" I said, grabbing a handful of my crotch.

"I hear you there" he said, looking drunkenly down at his lap. His precum was now creating a dark spot near the pocket of his jeans.

"I can guarantee you will get off in there" I said

"I don't know" he said.

"It's ok, we can just go back to the hotel, as long as you don't mind me rubbing one out. I'll just call another car" I said.

"No, wait ... it's ok" he said, steeling himself. He rubbed his hand over his jean's covered dick. I don't think his dick went down much since the strip club.

"You sure? You might see some pretty wild things in there" I said.

"Let's do this before I chicken out" he said.

I noticed him fiddling with his wedding ring like he was trying to take it off.

"And whatever happens we keep it between us" he said conspiratorially.

"Absolutely, what happens in Vegas," I said.

"Stays in Vegas" he repeated.

I was sobering up a bit and now was beginning to think better of my choice.

"Ok, but if you want to leave at any point, just tell me, I won't be upset ok" I said.

"Ok, ok! I get it, now are we going in or what" he said.

We headed inside. There was just an entryway with an older gentleman sitting behind a plexiglass barrier.

"Entry for two" I said.

"Two rooms or just lockers?" He asked, grabbing a couple of towels. Daniel looked at me with puzzlement on his face. This was a bad idea, I thought, but it was too late to back out now.

"Lockers I guess" I said.

He said the price and I handed him cash. He gave me two keys on stretchy plastic rings and buzzed us in. Inside there was a room full of lockers and the strong smell of chlorine cleaner and musk.

"What are we doing exactly?" Daniel asked, looking at the towel I placed in his hands.

"Strip down and put on the towel" I said. This was also my first time, so I wasn't at all clear what to expect.

A man came in wearing just a towel and eyed us intensely.

"Is this some kind of spa?" He asked.

"Something like that" I said. Where a spa had soothing, peaceful music playing, this had the beat of a nightclub pounding through the walls. I began to strip off my clothes, knowing we were being watched. Daniel began to strip as well, but nearly fell over as he attempted to step out of both legs of his jeans at the same time. His semi-hard dick pushed against his underwear, which showed precum stains. He waited for me to drop my underwear, then followed my lead. I marveled at the shining head of his cock as it dripped out more precum. The man in the corner continued to watch us as I wrapped my towel around my waist and beckoned Daniel to follow me into a dark passage. The place was lit indirectly, so things glowed in the dark. The first room we came to was a shower room with nozzles on the walls. There was a large black man standing at the shower, his huge ebony dick hanging down as the water cascaded down his body. We both couldn't help but stare at him. He was 250 pounds of pure muscle.

The man looked over at me and smiled. His white teeth glowed a shocking blue in the dim light. He looked like he was built to fuck and while I'd found a new appreciation for getting fucked by Evan's big dick, his was in a whole different weight class. Besides, I think that was more action than Daniel could handle his first time out.

I smiled back and tried to convey my apologies, I didn't want him to think I didn't find him incredibly hot, I doubt my little nod accomplished my aims.

The place was like a maze, with odd corridors leading off into dark corners. I was a little disappointed that there weren't as many people here as I expected. The ads made it out to be this Roman orgy every night. We passed an empty room with a tv playing a porn video. Daniel looked up at the screen showing two guys fucking, the one guy tied down and gaged, the other in leather and boots.

I led him down another dark corridor, he kept close as if I were his shield from danger. I spotted the guy we'd seen in the locker room slip into a room ahead of us. I looked in to find he'd disappeared. Then I spotted the holes. Bingo, this is it, I thought.

"There you go, a glory hole" I whispered to Daniel, talking in a normal voice seemed inappropriate, like we were in church.

I stepped up to one of the holes and aimed my dick through the opening. There was a shuffling behind the wall and then a warm wet sensation engulfed my dick.

"Is there someone in there" Daniel asked.

"Mmmm" was my reply as the man expertly sucked my dick.

"Fuck!" He said, watching me hump the stranger's lips.

"Go ahead stick it through" I told him. He hesitated for a moment, then pulled open his towel. His dick jumped up and smacked his abs. He inspected the hole as if it might bite his dick off. The ring around the hole was padded and soft, so there was little chance of bodily injury.

He stroked himself a few times, building up his courage, then slipped his dick through the hole next to mine. I felt my dick slip from the warm mouth, replaced by a hand stroking me.

"Oh fuck!" Daniel yelped and jumping back from the wall in surprise. He regained his composure and slipped his dick back in again. This time, he purred in delight as the mouth presumably began to work his dick over. I envied the guy behind the wall sucking this straight guy's dick. There was still time, if not tonight, then hopefully before the trip was over I'd have that beautiful cock in my mouth.

Though I enjoyed his mouth, his hand was lacking. He was so focused on sucking Daniel, he neglected stroking me. As if hearing my thoughts, I felt his mouth on my cock again. Daniel looked over at me while he waited for his turn again. His face was aglow in revelation.

I pulled out and watched his face light up as the man pleasured his dick like it probably had never been pleasured before. I was surprised he lasted so long as the minutes ticked by. I knew it was getting late, but I wanted to explore some more. I couldn't leave Daniel alone, and I didn't want him to cum before we both got a chance to enjoy what this place had to offer. I worried the moment he came straight, married man guilt would put an end to the fun.

I tapped him on the shoulder, and he jumped back in fright.

"Sorry," I said. "You want to explore some more?"

"Uh" he said looking down at his wet dick on the verge of release. He struggled for a moment, then stepped back and followed my lead.

I tied up my towel and whispered a thanks to our friend on the other side of the wall before we headed out.

We came to a tiled room with more showers and a glass door on one wall. I pulled off my towel and put it over my shoulder, then opened the door. A blast of warm air hit me as I entered the dimly lit room beyond.

The air was thick with steam and musk. Two figures sat next to each other on a tile bench. From the state of their dicks, it was clear we'd interrupted them in the middle of something. Thier dicks glistened with spit in the dim light. They eyed us as we took the bench across from them. Daniel tried to cover his clearly excited genitals, while I opened my legs and showed off my growing member.

They were both middle-aged and a little overweight but no more than Daniel. They were hairy and thier dicks were average, maybe five or six inches, I estimated. Both were cut with big thick heads and heavy looking balls. Daniel gave an audible gasp as they started to stroke their dicks openly. I noticed both wore wedding bands, though I doubted they were married to each other. I could have sworn one of them was the speaker at one of our sessions, but in this light it was difficult to tell.

Daniel's eyes were wide as they shifted from one guy to the next, then back to me. I began to stroke my cock along with them. From my angle, I could see Daniel was clearly hard, but he hid it from the guys across from us behind his arm. The guy across from me was eyeing my cock and licking his lips.

"Fuck!" Daniel gasped as the guy on the left knelt down in front of me and took my dick down his throat in one shot. Daniel stared in disbelief as he began to suck my dick. To my surprise, he was an expert at sucking dick.

I leaned my head back and let him take control. He'd bring me to the edge, then back off and play with my balls while I cooled off. I was so lost in the feeling, I forgot Daniel was sitting next to me.

When I opened my eyes and looked down, I saw the other guy's head in Daniel's lap. Daniel was whimpering in delight as the stranger expertly sucked his cock.

The guy sucking me stood up and brought his dick within inches of my face. It wasn't a long one but had decent thickness with a tapered cut head. I leaned forward and licked the precum from the tip, then sank down his shaft until it jabbed the back of my throat and my nose was buried in his pubes. He swayed and held the back of my head as he began to fuck my face.

A thought dawned on me, what if the other guy expected the same from Daniel. I looked over and, sure enough, his partner was on to his feet, dick looming in front of Daniel's face. Daniel's had a look of what I can only describe as disgust, terror and, to my surprise, curiosity on his face. I was about to come to his rescue and suck the stranger off for him when he moved. I choked on the cock in my mouth as I watched in slow motion his tongue reach out and tentatively lick the anonymous cock in front of him. My eyes grew wide as he opened his mouth and devoured it. I nearly shot my load hands free at the sight of it.

I realized I had stopped sucking the dick in front of me and merely had it in my mouth, drooling down the shaft. Satisfied that Daniel wasn't freaking out over the turn of events, I went back to lavishing the hard pole in my mouth. He began to get more into it, holding the back of my head and fucking my face. I tasted precum and felt his balls tightening.

"I'm getting close" he whispered hoarsely. Though I wanted to swallow his load, I worried what kind of precedent that would set for his buddy. I reluctantly pulled back and stroked him furiously.

"Oh fuck!" he whimpered as hot blasts hit my face. I licked my lips and tasted his acrid cum as the last of his load dripped down my chin.

"Fuck!" He said backing away. I looked over a Daniel who was enthusiastically going to town on the stranger's cock. He used his hand and his mouth to bring the stranger to, then over the edge.

"Oh fuck!" was all the warning he was given as I saw the shaft expand, flooding Daniel's mouth with his load. Daniel got a panicked look on his face for a moment, but didn't back away. He let the stranger finish cumming in his mouth, then turned his head and spit the contents onto the tiled floor, where I'm sure it joined millions of fellow ill-fated sperm. I sat back in stunned silence until I felt lips on my dick once more. I ran my fingers through the stranger's thinning hair as he worked my dick.

"Oh shit! I'm cumming!" My voice rang off the hard tiles as my pent of load flooded the stranger's mouth. He continued to suck me, getting every last ounce of cum I had to offer and swallowing it.

I looked over and saw Daniel, he'd continued to lick the stranger's softening cock with a greedy, fascinated look on his face. Finally, the stranger pried him from his oversensitive cock and stepped back, a string of spit and residual cum connecting them for a moment before the tension broke.

Before he could bend down a take my prize, I leaned over and engulfed Daniel's dick in my mouth. I could taste spit and precum and smell the strong musky scent radiating off his balls. I knew he wouldn't last long as his hips bucked off the tiled bench. His hand gripped the back of my head as he pushed me down on his cock to the root. It took all my effort not to gag on it, as he jabbed the back of my throat. I felt the first searing hot spray hit my tonsils. I backed off a bit, working his sensitive shaft with me tongue as I gripped his base tightly. His balls churned as another hot spray filled my mouth. It was like drinking from a firehose, the cum kept squirting onto my tongue. 5, 6, 7, I lost count after that. I did my best to swallow as he held my head tight and poured months, perhaps years, of frustration down my gullet. He whimpered and moaned as his dick became overwhelmed with pleasure. I milked the last of his load from the shaft until it formed a bead at the piss slit and sucked it down as his abs spasmed in delight and over stimulation.

"Fuck!" He called out to the now empty room. At some point, our friends must have walked out, but I hadn't noticed, I was so engrossed in my task. I sat up and leaned back against the warm tiles and basked in the afterglow, my mouth, and tummy full of sweet saltiness.

I glanced over at Daniel, his softening dick rested on his thigh in a pool of cum. I wanted to get the bit I missed, but wasn't sure what his mood was post nut.

He looked over at me and got this weird expression on his face. Oh no, here we go, I thought, bracing myself for the worst. Then a grin crept across his face.

"Fuck!" Was all he said. I nodded my agreement.

"I've never had a blow job that good in my life" he said. I welled with pride, then wondered if it was from me or the guys who were blowing him before me.

"Guys just know what feels good from experience" I said.

"I can't believe I never did that before" he said. He looked down with a guilty look on his face. I understood his mixed emotions. He'd just cheated on his wife, with multiple guys no less, and sucked cock for the first time in his life. It was a lot to take in.

"Get cleaned up and head back, or are you ready for another round?" I asked. From the sleepy look on his face, I had my answer. "Maybe let's call it a night" I answered for him.

"Yeah, what time is it anyway?" He asked.

"I have no idea" I said. There were no windows in the place and no natural light. It could have been the middle of the afternoon, and it would have looked the same in here. I figured it must be incredibly late or incredibly early. We had to be up for sessions in a few hours.

I got up and offered Daniel a hand up. Our towels were soaked from sitting in the steam. The air felt chilly when we left the heated room. The warm shower felt nice after the shock of cold. The guy from the locker room and glory hole was showering and stroking himself, a few nozzles down. I had a pang of guilt for leaving him high and dry, but I think Daniel was ready to get out of there.

We did our best to dry off with the damp towels and got dressed. A couple of new guys were milling around the locker room looking at thier phones. I called for a lift and we waited outside.

We both nearly fell asleep on the way back to the hotel. I downed some water to stave off a splitting headache that was forming and tried to get some sleep. Getting up the next day, no, later that morning by now, was going to be hell, but it was all worth it.

Chapter 26
Jail Cell

My alarm went off, and I smacked my phone to silence it. My head pounded. I rolled over and looked at Daniel's bed. He was on his back, a large mound tenting out the thin sheet covering his crotch. Did we really end up at a gay sauna, or was that all a drink fueled dream?

Daniel stretched and yawned, running his hand down his body to grab hold of his morning wood.

"Morning" I said.

"Morning" he said, looking over at me. I wondered if there would be any change in his demeanor now that he'd had a night's sleep to clear his head. To my relief, he grinned and pulled down the sheet, showing off his hard dick.

"I can't believe we did that last night" he said.

"I know, guess you can't call yourself a straight guy anymore" I suggested.

"Huh?" He asked.

"Once you get a taste for cock you can't go back" I teased him.

"I got caught up in the moment!" he said, looking a bit offended.

"I'm just teasing you, I don't go in for labels. You did what you wanted and enjoyed it" I said. He nodded his head in agreement.

"Why don't you come over here and help me do it again." He said, grinning and holding up his dick. I was rock hard in an instant, as I sprang out of bed and jumped on top of him. I straddled his chest and brought my dick up into his face.

He looked up at me then back down at it, then grabbed hold of it, stroking me in front of his face. I leaned forward, pressing my head against the wall, and fed him my dick. He was surprisingly good at it for a beginner. What he lacked in experience, he more than made up for in enthusiasm. He stroked my shaft while he wet my head with his lips. I knew I had to piss and probably wouldn't have been able to cum, but he was doing something to me.

I pulled out of his mouth, letting some drool run down his chin, and I scooted back down his moderately hairy chest. I felt his dick hit my crack and press into the cleft. I knew we didn't have time for fucking, and I wasn't sure he'd be up for it anyway. I pushed up and let my dick glide along his like crossed swords. I licked and kissed down his chest and abdomen until I came to his neat pubes. I licked around the base of his shaft and then licked his hairless balls.

I licked up his shaft and then popped his head into my mouth. I rolled my tongue around his head and sensitive shaft until I heard my alarm blaring in the background.

"Shit, we'd better get ready" he said.

Just then his phone rang and he jumped up to grab it.

"Hey honey, we were just getting ready to head down for breakfast" he said.

"Sorry I didn't write, we were at dinner then the reception, and it got late. I didn't want to wake you" he said.

"No, it wasn't like that, I was out with my coworker" he said my name.

"I know I should have let you know. I'm sorry I worried you" he said, twisting his wedding band nervously.

I felt bad for putting him in this situation. I got up and left him to finish smoothing things over with his wife while I went to the bathroom. A short time later, I saw him in the mirror, still naked but only semi-hard.

"Everything ok?" I asked.

"Yeah, she just gets like that when I go away, acting like I'm cheating on her all the time" he said. Well, she's not wrong this time, I thought but didn't say. My face must have given the thought away.

"I know, I know, but last night was different. It's not like I was going to run off with any of those guys. It was just some harmless fun, right?" He said. Whatever way he justified it was ok with me. A victimless crime didn't really exist, but then again, it was a crime to not take care of that beautiful cock regularly. There were plenty of men, myself included, who would volunteer to do it.

"Wish we had more time" I said, nodding to his half-hard dick.

"Me too" he said, grinning.

We got dressed and headed down to breakfast.

"You think we could go back to the spa after dinner tonight?" He asked.

"If I can stay awake I'm game if you are" I said. I was surprised at how eager he was.

"Ok cool" he said.

I went through the motions of taking notes during the sessions, but I couldn't help my mind wandering. I couldn't wait for dinner to be over and for us to head out.

"How's it going?" Blinked the message notification from Evan.

I was hesitant to tell Evan for some reason. I knew he was having fun with Nat and Jake while I was gone, but still, I felt a little guilty about what had happened with Daniel.

"It's going" I replied.

"Jake is coming over so we can watch the game" he wrote back. It was like he was asking my permission without seeming like he was asking.

"Cool, is it just you guys?" I asked.

"Yeah, Nat's mom is in town and Jake wants to make himself scarce." He wrote back.

"Lol, have fun" I wrote.

"You too" he replied.

The day dragged on until, finally, we finished dinner and headed back to the room to change.

"I've been thinking about this all day" he said when he dropped his pants and his semi-hard dick sprung out.

"I can see" I laughed. Though we had a drink or two at dinner, tonight couldn't be explained away by overindulgence. He seemed genuinely excited to go back.

I called a car, and we arrived a little earlier than last time. The parking lot was full, which was a good sign. He paid for the lockers this time and we headed in. There were several guys in the locker room getting undressed. I stripped down and waited for Daniel to finish. He stood at his locker, texting his wife.

"All good?" I asked.

"Yeah, just told her I was going to bed early since tomorrow was the last day" he said. I was conflicted, it was having so much fun for Daniel it was sad to see it come to an end, but I was also looking forward to going home again and seeing Evan. I'd genuinely started to miss him. I pictured him at home with Jake right now, his big cock slipping into Jake's hairy hole. Though I had my pick of guys in the rooms beyond and Daniel, I'd give anything to be home with them right now.

As if he read my mind from miles away, my phone lit up in my locker. I picked it up and saw a video clip in the chat from Jake. I played it. There was Jake's adorable face filling the screen.

"Hey, wish you were here with us, hope the conference is not too dull." He said. I felt self-conscious having the sound on as I looked around the locker room. The others had left to roam the maze of rooms anyway.

Jake turned the camera around to find Evan standing over him. He panned the camera down Evan's bare chest and abs until it rested on Jake's cock, floating in front of Evan's abs as they flexed behind it. He lowered the camera to show Evan's dick pounding away at Jake's hairy hole. The camera swiveled back to Jake's face with a broad grin on it, then the video ended.

"Fuck! Are those your neighbors again?" Daniel asked from over my shoulder. His close proximity, startled me.

"Yeah, that is Jake, the father of two" I said.

"And he's getting fucked?" Daniel asked.

"Don't knock it till you've tried it" I said.

"I think I'll pass" he said.

"Your loss" I said.

"Lead on" he said. I closed my locker, and we headed into the dark passage.

This time we explored in the opposite direction. It almost seemed darker here. Ahead of us was a set straight out of a prison porn. There were bars and a cell door, and bunk beds to one side. Hanging from the other side of the room were a pair of slings.

"What are those?" Daniel asked, pointing to the slings.

"Want me to demonstrate?" I suggested.

"I don't know" he hesitated.

"Here I'll show you" I said, not at all confident I was going to be able to. I climbed into the leather bucket seat awkwardly, nearly falling out as I did. I felt extremely vulnerable hanging with my ass out as I raised my legs and showed Daniel my ass.

"Guys get fucked in these?" He said. I pulled open my cheeks to illustrate the point. He looked at my hole for a moment that looked away as if he were supposed to be disgusted, but then looked back again. I took a risk.

"You wanna try?" I asked.

"What fuck you?" He asked.

"You can if you want" I said.

"I don't know" he said but didn't pry his eyes away.

"I've never been fucked in a sling before, I've heard it's out of this world." I said.

"No thank" he said.

"If you'd rather, I can fuck you," I joked.

"Definitely not" he said, looking around anxiously.

"If you're not going to, I will," came a gruff voice from the cell door. There was a large man clad in a leather harness and boots standing there stroking himself looking at my hole. I sat up, startled by the stranger.

"Damn, I take that back, I don't want to fuck you, I want that dick in me" he said looking down at my hard cock.

Daniel looked back and forth between us, his towel still cinched up around his waist. The big man strolled in and nodded at my dick.

"May I?" He asked.

"Go for it" I said. He leaned in and slipped my dick into his mouth. His mustache tickled my pubes. Normally, I wasn't into mustaches, since I figured if you can grow a full mustache why stop there, a beard was far sexier. But it fit him for some reason. Maybe it was the accompanying dark scruff that gave him a biker gang look. That and the leather harness that crisscrossed his chest and showed off his thick pelt and black hair.

He was an expert cocksucker, with no gag reflex that I could trigger, and trust me I tried. He deep throated me so deep he was licking my balls while my head was halfway to his stomach.

"Fuck, that's a nice one!" He said as he stroked my thick wet shaft. "You into fucking?"

"I am. Especially big hairy asses like yours," I said.

"Let's trade places then," he said. I got up with some difficult and let him take my place. He seemed to slip into the sling naturally. The straps creaked as they bore his weight. His lifted his legs into the straps so that his ass hung over the edge, open and ready for a good pounding.

Daniel stood by and watched, his mouth slightly open, his towel distended at the crotch. There were packets of lube and condoms on a side table. I grabbed one of each. I wanted some things in Vegas to stay in Vegas. I rolled down the condom and slicked it up with lube, then inserted a finger in the stranger's hole. He felt velvety soft inside. His fat, stubby cut dick stuck straight up from a thick nest of hair. His balls seemed to almost be an extension of his crotch, they hugged so close to him. The only thing that differentiated them from his legs was the fact that they were covered in hair and two shades darker than his tan skin.

I grabbed hold of his legs and pressed my dick into his open passage. I let gravity pull him down my shaft until my pubes rested against his tight ball sack. Even with the condom, he felt incredibly soft and warm inside. I was actually grateful for the thin latex, as it kept me from shooting my load too quickly.

I looked over and Daniel stood fondling himself through the towel while watching in stunned curiosity. It was tricky at first to get the rhythm of the swing right. I realized I had to just stand still and let the pendulum motion do the work for me. I could imagine Evan fucking me in one of these, and thought I might have to buy one for home. Though I was with these two hot men, my thoughts kept going back to Evan. I must really be failing for him, something I had never expected. I hovered on the edge of orgasm, imagining I was the one in the sling getting pounded.

The bear of a man grunted as I pinched his nipple and punched his chest.

"Fuck yeah!" He said in response. He was looking down at something to my side.

I looked over and saw Daniel had take off his towel and was now stroking his cock openly to the spectacle of men fucking.

"You want to give it a try?" I asked. He looked up at me and backed away, then looked down at my dick embedded in the stranger's ass.

"His ass feels amazing," I added as further enticement. He stared at my dick going in and out of that slick hole without looking away. His dick dripped precum in a long strand toward the floor. I pulled out, leaving stranger's hole open and waiting for Daniel's dick to fill it.

"Come on, you know you want to" the stranger said.

I opened a condom and stooped in front of Daniel. I licked up a string of his precum, then sucked his dick into my mouth. I realized then, as I looked past him, we had a growing audience at the bars of the cell.

I slipped the condom into my mouth and rolled it down his shaft with my teeth. I lubed it up and then stepped back to give him room. He hesitated, then gave a nervous laugh, the kind when you do something for the first time you're so excited your whole body shakes.

He grabbed hold of the bear's legs and tried to press his dick into the hairy hole. He aimed too high and missed the opening. I reached down and aimed him in properly. His eyes rolled back in his head, the whites glowed in the black light.

"Oh fuck! I can't believe I'm doing this" he said as he took a couple tentative strokes.

"Feels good, huh?" I said.

"It feels amazing" he said, picking up the pace.

"That's it straight boy, fuck this faggot hard," the stranger growled, somehow picking up on the fact that he was straight and a virgin at fucking guys. I noticed one of the bystanders walk past and get up in the open sling. He was a younger guy, which was a surprise in a place like this. I recalled seeing a sign at the front that said 18-25 free, I figured to encourage young blood. I guess it worked in this case.

He was shaved smooth from head to toe. His laid back in the straps like a pro. His soft white skin was covered in patterns of tattoos. They glowed in the black light like a psychedelic painting. His ass was wide and hairless and his dick was long and slender with an intact foreskin that pulled back from below his head like curtains on a window. He nodded for me to come to him. Though he wasn't my usual type, something about his slender, almost feminine frailty contrasted with the over the top masculinity of the setting.

He reminded me of Natalie if she had a dick and no breasts. Daniel was looking over at him as well.

"Fuck me daddy" the kid said to me, pulling apart his cheeks to show his little pink hole winking back at me. I stepped up to him and sank my dick into him. His body writhed in pleasure as my dick stretched his hole wide. As I pulled out, I could see his skin tug at my shaft and prolapse out. His ass felt like it was trying to suck me back in.

His dick bounced and swayed with the motions of the sling. I wanted to breed this boy so badly and fill him with my cum. Daniel was watching me fuck the boy, timing his thrusts into the bear with mine. Several more guys gathered around us, watching and stroking their cocks.

"Oh fuck!" Daniel yelled as he pounded the bear's hairy hole a few more times, then slowed and finally pulled out, the condom heavy with his load.

"Please daddy, breed my hole!" The boy said, reaching down and tugging at the condom. He pulled it off as I pulled back, his raw ass beckoning me. I thrust forward into his warm, wet slit. Without the condom to dull my senses, I knew I wouldn't last long. I pounded him deep and hard.

"That's it, fuck me! Use my hole!" He said, stroking his cock in time with my thrusts.

I began to erupt inside him, filling him with my cum. His abs contracted, and his dick jumped as it began to launch his load all over his chest. His ass milked the rest of my load from my shaft as his load continued to fly all over the place. I'd never seen so much cum. A man next to me grunted and added his load to the boy's chest.

I stayed inside him as he thrashed out the rest of his load, violently impaling himself on my spent cock. When I pulled out, my dick was instantly replaced by one of the spectators.

Daniel and I stood back and watched as each man took a turned breeding his hole or depositing a load on his face or chest. He reveled in it, smearing the cum over his skin like serum. The full condom still hung from Daniel's impossibly hard cock as he took in the scene of debauchery before us.

The kid came again, depositing nearly as much cum on his belly as he had done the previous time. His body flailed with each eruption of pure ecstasy. The bear, now recovered, stood and waited his turn. He smiled at the two of us as he slipped his dick into the young man's hole.

"That's it son, take daddy's load!" He said as he added his seed to his hole with a growl.

I pulled the condom off Daniel's dick and tossed it in the trashed as we headed to the shower.

"That was so fucking hot!" Daniel said as we rinsed off the cum and sweat.

"Yes, that was incredible" I said.

"I can't believe I actually fucked a guy" he said.

"You seemed to enjoy it" I said.

"I'm kicking myself for not doing it sooner" he laughed.

We finished getting dressed and headed back to the hotel. I was out before my head hit the pillow.

Chapter 27
Strange Bedfellows

I woke to find I wasn't alone in bed. For a moment, I thought I was home in bed with Evan tucked in behind me. But this was not my bed and that was not Evan's crack my dick was now resting in. Daniel must have slid into my bed sometime during the night, and now I was spooning him in the early morning hours.

He stirred next to me and pushed out his ass as he stretched. My dick was already hard and rubbing up against his hole. He seemed to be awake but didn't pull away as I would have expected a straight man to do.

"Morning" I ventured.

"Hope you don't mind, I was cold" he said. I very much doubted that he'd climbed into my bed just to share body heat. Sure, the a/c seemed to be stuck on full blast, but that was a flimsy excuse.

"You sure that's the only reason?" I asked.

"Well ..." he hesitated, and I felt his sphincter clench on the back of my dick. Was he really looking to get fucked? I thought that highly unlikely, but here we were.

"We leave today, and I may never get another chance like this" he finally said. I heard the longing in his voice, this was not the same man I'd met a few days ago. He was showing a vulnerable side that I think he rarely showed to anyone.

"I saw how that kid was last night, he looked like he was blissed out of his mind" he said.

"He may have been on something" I joked.

"True, but I doubt that was all of it" he said.

"I know I was just teasing. But seriously getting fucked is something you have to kinda build up to. I remember my first time, it hurt like hell" I said.

"So why'd you ever do it again?" He asked.

"It took me a while to do it again, but when I did, and I got past the pain and the strangeness of it, I suddenly felt something I'd never felt before. It made me cum harder than I'd ever cum in my life." I said.

"I've been curious for a long time, I've just never had the opportunity" he said.

"If you are sure, I'm willing to give it a try, I just can't guarantee it will be successful. I've had guys take a look at my cock and back out at the last minute" I said.

"I'll let you know if I want you to stop" he said.

I moved down under the sheets and found his hole in the dark. I pulled apart his cheeks and licked him.

"Oh fuck" he said, pushing his ass out for more. I licked and sucked his ass as he squirmed under me. His ass ring was clamped tightly closed at first, but gradually I was able to push the tip of my tongue inside him. He gasped for air and reached back, pressing the back of my head, my tongue jabbing his ass.

I pulled back to gasp for air when he let me up. I looked down at the wet hole and the bit of hair matted down around the edge. I poked it with my finger, testing to see how ready he was.

"Mmm" I heard him say as my finger slipped inside him. He must have had some experience to not resist at all.

"You sure you've never done this?" I asked.

"No never, why?" He asked.

"I expect a bit more resistance." I said, shoving a second wet finger in.

"Feels good actually" he said. A straight guy who is a natural bottom, there is a mythical creature for you. Then I thought about Jake and realized lightning could strike twice.

It was only when I had 4 fingers shoved up his ass that he showed any sign of discomfort.

"I don't have a condom" I said, realizing he may not want to risk going bare.

"I want to feel you like that kid last night" he said, rolling onto his back. His dick jumped up, landing on his abs and leaving a puddle of precum. I got up and rummaged in my suitcase for a small bottle of lube. I honestly didn't expect to use it but has brought it along just in case.

I lubed up my dick, then slipped a slick finger back in his hole. I bent forward and licked the head of his cock while I lined up my dick up with his hole. I pushed his legs back and looked into his face. He looked back with an intense expression on his face. My head slipped inside him. His eyes grew wide as I held his ass open. Slowly I slipped in deeper. His sphincter tightened and his jaw clenched.

"Relax" I said. He took a deep breath and nodded. I leaned in and licked his nipple, then lightly bit down on it to distract him. I slipped in deeper.

"Fuck!" He said, holding my head to his nipple. I licked around his chest, then came to his armpit and gave it a good tongue bath. I could taste and smell is deep masculine scent on the long hairs.

I took hold of his hand and moved it to the base of my dick now pressing against his balls.

"You're all the way in!" He laughed in astonishment. I nodded. I took a few tentative strokes inside him, poking at his prostate.

"Oh shit, what was that?" He asked, his eyes wide and his chest heaving.

"You're p-spot" I said as I poked it a few more times.

"Oh fuck I'm seeing stars" he said, slamming his head back onto the pillow.

His ass was wide open and ready for me. I grabbed his legs and pulled forward, slipping in and out of him slowly at first but building up speed. I added some more lube, then started to pound him. His dick was hard and dripping precum. I leaned in and licked it from his piss slit.

His ass gripped my cock tightly with each stroke, sending waves of sensations up my spine. My balls tightened and readied to shoot my load.

"I'm gonna cum!" I shouted as I worked into a frenzy.

"Come in me" he said, grabbing my ass and pulling me in to him deeper.

"Fuck!" I growled as my hot load filled him.

"Oh fuck! I felt that" he said.

I grew light-headed and leaned forward into his chest. His dick poked me in the abs, leaving a slug trail on my skin. I pulled out of him and scooped up some of my cum spilling out of his ass. With it, I slicked up his pole and applied some to my ass. I sat down on his cock to the root.

"Oh shit!" He cried as I began to lift myself up and slam down on him. I impaled myself on him over and over until my calves burned from the effort.

"Oh fuck I'm cumming" he said. He didn't have to tell me, I could feel the hot stream inside me and see the look of bliss on his face. I collapsed onto his chest with his cock still pulsing in my hole.

I leaned forward and kissed his lips. I suddenly felt like I'd crossed a line. Somehow, fucking him and then riding his cock to completion was less intimate than a simple kiss on the lips. He screwed up his face in surprise at my gesture.

"I'm sorry" I said.

"No ... it's ... ok, really" he said, leaning up to plant and kiss on my lips. I kissed him as he let his head rest on the pillow. Our tongues wrestled until his dick slipped out of my hole and I rolled onto my side next to him.

"So, how was your first time getting fucked?" I asked.

"Better than I imagined, honestly" he said, reaching back and feeling his open hole.

"So you'd do it again?" I asked.

"In a heartbeat" he said. "I can't believe I waited this long to try."

"Once you realize how much you enjoy it, you keep going back for more" I said.

"Too bad we live so far away from each other" he said.

"I know, it's a pity. I bet you would love Jake and Evan" I said. A melancholy came over us, knowing our time together was coming to an end. I took comfort in the fact that it was ending in such a high note.

"Hopefully, we can come back next year" I said.

"I will definitely request it" he said.

"Maybe I'll drag Evan and Jake along" I said, imagining what it would be like to have a week in Vegas with the three of them. I did miss them and my own bed.

We reluctantly got out of bed and got ready for breakfast and our last set of sessions. The conference was winding down already, the exhibit hall was being packed up. After the morning sessions, everyone would be leaving to go thier separate ways. I said goodbye to my boss and other coworkers at lunch before Daniel and I headed up to our room to pack.

We stripped out of our khakis to change into something more casual. I looked over at Daniel's dick one last time. He reached over and grabbed mine.

"One more for the road?" I asked. He nodded and dropped to his knees. I felt his warm mouth on my soft dick. It slowly grew inside his mouth so that when he pulled it back out, I was fully hard.

"Damn, I'm gonna miss that dick" he said.

"I'm gonna miss this one as well. I said, pushing him down onto the bed. I turned around and got my dick in his face, and I went for his dick in a sixty-nine position. He sucked my dick into his mouth and grabbed my balls. Having fun so much in the last few days, I wasn't sure I had another load to give him. Poked his hole while I deep throated his dick. He did the same to my hole. Suddenly, I felt my dick slip from his mouth as he shifted position. Then I felt his tongue on my ass. I let go of his dick and reached for his ass as well. We licked and sucked each other's asses until my phone chimed in the background. It was time to go.

We stood up and stroked our dicks, watching each other. He took long strokes from the base while I rubbed the sensitive skin by his frenulum. His breathing became heavy and suddenly a blast of cum shot out and landed on the top of my cock. I grabbed his cock and put it on top of mine as the last of his load oozed out onto my dick. Using his cum, I stroked myself to completion, my load landing in his neatly trimmed bush. I leaned in and kissed him deeply, knowing this was our chance to do it.

We cleaned up quickly, packed and raced to the lobby to catch a lift to the airport.

"Thank you for everything" Daniel said as he turned and gave me a hug. I wanted to kiss him, but my boss was around here somewhere, and I didn't want either of us to have to explain that. I waved as he headed down the gangway to board his flight. I had another hour until my flight.

I found a seat to watch the planes and wrote to Evan to let him know when to pick me up.

"I've got some great news when you get back" he wrote.

"What is it?" I asked.

"I'd rather tell you in person" he said.

"Ok, see you in a few hours" I wrote as I settled back in the uncomfortable seat and watched Daniel's plane taxi away from the gate.

Chapter 28
Bombshell

"He wants me to join his crew as his mechanic!" Evan said excitedly as we pulled away from the airport pickup line. I'd asked him how the interview went. My heart sank. So many conflicting emotions flooded my mind.

"That's great" I said, trying to be happy for him but knowing it would take him away from me.

"You can finally have me out of your hair" he said.

"I don't mind you being here" I said, my tone betraying my feelings.

"It's a six-month contract, I'll be back. You could always come with me!" He said, lifting my sagging chin.

"What would I do on a yacht?" I said, rolling my eyes.

"I don't know, you're a pretty good cook" he said.

"I can't just quit my job and go sailing around the world" I said.

"Why not?" He said, looking a little crestfallen.

"I have a career and family here, I'm not sure, I'd be able to work from the middle of the ocean." I said. It was tempting to run off and escape the world with him, but I have bills and a mortgage to pay. I couldn't give it all up so easily.

"Oh ... I just thought ..." he said, suddenly realizing how impractical the offer really was.

"What about your daughter? Don't you want to see her?" I asked.

"At this rate, I won't ever get to see her. She's got some lawyer now putting up all these roadblocks. She says I need to pay child support, in order to see her. I don't make enough money to support myself, much less pay her. If I take this job, I'll have enough money to start a proper company when I get back. Then I'll be able to help support my daughter."

"Lawyer's suck" I said. Knowing several lawyers who give pretty decent blow jobs.

"When would you be leaving?" I asked.

"Every year he migrates south before the weather gets colder, so in the next couple of weeks. The first stop will be in the Caribbean, then over to the mediterranean." he said, renewing his excitement. I was happy for him.

"It sounds like an amazing opportunity." I said, trying to muster all the enthusiasm I could. He looked at me, seeing through the facade.

"These past few weeks have been the worst and best of my life. I have you to thank for helping me when I needed it most," he said, pulling me into a tight embrace.

Tears began to flow as I lost my stoic composure. I gripped him tightly, not wanting to let go.

"It won't be forever, I'll be back" he whispered in my ear. It renewed my hope. Six months wasn't that long, after all, but a lot could change in that time.

"I'm truly happy for you. You can't pass this up" I said.

He kissed me softly on the cheek and looked into my tear stained face.

"I'll miss you" he said, sensing something bordering on love in his voice.

"I'll miss you too" I said, smiling through my tears.

"You sure you're ok with this?" He asked.

"Of course" I said. He kissed me and pushed me back into the sofa. His strong arms enfolded me. We kissed passionately, feeling the clock ticking on our time together.

He sat back and pulled off his shirt, exposing his chest, the blond hairs lit up by the soft light of the table lamp. He lifted up my shirt.

He dove down and licked my nipple, biting and teasing it. I writhed under him as my dick grew hard and pressed into his crotch.

He stood and dropped his shorts. He never wore underwear, so his hard cock flopped out and floated in front of him. I twisted around, so I was on my back facing him with my head hanging over the edge of the sofa. He came forward and pushed his cock down so it sank into my mouth. I sucked his dick, trying to get as much of him as I could down my throat.

He bent his legs and did mini squats, fucking my throat from above. Then he leaned forward and pulled my shorts up my legs and off. My dick hung down in front of me, aided by gravity. He leaned in and took me in his mouth. I licked and sucked him as he did the same to me.

He pulled his dick from my mouth and stepped forward, so his ass was hanging over my face. I pulled his cheeks apart and dove in, sucking his pucker. He gasped and leaned forward, attempting to reach my hole. I was teetering on the edge of the sofa, but he was able to reach it with his tongue. He licked my hole as I stuck my tongue into his.

He stood up and grabbed my head, pressing it into his crack with such force I thought he'd break my nose. I pressed an inch of my tongue into his hole and kept it rigid, fucking him with my tongue. He grunted and stepped back.

I looked up at him upside-down, wondering what would happen next. He turned and headed to the stairs, wagging a finger at me to follow.

I jumped up and ran to the stairs, then stopped as light faded from my eyes, replaced by stars. I grabbed the railing and held on as the stars faded and light returned. I'd stood up too quickly, and all the blood that had rushed from my head. The room spun for a moment. Evan had already reached the top of the stairs, and I heard him heading away from the bedroom.

I heard the back door open and close. I recovered my senses and followed him up and toward the back door. I stepped out into the cool night air, looking around to see if any neighbors were about. I didn't really care if they saw me naked ascending the stairs.

Evan had already reached the top of the stairs and had disappeared. I followed, up the stairs, bathed in the cool of the evening and the glow of the moon.

In the soft light, I saw him on the sofa on his back. He waved me over to him. I climbed on top of him as he pulled his legs back. Our dicks rubbed against each other as we kissed under the stars.

"Fuck me" he said softly. I was taken aback by his request. My previous attempt to fuck him didn't go so well. We'd not attempted it again after that.

"Are you sure?" I asked. I wished we'd been in the bedroom, where there was at least some lube handy.

"Yes, I want to feel you inside me" he said, pulling his legs back further and exposing his hair - covered hole. I got down below him and licked his hole, spreading as much saliva on it as my dry mouth could muster.

I started to stretch him out with a few fingers, getting more excited and nervous about fucking him every second. He pulled my hand away from his hole and grabbed for my dick. He pulled me up and pressed my head to his hole. I spit and let the thin line fall into his ass, just above his hole. It seeped down into his crack just above my head. He grabbed my ass and pulled me forward. My dick pressed into him, meeting considerable resistance.

In the dim light, I could see him gritting his teeth in pain as my dick invaded his tight hole.

"Maybe I should stop" I said, but he held my ass tightly, not letting me back away.

"No, we're doing this" he said, showing his commitment by pulling hard on my ass and shoving my dick into his hole.

"Oh fuck!" he wailed as my head popped inside him. I wanted to pull away, but he held tight despite the look of pain on his face.

"We don't ..." I started to say, he glared at me. I waited, feeling his ass clench around me.

"How do you and Jake do it" he asked between short tight breaths.

"We've had more practice," I said, taking hold of his softening dick. All his focus was going on opening up for me and enduring the pain I was inflicting on him. I pulled back and gathered what little spit I had left and let it fall where my dick met his hole. I pulled back and pressed forward a few times, letting the spit slip between us. It seemed to help somewhat as I slipped in another inch. He took in a sharp breath as I felt him clench down.

"Just relax and try to push out. I know this may sound gross, but pretend like you are pushing out a massive turd," I said, realizing just how unromantic it was. Though I love gay sex in all its forms, anal sex has its pitfalls.

His ass unclenched and I slipped in deeper.

"Oh fuck!" He said, but this time it was not an exclamation of pain. His mouth fell open, and his eyes rolled back. I must have hit something. I pressed in gently then pulled back ever so slightly. He grunted again and his dick, which had until this point rested in the basin where his pelvis met his leg, began to rise.

I poked at his prostate a few more times, noting the corresponding jump in his dick. A wet bead of precum began to form in his piss slit. I bent forward and lapped it up. His eyes shot open as he felt my dick shift inside him and the action of my tongue on his head. I grinned and leaned down to lick his shaft up to the moist head.

"Oh fuck" he whimpered as his dick jumped again, spilling more precum for me to lap up. Before either of us realized it, I was fucking him. It wasn't deep fucking like with Jake, who seemed to want it ever deeper and harder. I was content to take short strokes inside him, feeling how he gripped me and how my head pressed into him. Being partly out of him also lent itself to me sucking him simultaneously. I could only reach the top two inches, but it was enough to stimulate his frenulum.

He moaned and ran his finger through my hair as I continued to stimulate him from both ends. He was so tight my dick was already twitching ready to shoot my load. I focused all my attention on his dick, I wanted to feel him cum while I was still inside him.

He balls tightened, and his ass clenched down. That sent me over the edge. I pushed in deeper and began to unload my balls into him. He whimpered as my dick slipped in deeper.

"Oh fuck!" He cried. Suddenly, my mouth was full of warm wetness. I drank his load as his ass massaged the rest of my load from me, deep inside him. Our cum bonded us together, a part of me in him and a part of him in me.

My dick slipped out of him, and I let his legs stretch out and connect with the deck. I sat down next to him and pulled him toward me, my chest meeting his strong shoulders. We sat looking up at the stars while I softly stroked the hair on his chest. Time stretched out before us. I savored this moment, knowing this would have to sustain me in the months to come.

Chapter 29
Parting Gift

"I still can't believe you're leaving" Jake said.

"I'll be back, it's only six months" Evan said. To me, it seemed like an eternity. Jake had planned this little get-together when he heard Evan was shipping out. In fact, he was leaving the next day, this would be our last weekend together for a while. Nat was visiting her parents out of state with the kids, so it was just the three of us hanging out in Jake's yard. He had the grill going with a few premium steaks on it. My stomach growled in anticipation of the mouthwatering feast.

"How was the other night?" I asked. I both did and didn't want to know what they got up to with Nat while I was away on a work trip.

"Oh shit! It was amazing," Jake said. I felt a slight pang of jealousy when I saw Evan grin and shake his head.

"I think Nat is even more of a freak than you are" Evan said to Jake.

"You see where I get it. Until I met her I'd never even thought about any of this stuff, and now I can't get enough" Jake said.

"I can't believe she took us in both holes, I've never done that before" Evan said.

"What?" I asked.

"I was fucking her when Jake here gets up behind us and starts fucking her ass" Evan said.

"Oh, really?" I said.

"Yeah, felt so good with both of us inside her, pounding away. I think she came like three times in a row" Jake said.

"I've only seen that in porn" I said.

"You look at straight porn?" Evan asked.

"Mostly bisexual porn, I like it for the guys," I said.

"I love male male female porn," Jake said with a laugh. "Lately, I've been watching more gay threesomes"

"I love those too" I said.

"There is this one where the these two guys fuck this one guy at the same time" Jake said.

"You mean two dicks in the ass? How is that even possible?" Evan asked.

"I've never done it before, but it's possible." I said.

"No fucking way" Evan said. Jake was surprisingly quiet, like he had something he wanted to say.

"It doesn't look easy, but it's possible" I said.

"I'm not sure I'd want one dick inside me, much less two" Evan said. I'd not told Jake about fucking Evan. I got the impression he didn't want Jake to know.

"I want to try," Jake finally said. We both stared at him in shock.

"You for real?" Evan asked. All this talk had made his dick begin to poke up against his shorts.

"Ever since we both fucked Nat, I've been curious what it would feel like," Jake said, blushing. It took a lot to make Jake blush.

"I don't know, I think you have to be pretty well-prepared for something like that" I said.

"How would that even work?" Evan said, pinching his dick inside his shorts.

"It might take some trial and error" he said. "But I've been practicing."

I remembered seeing a dildo shaped like a garden gnome in a shop in the red-light district in Amsterdam and thinking who could possibly stick that up their ass. I saw it as something more comical than practical. Now I pictured that same gnome in Jake's hairy ass and had to suppress a fit of giggles.

"You're serious?" Evan asked. Jake nodded gravely. Evan downed the rest of his beer and crushed the can.

"Ok, let's do it" he said standing up to head inside. His shorts were tented where his hardening dick was pushing out of the pocket.

"Are you sure?" I asked Jake.

"When am I going to get another shot at two dicks like yours." He said.

"You could wait till he gets back" I said. I was trying not to think about him going and focus on the few hours remaining.

"I hope he does come back, but six months is a long time to wait." He said.

"Hope you have lots of lube" I said.

"It's all set up downstairs" he said grinning. So he'd been planning this.

We headed down to the basement to find a beach towel laid out over the ottoman and a bottle of lube sitting on top of it. Jake had stripped off his shorts and shirt before we'd finished descending the stairs. His hard dick bounced as he took his place on the ottoman. Evan and I looked at each other a moment, then began to strip.

Jake waited for us, looking back and forth between our hardening cocks, his eyes growing wide. It looked like he might be having second thoughts. It's one thing to imagine being fucked by two massive dicks, it's another to have those dicks in front of you.

Jake started out sucking Evan's dick. I stroked myself to full hardness, watching him slick up Evan's shaft. He felt around the base, like he was measuring it and doing calculations of diameter and volume in his head. His untouched cock was slick with precum dribbling out of his foreskin.

I knelt down and started sucking his dick, tasting the nectar he was producing. It was clear he was very excited because after a few minutes of him sucking Evan and me sucking him, he pushed my head away.

"I'm getting close" he said quietly. I reluctantly let go of his slick cock, tickling his hairy balls a little before I stood up.

I stepped up next to Evan and placed my arm over his shoulder. He looked over at me and smiled. I couldn't believe we were doing this. Jake spit out Evan's dick and began to slick up my dick the same way. His warm wet mouth felt incredible. He took turns sucking us until both our cocks were dripping with spit. Then he turned and got down on all fours on the ottoman, pushing his ass up in the air.

"What is that!" Evan said, pointing at a red rubber plug protruding from his hole.

"You've never seen a butt plug before?" Jake said casually.

"No" Evan said looking at it then looking away. "You've had that sticking in your butt all this time?"

"Since I took a shower earlier" he said.

"Doesn't it hurt?" Evan asked.

"I had to work up to it with smaller ones first, but no, it actually feels really good" he said.

Evan shook his head and I knew he was thinking what he had told me before, "he is a freak". He wasn't wrong. For a married man, he was more than a little open-minded.

He reached back and pulled at the plug. Evan looked away at first, then couldn't help but look back as curiously got the best of him. It grew wider as he pulled it, stretching out his hairy ring until it pulled free with a slurp.

"You should try it" Jake said, holding up the clean but glossy rubber plug. It was nearly as wide as my fist at the large end, tapering to a point in stages. Jake wasn't kidding when he said he's been practicing for this.

"No thanks!" Evan said, looking away from the plug, clearly grossed out by it.

"I've also been practicing with this" Jake said, reaching inside the storage area in the ottoman to pull out a massive black dildo.

"The fuck? How'd you fit that thing?" Evan said on seeing the latex log he was holding.

"Trust me, it will fit. I once saw a guy take an arm past the wrist" I said holding up my arm with my other hand making a ring around my arm where he'd managed to take the fist.

"It's true, I've been using it for a week now, in addition to the plug" Jake said. This guy is more gay than I am, I thought.

There seemed to be this weird awkwardness, like none of us were sure how to start. It seemed too clinical somehow. Jake looked at us expectantly. I nodded to Evan, who nodded back at me.

I'd actually never double penetrated anyone before, and I'd certainly never been double penetrated. Evan alone was my limit.

Jake grabbed hold of me and pulled me down on top of him on top of the ottoman. He kissed me deeply while drawing up his legs around my back. I kissed him back, grinding my cock against his as we kissed. Evan stood over us, his heavy dick floating in front of my face. Jake and I both went for it. Him licking Evan's balls while I focused on his dick. I licked up Evan's treasure trail while Jake took over sucking Evan's dick.

"Fuck me" Jake said between slurps. I sat back and pulled him to the edge of the ottoman. I grabbed the lube and slathered my dick with it. I don't think I really needed it. His hole gaped open at me, already slick with lube. My dick slipped inside him easily. He was much more loose than the last time I'd fucked him in our usual spot by the water. I was able to take long wet strokes from tip to root with ease. He had been preparing for this.

I fucked him until I felt like I was getting close. I didn't want to finish too soon, so I pulled out and tagged Evan in. Jake let go of his cock as Evan stepped back and went around the ottoman to grab hold of Jake's legs. I watched as he too slipped inside Jake with ease.

"Fuck!" Jake whimpered, feeling Evan's thick cock penetrate him deep. I'd never tire of watching these two fuck. I tried to picture how

I might add my dick to Evan's, but there wasn't a good angle in this position.

I got down behind Evan, watching his dick going in and out of Jake's hole. Evan's hole was right there in front of me, looking so inviting. I leaned in and drilled it with my tongue. Evan gasped and pushed his ass out for me to lick deeper.

He paused fucking Jake to enjoy my tongue in his ass. Jake seemed oblivious to what was going on behind Evan. He had his eyes closed, and his legs pulled back in pure bliss at Evan's thick cock buried deep inside him.

I grabbed some lube and slathered it on my finger, which I then shoved in Evan's ass. I'd fucked him a few more times since that first time, so he was started to get used to having things up his ass. I think he was as surprised as I was how much he was enjoying it.

I got up and slicked my dick with some additional lube before getting up behind him. Evan looked back as my head mashed into his hole.

"Oh fuck!" he said as I sank into him slowly.

"What the fuck? Is he fucking you?" Jake asked, looking up into Evan's face, then back at me behind them.

In answer, to him, I slammed into Evan so hard, it made him slam into Jake.

"Fuck!" Evan cried out.

"Damn! Is this your first time?" Jake asked. Evan shook his head shyly, looking embarrassed to be enjoying a dick in his ass.

"Why didn't you tell me?" Jake scowled at me over Evan's shoulder.

"He made me swear I wouldn't. See, I can keep a secret" I said.

"Fuck! See what I mean?" Jake said, his face lighting up at the revelation. Evan was lost for words but nodded his head in agreement. I took a few deep strokes, sending Evan's eyes rolling into the back of his head. He grunted and fell onto Jake's chest, pushing his ass up to accommodate more of me. In the process, he folded Jake in half, raising his ass off the ottoman. I felt Evan's ring tighten around me and sensed he was getting close. I reluctantly pulled out, knowing how much Jake wanted to have us both fuck him. Evan also pulled out with a loud slurp as Jake stood up.

"Why don't you lay here," Jake told me, pointing to the ottoman. I figured out how we planned his attempt. I'd seen it in a porn video. I laid down on my back with my dick sticking straight up. Jake slicked up my dick with another generous portion of lube. Then he straddled me and sat down on my cock. He sunk to my root instantly. He felt incredibly open, his velvety cavity hugging my dick. Evan watched my dick disappear inside Jake while stroking himself.

"Fuck, that feels good" Jake said, wiggling his ass around my pole.

"What do I do?" Evan asked, looking a little lost.

"Slide your dick in over his like you did with Nat" Jake said.

Evan moved closer, still looking a bit dubious. Jake squirted some more lube onto his already wet dick, pulling him closer to his ass. Evan pushed his dick down, so his head touched my shaft. I felt him slip in.

"Oh shit" Jake yelled, pushing Evan back out.

"Sorry, we don't have to..." Evan said.

"No It's ok. just take it a little more slowly" he said.

I held my dick in place, feeling Jake's ass squeeze it as he prepared for another try. I felt Evan's hot shaft rub up against mine. Jake tightened around me as Evan slipped forward along my shaft. I saw Jake's face crunch up in concentration and his jaw clench in pain.

"Relax and breath" I told him. His eye's opened and his pupils almost looked dilated. He took a few deep breaths in and out slowly. I felt Evan creep forward a little more. My dick pulsed as he moved up my shaft and touched the sensitive skin of my frenulum. Jake reached back and felt his hole stretched around both of our cocks.

"Holy fuck!" He said with a wide grin on his face. "I wish Nat was here to see this!"

He reached down and grabbed his phone from his shorts, handing it to Evan.

"Can you take a video for her?" He asked. Evan took the phone and fumbled to find the video control. He held the phone up and swept it from side to side, getting a few good angles of both our dicks buried inside Jake's very stretched hairy hole.

He continued to film as he took a tentative stroke forward and back. His dick popped out of the tight opening.

"Shit" he said, putting down the phone and attempting to jam his dick back inside. This time I slipped out while he got in. After a few awkward moments, we both managed to get back inside him.

I held still while Evan began to tentatively fuck Jake. I felt his dick slide smoothly over my dick. Jake grunted, and his eyes rolled back in his head. Jake's legs began to buckle, and he fell forward onto my chest. I could feel his perspiration glue us together. I stroked his hair gently as Evan started to fuck him. I loved the feeling of his cock sliding up along me while we were both held in Jake's warm, wet cavity. My balls tightened, and I knew I was moments from releasing my load. There was nothing I could do to prevent it, I couldn't change the pace of Evan's relentless strokes.

"Oh fuck!" I cried as my abs tightened, and my load shot inside Jake.

"Oh shit!" Cried Evan as he slammed into Jake hard. I felt the warm jets against my sensitive skin. I reached up and pulled them both closer as Evan's shook and drained his balls into Jake's hole. I wished it was my hole he was unloading into. I hoped there would be time for that before he left.

Jake let out a guttural howl as his dick began to erupt between us. Warmth spread across my abs and chest as his ass clamped down on us. The weight of both of them bared down on me. I held them in my arms, our breathing slowing and syncing up.

Evan pushed off and with a grotesque slurp pulled out of Jake's hole. I felt warm wetness oozing down my balls. He fell onto the sofa beside me, his softening dick resting in the groove of his abs.

Jake relaxed and fell against me, causing my dick to slip from his stretched hole. A flood of our cum poured out into me, like a broken levy. He sighed and let his full weight bear down on me. I stroked his hair as a looked over at Evan.

Jake stirred and looked over at him as well. No one spoke a word, too many thoughts and feeling to express in that moment. I reached out and touched Evan's cheek where the soft hairs of his beard encroached on his freckled skin. He turned and kissed my finger, smiling. I wanted this moment to last forever. We stayed like that until I felt I was drifting off to sleep.

"Get cleaned up" Jake suggested as he shakily stood stretching his legs. He offered me a hand up, and I reluctantly stood, his cum funneling down to my slickly pubes. I extended and hand to Evan and pulled him up. Before he turned to go upstairs, I pulled him into an embrace and kissed him deeply.

"Ugh, you got his cum all over me" he said smiling and laughing.

As we followed Jake up the stairs, I reached out and felt his stretched hole. It was gaping open and dripping cum, our cum.

We took turns showering in the too small for more than two at a time bath. And I toweled Evan off. Reluctantly, Evan and I got dressed.

"I'll see you off tomorrow" Jake said as he gave Evan a hug. Evan pulled Jake into a kiss, which I don't think Jake was prepared for. His eyes grew wide and then relaxed as they shared a deep kiss. I realized this was more than just buddies getting off together, there was something more building between us.

"I'm gonna miss you" Evan said.

"Me too bud," Jake said, his eyes getting glassy. I blinked back tears, trying not to think about tomorrow.

Chapter 30

Bon voyage

The bed was empty for the first time in weeks. I expected him to walk in the door any moment, like he'd just been finishing up in the bathroom. I rolled onto my side and hugged the pillow, his pillow, and caught a whiff of his scent.

After the crazy night with Jake, Evan and I had fallen asleep holding each other. His arms wrapped around me, his soft dick pressed against my ass. I tried to hide my tears.

"Please don't cry, you'll make me cry" Evan said, and I felt wetness on my shoulder. He hugged me tight as we fell asleep.

In the morning, I woke, feeling the bed moving as Evan shifted beside me. During the night, he'd rolled onto his side, and I'd tucked myself up against him. My morning wood was pressed into his crack. I couldn't tell if he was awake yet, but he was pushing his ass back against my dick, rubbing his cheeks against it ever so slightly.

I rolled my hips forward and pressed in against him. He stirred and pushed back more forcefully. My head rested in the valley of his ass, directly over his hole. He pushed back, and my head pressed into him. I pulled away, not wanting to hurt him. When I did, he shifted back toward me.

I nuzzled my chin against his shoulder, and he opened his eyes and looked back at me. He nodded and pushed back against me. I gave him a questioning expression. He nodded again.

I crawled under the covers so that I was facing his ass. I took a tentative lick up his crack. He gasped when I touched his hole with my tongue. I pulled his cheeks apart and licked deeper, drilling his hole with my tongue. He whimpered and pushed up his hips to meet my tongue. I sucked on his hole and lightly bit down on it. He gasped. I continued to work his hole with my tongue until my face was covered with spit.

I reached over to the nightstand and found the lube. I slicked up my dick and gently pressed a lubed finger into his ass. He didn't protest. I added a finger and wiggled them around inside him, looking for his prostate. He moaned and pushed his ass up against my fingers. I got back in behind him and pressed my lubed head against his hole.

"Are you sure?" I asked.

"Yes," he said, "I now understand that look Jake had on his face when we fucked him, it was like he was high out of his mind" he said.

"Once you know that feeling you can't get enough" I said, pushing in gently. I slipped inside him only an inch and waited for him to relax. Minutes went by as I painstakingly entered him as slowly as I could. He only stopped me once and only for a minute when I was halfway into him. Finally, I felt his soft hairs press into my pubes and knew I was all the way in.

"Fuck" he said when I bottomed out, pressing in deep and flexing my dick. I kissed his neck and reached my arms under him, holding him close. I stayed inside him like that, feeling my cock pulse as he clamped down on me. I'd never felt so connected to him than in that moment. He was letting himself be vulnerable for me. I gently began to fuck him, just a slight in and out movement of my hips at first. He pushed up his ass to meet my strokes. The movement built until I was pulling out and pushing back in a few inches. I wanted to see his face, wanted to know what I was doing to him. I pulled out nearly all the way, then pushed back in a few times before I pulled out completely.

"What's wrong?" He asked.

"Flip over" I said. He rolled onto his back, his dick was only semi-hard. I bent down and slipped it into my mouth, bringing it to life. It grew and expanded against my tongue. I tasted his precum forming. He pulled his legs back. I stopped sucking him and looked up into his face.

"Fuck me" he said, exposing his open ass. I scooted forward and found his hole once again. I added more lube and slipped my head into his waiting hole. His eyes widened as I slipped back inside him more quickly this time. I was afraid I'd hurt him when his hands went up to my side. Instead of pushing me away, he pulled me closer. My dick pressed in until his balls rested against my belly.

I leaned forward and kissed him, feeling his dick pressing into my abs. His beard scraped at my lips, and I kissed him and sucked his tongue into my mouth. Our need built as I began to fuck him with long deep strokes at first. As our passion grew, my strokes became shorter and quicker. My orgasm raced towards me. There was no stopping it, I could feel it building. Even if I stopped fucking him and held still, I would have cum just from the mere fact I was inside him. His eyes lit up and a smile creeped along his face. His lips curled into an oval as I rammed my cock into him hard now. He encouraged me with his hands on my ass, pushing me forward into him. My balls tightened and churned as my load built inside them.

"I'm going to cum" I whimpered as I ravaged his hole. He beamed up at me, his dick leaking precum all over his abs and mine as it jabbed into me with each thrust.

"Oh fuck!" I yelled as cum shot up my shaft and into him. I kept shooting as if I were draining my entire supply into him. My cock jerked wildly as I filled him with my seed. I saw stars come out before my eyes. I collapsed onto his chest, my dick still buried in him.

He hugged me and ran his hands along my back gently as waves of pleasure dispersed and faded. My heartbeat began to calm, and I felt his hard dick pulse under me. I grabbed hold of him and rolled us both across the bed until his was on top of me. In the process, my dick slipped from his hole. He reached back and felt his opening with a look of giddy surprise on his face.

"Your turn" I said, pulling my legs back. Normally, I didn't like getting fucked after I'd cum, but I wasn't going to pass up this opportunity. I wanted his seed inside me, like mine was now inside him. He grabbed the lube and slicked up his pole and my hole. He jabbed my opening a few times in haste to enter me. I didn't care, I nodded for him to do it. He held his cock by the base and pressed it into me. I winced in pain for a moment as he slipped in much less gently than I had done for him. The pain passed, and I felt him fill me up. No one had ever filled me like him, he was by far the biggest to ever fuck me. He started to take a few strokes inside me. He leaned in and kissed me as he pounded my hole, nearly biting my lip.

He laid waste to my hole with quick, jerky strokes. I knew he wouldn't last long.

"Oh fuck!" He said pounding me hard with deep strokes. I felt a warm sensation flood me as his balls drained inside me.

"I love you" I said softly. I don't know what came over me. I regretted it the moment I said it. I was caught up in the moment. I did love him, I just didn't think he felt the same way. There was a long pause as his dick drained inside me, and he looked down at me. I looked away, embarrassed at what I'd confessed to him.

He reached down and gently turned my head to face him. Our eyes met and locked onto each other. I saw deep love and longing in those eyes. Finally, he whispered. "I love you too" and fell into my arms.

Tears streamed down my face as he fell on my chest. We held each other as his dick softened and slipped from my hole. I let my legs fall to his sides and stretched them out, the pain of holding them up so long, diminishing.

I knew our time was growing short, but I held on to the moment. I would soon be dropping him off at the boat to share a tearful bon voyage with Jake by my side. I'd watch the ship release its moorings and begin to move away. I'd see Evan waving to us from the deck as he grew smaller and smaller until the boat disappeared around the jetty and headed for open water.

"What's that?" Jake asked.

"A postcard from Evan" I said, turning over the card to look at the message.

"He must have sent it from Greece." I said.

"And it's just getting here now?" Jake asked, fetching his shorts which he'd discarded as soon as we'd gotten in the door.

"You can sail across the ocean faster than the postal system can deliver a post card" I said.

"He just messaged, they're already in the bay" Jake said, as he slipped his shorts back over his used ass.

"We've got some time," I said as I headed upstairs to clean up. I was both excited and nervous to see Evan again. Six months had gone by quicker than I expected. When he had a signal, we'd been able to chat from time to time. He told me the owner of the yacht was a nice guy, wealthy, retired and gay. The crew consisted of a skipper and first mate, a chef and porter in addition to himself. All younger guys and all picked for their bodies in addition to thier skills. He was ok with the arrangement given the money he was making. The owner never took advantage of them, but he certainly didn't mind having a lot of eye candy around. Evan did basic maintenance and upgrades from time to time, but had a good deal of free time to enjoy life on the water and the places they'd stop in.

When they were at sea, nudity was strongly encouraged. Evan would strip down and sun bathe on deck with a few of the crew. The owner would occasionally join them. He was in decent shape for an older guy. He'd sent me a few pics of the other crew. I was beginning to regret not joining him after all.

I tried not to feel just a little jealous about him being on a boat with these hot guys. I assumed things were going on between them, but Evan kept quiet about it and I didn't ask. He seemed so happy in his element at sea.

"You about ready?" Jake asked. "Nat is going to meet us at the dock".

"Almost" I said, pulling on my shorts. It was warm for early May, and the sun was bright and the sky a crystal blue. I was more than a little nervous about the reunion. Both excited to see Evan, but nervous about where our relationship stood.

I saw a deeply tanned figure come down the gangplank. I almost didn't recognize him with the neatly trimmed beard. He rushed up to me and grabbed me around the waist, pulling me close.

"I've missed you so much" he said, his bare chest pressed against my teeshirt.

"I missed you too" I said, tears of joy forming in my eyes. It all came flooding back. My fears fell away, holding him. I didn't know what the future might bring, but I knew for this moment I was his and he was mine.

Don't miss out!

Visit the website below and you can sign up to receive emails whenever Kevin Davis publishes a new book. There's no charge and no obligation.

https://books2read.com/r/B-A-WAVX-XYDSC

BOOKS 2 READ

Connecting independent readers to independent writers.

Also by Kevin Davis

Jason and the New Argonauts
Beasts of Gaea

The Quarterback and His Son
Backcountry
The Roommate
Homecoming

The Salesman
The Salesman

Standalone
The Compound
Helping out my Straight Neighbors

About the Author

Kevin Davis began writing short stories growing up and wrote his first novel at age 17. He was accepted into the writing program at university. He took a break from writing to pursue a career in IT but continued to write and journal about his experiences. He began writing erotic fiction based loosely on his journals and reminiscences for blogs and on Reddit. With the encouragement of his fans, he expanded these stories into full-length novels. His character-driven stories propel the reader into worlds of steamy sex and forbidden desires, leaving readers demanding more. You'll not only find hot man on man sex in his stories, you'll also find touching stories and compelling, relatable characters. ***Contact the author at blueiguanapress@gmail.com***

Read more at https://linktr.ee/blueiguana.